The Devil's Game

ALSO BY SEAN CHERCOVER

The Trinity Game

Trigger City

Big City, Bad Blood

Eight Lies (About the Truth): A Collection of Short Stories

The Devil's Game

A novel

SEAN CHERCOVER

f THOMAS & MERCER

Text copyright © 2015 Sean Chercover

Published by Thomas & Mercer, Seattle

www.apub.com

Amazon, the Amazon logo, and Thomas & Mercer are trademarks of Amazon.com, Inc., or its affiliates.

ISBN-13: 9781477828663
ISBN-10: 1477828664
Hardcover ISBN-10: 1503944573
Hardcover ISBN-13: 9781503944572

Cover design by Marc Cohen

Library of Congress Control Number: 2014958622

Printed in the United States of America

For Holly Chercover,
friend, sister,
co-traveler through the wild ride of childhood

And Alexander "Sasha" Neyfakh (1959–2006),
who fought deadly microscopic critters
on behalf of the whole human race

"There have been as many plagues as wars in history; yet always plagues and wars take people equally by surprise."

"But what does it mean, the plague? It's life, that's all."

"On this earth there are pestilences and there are victims, and it's up to us, so far as possible, not to join forces with the pestilences."

—Albert Camus, *The Plague*

1: DON'T FEAR THE REAPER

Red Ridge, West Virginia

*T*oday is a good day to die.

Daniel Byrne handed the counterfeit identification card to the soldier behind the metal desk. To the left of the desk, another soldier stood blocking the solid-steel inner door. Mounted to the cinder-block wall beside the door was an electronic palm-print reader. A third soldier—the one cradling an assault rifle—stood behind Daniel, blocking the larger metal door through which he'd entered, and which he knew was the only exit. They wore plain green uniforms, no identifying patches or insignia.

Today is a good day to die. But I've decided to stay alive until tomorrow.

The soldier at the desk examined the forgery, which identified Daniel as Colonel Walter Pomerance of the Defense Intelligence Agency, then tapped on the computer keyboard and looked at the screen. His mouth twitched once and he became very still. The sentry stationed at the inner door moved his hand an inch closer to his holster.

The soldier at the desk said, "Sir, there's no record—"

"Typical," snapped Daniel. The persona he'd created for Colonel Walter Pomerance was that of an insufferable bastard—he would play the role all the way, whatever the outcome. "Is it too much to presume your computer is at least capable of providing you the phone number of the Pentagon?" He resisted the urge to adjust his uniform. Putting ice in his voice, he added, "Don't waste my time . . . Sergeant." Forcing that last word, having no way of knowing if the man was in fact a sergeant.

During the pre-insertion briefing, Raoul had told him the one behind the desk would be a sergeant and said to address him by rank. Daniel had just bet his life on the accuracy of that intel—intel provided by a man he'd known less than three months.

He raised his left wrist and pressed the button on the side of his watch—starting the chronograph—and shot the young man a look. From the soldier's perspective, the move would scan as an ego-driven high-ranking officer tossing his clout around. But Daniel needed to track time. From the moment the soldier had entered Daniel's cover name into the computer, he would have one hour. That is, if the Foundation computer geeks, tapping away furiously 538 miles away in New York City, were successful.

If they were successful, the phone call would be intercepted by the Foundation, who would also take control of the local computer network and upload the military file for Daniel's legend—not a complete file, because much of the fictional Colonel Pomerance's file would be classified even above the level of this place, but a file even more impressive for what was redacted than for what it contained. Colonel Walter Pomerance was a very powerful DIA spook.

Not a man whose time you wanted to waste.

Daniel watched a half-dozen seconds tick by—he loved the smooth micro-ticks of his new watch's automatic movement—and when none of the three soldiers put a bullet in his head, he figured the guy was really a sergeant. He dropped his wrist to waist level.

The room was a perfect square, twenty feet wall-to-wall. No furniture beyond the steel desk and single chair, nothing on the desktop but the computer and a telephone. LED light fixtures set into the ceiling, protected by thick sheets of clear bulletproof Plexiglas. Nothing on the walls. No military shields or symbols, no flags, no official portrait of the commander in chief. Of course, there wouldn't be. Officially, this facility, which ran twelve stories down into the earth, did not exist. Black ops, according to the case file Daniel had spent two days studying. It had once been a coal mine, and hundreds of West Virginia men and boys had died here in the early 1900s. How many men died here now, and what they died of, was not in the case file.

The sergeant at the desk picked up the telephone receiver and pressed a speed-dial button. He offered a verbal passphrase, paused for confirmation, and began to explain the problem. There was nothing Daniel could do now but act inconvenienced and wait for it to play out.

And breathe.

He took his mind back to the zazen meditation that had started his day. Sitting *seiza*—kneeling, sitting on his feet with his back straight and his hands cupped together in his lap—on the impossibly plush royal-blue carpet of the Greenbrier Hotel's Congressional Suite. Counting breaths, mentally tuning out the riotous floral print that assaulted him from the draperies, headboard, duvet cover . . . the smell of coffee beckoning from his room-service breakfast table . . . the sound of a distant woodpecker working to find its own breakfast. Tuning out thoughts, worries, fears about the day ahead. Tuning in to counting breaths. Then moving past counting, tuning in to breathing itself.

Tuning in to the *now*.

In the previous three months, Daniel had become an exceedingly proficient meditator. Any decent Buddhist will tell you that meditating is not about grasping for proficiency, but Daniel was not a Buddhist, decent or otherwise, and the daily practice was not religious in nature. It was part of his job.

Having spent ten years in his previous job as a Roman Catholic priest, he was familiar with meditation, knew much about the Zen sect of Buddhism, but he'd never *practiced* zazen meditation until after he'd quit the priesthood. He'd learned it as part of his training at the Fleur-de-Lis Foundation.

For the Foundation, it was simply about brain chemistry and best practices, nothing more. Operatives who meditate solve problems faster, shoot straighter, stay more focused under stress, and recover faster from injury. So they were trained to meditate and were expected to continue their practice in the field.

And they were trained to end each morning's session with this intentional thought:

Today is a good day to die. But I've decided to stay alive until tomorrow.

An elegant phrase. An acceptance of death, followed by the simple decision to see the day through, with all that such a decision implies. Daniel liked to think of it as a set of instructions to his subconscious.

The sergeant pinned the telephone receiver between his shoulder and ear, reached for the mouse, and spoke into the mouthpiece. "I'm reloading the screen now, sir." A small wave of relief rolled over Daniel. They'd successfully hijacked the phone call, but that was just the first link in a chain of events that needed to be perfectly calibrated. The computer system had exponentially stronger firewalls. If the Foundation hackers were successful, Daniel's military personnel file and palm print were now being fed into the local network.

If they weren't successful, today would have to be a good day to die after all.

What a rush, thought Daniel as he waited to find out which.

2: GOTTA SERVE SOMEBODY

New Orleans, Louisiana

I t started with the running.

The month following Tim Trinity's death was a blur. Trinity's finances were all kinds of illegal, and he'd named Daniel executor of his will, so Daniel hired a team of absurdly expensive, white-shoe New Orleans lawyers to take care of business while he focused on the business of grieving.

Daniel's lawyers managed to win a battle royal against the IRS, helped no doubt by the fact that millions of Americans now believed Tim Trinity had been a prophet sent by God, or even the messiah returned.

Others believed Trinity had been the antichrist, but they were outnumbered by the optimists.

Tim Trinity's estate paid the federal government twenty million dollars in back taxes. Another forty million was allocated to pay for property damages and to cover the cost of police and EMS overtime stemming from the chaos Trinity's followers had caused in Atlanta, Memphis, and New Orleans—that account was to be administered by FEMA.

The lawyers then established the Tim Trinity Charitable Trust to distribute the remaining 120-odd million to New Orleans and the towns across the Southland where Trinity had worked his preacher grift for so many years. *For the general welfare,* Trinity had said in his handwritten will.

But as the first month bled into the second, things got harder for Daniel. Most of the administrative work had been handed off, leaving him with time on his hands just as he passed his thirty-fourth birthday. Which raised the question:

What the hell do I do with the rest of my life?

So he started running. Years earlier, when he competed in Golden Gloves, they hadn't called it running. Daniel's trainer, Father Henri, simply called it "roadwork." Daniel liked the term and still thought of it as roadwork. His boxing days were long behind him—he'd won the trophy at eighteen and retired from the ring—but during his years in the priesthood he kept in shape skipping rope and working with a heavy bag set up in his Rome apartment, and he tried to get in some sparring with the Jesuits at the Vatican boxing club whenever he was in town long enough.

Around the time he left the priesthood, those fighting skills had been called for once again, this time outside the ring. And now in the middle of a New Orleans summer, he returned to roadwork.

Running. And wondering what to do with the rest of his life.

Prevailing opinion said that in the middle of a New Orleans summer, sane people did their running on treadmills inside air-conditioned fitness clubs. But Daniel pounded it out on the heat-buckled pavement with the po' folk and the moneyed lunatics, sweaty street by sweaty street, reconnecting with the city of his childhood.

He'd lived his early years mostly on the road, traveling the Bible Belt with his uncle and legal guardian, the Reverend Tim Trinity, grifter at large. Trinity worked the tent revival circuit hard, about 275 days a year, homeschooling Daniel in that rusty Winnebago, but home base was always New Orleans, where they kept a house in Uptown. After leaving Trinity at the age of thirteen, Daniel lived in the Crescent City full-time, the archdiocese his legal guardian.

Daniel left New Orleans behind after graduating the seminary at twenty-three. For the next ten years he kept an apartment in Rome but lived mostly out of a suitcase. His world expanded to Africa, South America, Europe, Australia, Southeast Asia, each city, country, continent bleeding into the next.

Now he was back to home base. Hurricane Katrina had tried its damnedest to kill this town and idiot politicians almost finished the job, but neither succeeded. There was no killing New Orleans. Even with crooks holding sway in government like nothing had happened. Even with corporate America trying to turn the place into Las Vegas. All you had to do was get away from the tourist traps and into the neighborhoods.

The soul of New Orleans was intact.

By now, every existing video of the late Reverend Tim Trinity speaking in tongues had been analyzed and decoded and dissected by the media. It had been thoroughly established that Trinity had been speaking English backwards and that he had predicted future events with 100 percent accuracy. That was beyond dispute.

But nobody knew *how* he'd done it.

The autopsy revealed a brain tumor, which might (or might not) conceivably explain speaking backwards, but there was still no explanation for how he'd successfully predicted the future. Religious people said it was the work of God or Satan or the Cosmic Consciousness, while non-believers waded into the baffling math and unsettling metaphysical implications of quantum physics.

The Trinity Phenomenon remained a mystery, and Daniel figured the rest of the world could solve it without his help. Until that muggy Monday morning, this time running along Magazine Street. It had rained buckets all through the night until just before dawn, when the nuclear furnace in the sky took over, turning New Orleans into a steam bath, air both hot and laden, so thick you could feel the weight of water in your lungs and you were reminded that lungs are our gills and we were once fish.

One of many ways New Orleans connects us to the primal, to the truth about what we are.

It would be a slow run today, but that was fine. This run, on this morning, was finally the run to the bank. Daniel had held down the urge long enough.

Time to see what was on that damn laptop computer.

The laptop had arrived by FedEx a week after Trinity's death. Sent by Carter Ames, managing director of the Fleur-de-Lis Foundation.

Daniel ran to the edge of the Quarter, stopping to buy a padded backpack at a luggage shop on Canal Street. Then over to IberiaBank on Poydras, where he kept the laptop in a safety deposit box. He forced himself to complete the last three sweat-drenched miles of roadwork with the computer on his back, rather than going straight home with it.

Felt like a marathon.

Showered and shaved and cooled down, with a fresh aromatic pot of Community coffee at hand, Daniel powered up the laptop. The note Ames sent with it said: *Your uncle was not the only one.*

The Vatican had sent Daniel to debunk his uncle, but they weren't alone in trying to silence Trinity. There were others, some willing to go way beyond discrediting the man, and behind the

scenes, with their fingers in every pie, were two powerful organizations Daniel had never heard of before. The Fleur-de-Lis
Foundation had tried to help Daniel protect his uncle. As Carter
Ames told it, the Foundation was doing battle with an outfit called
the Council for World Peace.

Don't be fooled by the name, Ames had warned, *the only peace
offered by the Council is peaceful slavery.* Adding, with an attempt
at dry humor, *Mind you, they did get the first word right. When
did any group calling itself a "council" accomplish anything good?*

These two groups, under various names, had been fighting
for influence over world events for centuries. Both had operatives
embedded within governments, military forces, the intelligence
community, law enforcement, multinational corporations, univer-
sities, the media, and religious organizations of all stripes.

Incredible as it sounded, the story fit with some of the lingering
*why*s left unanswered by some of the stranger things Daniel had
bumped up against during his years in the field. He hadn't known
how much of Carter Ames's story to believe but if even half of it
were true, then there was an unwritten history behind the official
history of world affairs.

A shadow history of shadow governments.

A separate reality behind the one we know.

The laptop screen brightened and the machine automatically
launched the QuickTime video player. Carter Ames sat behind a
cherrywood desk, facing the camera. The angle wasn't wide enough
for Daniel to make out much of the room behind him. It was an
office, or maybe a well-appointed study. A large Mondrian canvas
dominated the wall behind the desk.

Ames was a trim man in his sixties—or if very fit, early
seventies—dressed in an impeccably tailored gray suit. He spoke

with a transatlantic boarding-school accent, somewhere between British and American.

"Good day, Daniel," Ames said. "During our brief time together, I said that if you walked the path, you'd learn the truth. You did walk the path, quite admirably, and now you shall have the truth." He paused to sip water from a glass on the desk. "What the media has been calling the Trinity Phenomenon is not, in fact, exclusive to your uncle. While Tim Trinity is the only case that has become public as a news story, whatever this phenomenon is—and let me be clear: We do not yet know what it is—has been happening to thousands of people around the planet in recent years, at an ever-increasing rate."

A bar graph filled the screen. *Confirmed Cases of Anomalous Information Transfer—Worldwide.* The graph covered the past twenty years, a bar representing each year. Around the millennium, the bars jumped from a baseline barely in the double digits up into the hundreds, climbing through the following years until it reached above nine thousand. "Of course, we haven't any idea the origin of the phenomenon"—Ames shook his head—"nor its purpose. But for good or ill, it is on the rise."

Over the next hour, Carter Ames narrated a presentation that included charts and graphs, scanned copies of affidavits and psychiatric evaluations, MRI reports, and video clips. The Trinity Phenomenon—what the Foundation called "Anomalous Information Transfer"—didn't usually manifest in backwards speech, as it had with Daniel's uncle. In some cases, subjects fell into a kind of babbling trance. Others spoke fluently in languages they'd never studied or even been exposed to. Some simply transcribed the voices they heard in their heads, or wrote down the dreams they had that felt like more than dreams.

But all *confirmed* cases contained information the subjects could not possibly have known. And they didn't all predict the future, as Trinity had. Some detailed events from the distant past that appeared in no history books and were known to very few. Others spoke of events unfolding half a world away, at the very time they were happening.

Carter Ames came back on the screen. "I realize it's a lot to take in, Daniel. The bottom line is, whatever the cause of Anomalous Information Transfer, this explosion of cases represents a seismic event in human history, and we believe the people of the world deserve to know about it. The Council for World Peace aims to keep it to themselves, and they have killed hundreds, including your uncle, toward that very aim."

Daniel hit the space bar to pause the video, and took a sip of his thick black chicory coffee. He put personal issues aside, focused on the facts. On a planet of over seven billion, nine thousand was a minuscule number. Even if, as Ames had suggested, the actual number was ten times the number of confirmed cases, that would still be ninety thousand out of seven billion. But if the trend line depicted on the graph continued for another decade, ninety thousand would become nine million. Whatever the cause—God, quantum physics, or something as yet unimagined—clearly the universe was trying to *tell us something*.

The very idea sent an electric charge up Daniel's spine. He put the mug down, tapped the space bar. He knew what was coming. Carter Ames was a smart man, he'd sunk the hook well.

The video resumed.

Carter Ames said, "Understand, the Foundation was completely unaware of the existence of AIT until the late 1920s, when our predecessors learned that the Council for World Peace—then called the Many Nations Alliance—was studying the phenomenon in Germany. The Foundation's own studies confirmed its existence, but with only a handful of cases to study, the studies went nowhere. The more important thing we learned was that AIT was not the appearance of a new phenomenon, but the reappearance of a very old one.

"It's always difficult when reading the tea leaves of ancient history, the records of pre-scientific societies, but we know Anomalous Information Transfer waxes and wanes throughout history. It goes virtually dormant for hundreds of years at a time but surges during times of great change—the fall of empires, when there are rapid shifts of power, or at times of depopulation due to widespread war or disease—sharp turns in the course of human affairs. We don't know if these pivotal changes *cause* AIT, or if the periodic rise of AIT triggers the societal changes, but we do know that they arrive together." Carter Ames sipped his water again, his expression turning grim. "Which does not bode well, since AIT is surging once again. We intend to do something about it, and I think you could play an essential role in our efforts."

Daniel had spent a lifetime looking into the faces of some of the most talented con artists on the planet, and more than a few lunatics, but looking at Ames, Daniel saw neither.

"And so I leave the ball in your court, Daniel. Let's talk about how we might work together, should you feel so inclined." The image faded to black, and a 212 telephone number came up on the screen.

When they'd met in person, Carter Ames had floated the idea that Daniel might become an operative for the Foundation, but at the time Daniel wasn't thinking past keeping his uncle alive. Then the Council silenced Tim Trinity with a bullet, preventing the world from learning whatever the universe was trying to tell us.

Now Daniel would join the game.

3: WELCOME TO THE MACHINE

New York City

In the Yorkville neighborhood on the Upper East Side of Manhattan, a half-dozen blocks south of Spanish Harlem and a block from the East River, a feat of architectural and engineering brilliance hides in plain sight. Thousands bustle past the thirty-two-story building each day without giving it a second thought. From the street, it looks like a quietly upscale condominium tower built in the late 1990s or early 2000s. But instead of the standard swimming pool, hot tub, chaises longues, and party deck with wet bar, the rooftop boasts a helipad and satellite relay station. And none of the units ever go up for sale because the Fleur-de-Lis Foundation owns the entire building.

The perimeter is like any upscale condominium tower. The apartments are used as housing for Foundation trainees, visitors, and staff members working round-the-clock assignments, and on the lower floors is office space for several Foundation-affiliated businesses. But inside the perimeter is a second building entirely. Windowless, electronically shielded, with its own elevators and stairwells, and running on its own separate power and ventilation systems.

The inner building is invisible to the outside world.

Daniel Byrne removed his headset as the AgustaWestland executive helicopter touched down in the yellow circle on the roof. He waited for the pilot's signal, then opened the door and stepped down onto the sizzling, sun-drenched surface, crouch-jogging to the man waiting at the rooftop door. The man gestured Daniel inside and shut the door behind them, cutting off the din of the decelerating rotor blades.

The man held out his hand and Daniel shook it. "Raoul Aharon. Pleased to meet you." Raoul Aharon looked about thirty-five, curly black hair, olive complexion, five o'clock shadow a few hours ahead of schedule. He wore black cargo pants and T-shirt. He was tightly muscled, his handshake firm with maybe just a hint of implied challenge. He stepped into a mahogany and brass elevator. "I'll take you to the director."

✤ ✤ ✤

In the lounge area of Carter Ames's expansive office, Daniel sat on a white leather Barcelona chair, drinking strong black coffee from delicate bone china. Ames wore a bespoke navy-blue suit over a powder-blue shirt, offset by a yellow Hermès tie, tied in a perfect Windsor knot. The Windsor had always seemed fussy to Daniel and he'd never learned it, but on the director of the Fleur-de-Lis Foundation it looked more than comfortable. It looked inevitable.

Carter Ames did not waste time on small talk. "Our training program is rigorous. If you quit during training or fail to graduate the program, we pay you a severance of fifty thousand dollars, you sign a non-disclosure agreement, and we part friends. If you succeed, you become a Foundation field operative. And we take good care of our operatives. The job comes with a six-figure salary, but that just goes straight into your retirement fund—the Foundation covers all of your living expenses while you are in our employ. We pay for everything. You will live well"—Ames sipped his coffee— "which is as it should be for a job that makes high demands on your life and carries the risk of an early death."

"Care to quantify that risk?" said Daniel.

"Eleven percent on average," Ames said without hesitation. "Eleven percent of our field operatives die on the job. Another 33 percent quit the game with various PTSD-related issues—what we used to so quaintly call burnout. We take care of their financial and medical needs, but of course we can't undo the damage." He was quiet for a moment, giving Daniel time to absorb it. "Still interested?"

"So only 56 percent make it to retirement relatively intact," said Daniel, a smile invading his face. "Hell of a sales pitch. Sure, I'm still interested."

"I thought you would be. Questions?"

Daniel eyed the large Mondrian he'd seen in the video Ames had sent him, the Picasso on the opposite wall. Originals. "Why didn't the Foundation put some skin in the game and really try to prevent my uncle's assassination? You've got the resources."

Ames nodded. "I don't mean to be impolitic or to minimize your personal loss, but the direct answer is Tim Trinity wasn't worth the investment of manpower or the risk to our top operatives. You saw the graphs, the trend lines. In the last year your uncle was one of—we don't even know the number . . . ten thousand? One hundred thousand?—let's just say *many* cases of Anomalous Information Transfer. His case was strange, but aside from the fact that it became a news story, it was not particularly special."

Carter Ames turned and lifted a file folder from a small stack on the side table. "To be perfectly frank, we were more interested in you than your uncle." He placed the file folder on Daniel's side of the coffee table. Printed on the tab was *Daniel Byrne*. "We've been scouting you for some time, and we're not alone in that." Ames refilled their cups from the silver coffee pot. "Anyone who spends ten years as a top-level Vatican investigator does not go unnoticed by the players of the game." He gestured at the folder, flashing professionally manicured fingernails. "You'll see."

"All right," said Daniel.

"Now there is the matter of confidentiality." For the first time, Carter Ames seemed a shade less than perfectly comfortable. "Perhaps the greatest sacrifice our members make, you will not be able to discuss the Foundation or the work we do with anyone on the outside. Naturally, that makes relationships difficult, and it's why we encourage friendships and romantic entanglements between Foundation members. If you're involved with a civilian and the situation becomes untenable, you can request that he or she be vetted and, if cleared, read in. But I'm afraid your lady friend, Miss Rothman, would not be cleared. For obvious reasons. I can only offer that, when the time comes to go public, we will offer her a head start on the rest of her colleagues in the media."

"We're no longer a couple," said Daniel, "but she's still a good friend, and I'll take you up on the head start."

"When the time comes, and not before. We're not in the business of causing mass hysteria. That would only play into the Council's hands. They've been far ahead of us on this from the start, and we're still playing catch-up."

"Understood."

"And we have to play catch-up a lot faster than we have been. You saw what happened with your uncle, the flood of information that came out of him—in a matter of weeks, he plunged the entire country into chaos. Imagine if the Council had exclusive access to not just one, but maybe dozens of sources like that. They could manipulate currencies and stock markets and wars and elections around the globe; they'd have influence over world events on an unprecedented scale. The world wouldn't stand a chance. So Anomalous Information Transfer has become the Foundation's top priority, and we need you on the AIT team as soon as humanly possible. Our training program normally runs six months, but I've asked Raoul to get you ready in three."

"I'm a quick study," said Daniel.

✚ ✚ ✚

When Raoul Aharon said they'd be having dinner in the commissary, Daniel naturally imagined a cafeteria. But the Foundation "commissary" was a large, elegant wood-paneled dining room complete with adjoining bar. The place would give the Yale Club an inferiority complex. But what really floored Daniel was the artwork—Degas and Toulouse-Lautrec and Miró and Dali and Hopper and Pollock and . . . too much to catalog.

"It rotates," said Raoul as they sat. "The art. They go on tour or long-term loan to all the top museums. The view changes regularly, which you'll come to appreciate. It's what we have instead of windows."

A waiter stopped by and took their order—crabcakes for Daniel, salade Niçoise for Raoul, and a half liter of Bordeaux to share—and then Raoul got down to business.

"Carter has decided to fast-track you through training."

"He told me."

"Did he tell you I argued against it?"

"No, he didn't mention that. Do you argue with him often?"

Raoul nodded. "And sometimes I win him over. See, the way it works here . . . discussion and debate are not only encouraged, they're insisted upon. Everyone's clear on chain of command, but it's less hierarchical than you might think—certainly nothing like it was back home."

"Israel?"

"Are you saying I have an accent?"

Daniel smiled back at him. "Slight."

Raoul drank some wine. "Yes, I was Mossad. Israeli Army Intelligence before that."

"Why'd you quit?"

"I saw the bigger picture. A moment comes to every intelligence agent worth a damn, no matter what country you pledge allegiance to . . . you realize decisions are being made far above your pay grade, far above your boss's pay grade, by men who do not pledge allegiance to nations, men playing a bigger game for even bigger stakes. And you don't even know your real role in it all. So you have a choice to make. You can pretend not to see it and go on doing their grunt work without knowing why, you can quit intelligence work altogether . . ."

"Or you can join the big leagues, play the bigger game."

"If you're good enough." Raoul gestured at the file folder Carter Ames had given Daniel, now on the table beside them. "For the record, Padre, you're good enough. I'm the guy who scouted you for Carter. And I'll try to get you ready in three months, but until you're ready, you won't go out in the field, however long it takes."

"Padre" was a friendly jab, the kind of ribbing men do to bond with each other, but it rankled Daniel more than he liked. "For the record," he said, "I was ex-communicated."

Raoul chuckled at that. "You forced the Vatican's hand, didn't give them any choice. You ex-communicated yourself."

"Fair enough," said Daniel.

"You were never sincere about the priesthood—"

"I was sincere about my work," Daniel cut in.

"No doubt. Great investigator, lousy priest, not much of a Catholic even. I'm not judging—believe me, I understand better than you think. Me, I'm an Israeli Palestinian love child who joined Mossad, so I know, things get complicated. My concern is not with your choices in the past. Everyone arrives here with a past."

"What is your concern?"

"We've never fast-tracked training before. For anyone. We can get you up to speed on what you have to learn, but we can't rush your assimilation into our culture. The Vatican is like most places—interdepartmental rivalries, turf building, compartmentalization of intelligence—not unlike the CIA and the wider intel community. And you were pretty much a lone wolf there. I mean, did you trust—I mean *really* trust—anyone beyond Father Nick?"

"Not really," Daniel said honestly. "There are only three people alive I'd trust with my life—one is my ex-girlfriend, one is a New Orleans voodoo priestess, and the third is a mercenary named Pat Wahlquist I met in Honduras." He toasted with his wineglass. "It's been a long, strange trip. And it turns out Pat's a Foundation ally. I figure if he trusts you, I can."

Raoul sipped some wine. "Good answer. Understand, the game we're playing here is life-or-death. Trust is essential."

"Carter already laid out the risks," said Daniel.

Raoul continued as if Daniel hadn't spoken. "Here, we trust each other, and we share information with each other. Look, we're not asking for a blood oath. You stay with the Foundation as long as you like, or as long as we like. You judge us by our fruit, as the Bible says. But it takes time to get to know each other, and you can't come in half-assed."

"You think I am?"

"It's what you did with the Vatican. You had a personal agenda, right? Becoming a priest allowed you to serve that agenda." Raoul locked eyes with Daniel. "My concern is that you have a personal agenda here."

"And that would be?"

"Revenge for your uncle's murder."

"I'm not in the revenge business," said Daniel.

"I hope not. Because the man who engineered Trinity's death is one of the Council's top operatives."

"We're talking about Conrad Winter, right?"

Raoul nodded. "And he's moved up in the world since you last saw him. He's been put in charge of the Council's efforts with regards to Anomalous Information Transfer. What's so funny?"

"Nothing," said Daniel, "just getting used to the term." Like the rest of the world, Daniel thought of it as the Trinity Phenomenon. Of course the rest of the world didn't know it was happening all over the place.

"Anyway, there's a good chance you and Winter will eventually cross paths and I have to know you'll keep your head. We've been at war with the Council a long time. Right now it's a cold war, and it's in everybody's interest to keep it that way. Even in a cold war there are casualties, but we do not issue kill orders on each other's field operatives. So if you came to us for that, you came to the wrong place."

"You don't have to worry about me," said Daniel. "I'm not the assassin type."

4: I AM THAT I AM

After reading to the end of the scouting report, Daniel flipped back to the top and re-read the executive summary—his vital statistics, known skills and relevant experience, and this one-paragraph conclusion:

Smart and resourceful. Doesn't play well with others and has a problem with authority. Adrenaline junkie—an asset if he can harness it, a huge liability if it graduates to a death wish.

Recruitment strongly recommended.

It was signed *Raoul Aharon.*

Daniel couldn't ignore the vulnerable feeling of intimate exposure to people who were strangers to him. He felt not violated but *formulated, sprawling on a pin . . . pinned and wriggling on the wall.* Such a feeling was itself obvious and undeniable evidence that Raoul had pretty much nailed it.

Looking past the initial discomfort of exposure, Daniel knew this was good news—it would've been a red flag if they'd gotten it wrong. But Raoul's concern was unnecessary. Daniel had no interest in coming in half-assed, and he wasn't chasing miracles, or death, or revenge.

He was chasing truth.

5: ALL OR NOTHING AT ALL

Your goal this morning is simple," said Raoul. "Your goal is to hit me." They were standing on the mats of the Foundation dojo, a large, windowless white room, brightly lit by an array of fluorescent tubes suspended high above. One wall held racks of wooden swords, batons, and daggers. On another, a framed black-and-white photo of an old bearded Japanese man. A heavy bag hung from chains in one corner. Away from the mats, a small but well-equipped fitness center took up a section of the cavernous room. Beyond that, a climbing wall loomed over everything, reaching to the thirty-foot ceiling.

Large black letters stenciled on the fourth wall read: *Somewhere in the world someone is training harder than you. When you face him, who will live?*

Both Daniel and Raoul wore traditional white cotton Japanese gis, with white belts.

"You might want to put on some headgear," said Daniel. "You know, I—"

"Golden Gloves wunderkind. Yeah, I know. I spent five years attached to Tokyo Station for Mossad, trained in several of the world's best dojos. A thousand dollars says you can't even touch my face."

"Maybe *I* should put on some headgear." Daniel smiled.

"I'll be gentle with you. Now shut up and hit me." Raoul brought his fists together in front of his chest and offered a quick and shallow bow, then stood with hands open and knees slightly bent.

Daniel presented, falsely, as a southpaw. Because Raoul was a righty, Daniel circled right, away from the man's power punch. Midstride, he stopped and shuffled his feet and threw a fast left jab.

The world flipped upside down and Daniel hit the mat hard, his left hand burning, wrist joint screaming, bolts of lightning shooting up his forearm, his face pressed into the mat. He double tapped the mat with his right hand, Raoul let go, and the pain eased.

Daniel took his time in standing, working his wrist around, holding his left hand in his right. "Perhaps we should start with me trying to snatch a pebble from your hand," he said.

Raoul didn't smile. "You were a fine boxer, Daniel. And we'll use those skills—footwork, hand speed, parry and counter—but in our world, if you're fighting, it's for your life. No gloves, no rules, one survivor. You only throw a knuckle punch if you're damn sure it's going to land on flesh and not bone. Opponent ducks his chin and you break your hand on his forehead? Now you're fighting one-handed and consequently you die. If I fail in my responsibility to train you properly, you die. So you can take your pebble, Grasshopper, and shove it up your ass."

"Hey," said Daniel, "I didn't—"

"At the end of each day, we gather for drinks at the commissary bar. That's when we joke around. You set foot in this dojo, you are all business. Got it?"

"Got it."

"Good." Raoul set his stance once more. "Again. Don't box with me, Padre, just hit—"

Daniel's right fist flew forward even before Raoul had finished speaking, but again the world flipped upside down and an elbow slammed into his nose on the way to the mat. Again lightning shot through his wrist and up his forearm as the lights above went in and out of focus. He tapped out and Raoul let go of his hand.

"Get up."

Daniel stood and used the sleeve of his gi to catch the blood dripping from his nose. "I had to try again," he said with a shrug. "Like you said, I'm a boxer—it's what I know."

"You came to me as a boxer. You'll leave as a street fighter, or you won't leave at all. Instead of knuckle punches, you're going to learn hammer blows, elbow strikes, you'll use your knees and shins and feet. You'll learn to scratch and claw and gouge and bite—whatever it takes to survive."

Raoul continued talking as he walked to a plastic cooler at the edge of the mat. "We take a multidisciplinary approach to fighting. We start with aikido and judo, but we borrow heavily from a half-dozen other martial arts as well." He opened the cooler, pulled a white facecloth from the ice water, and wrung it out. "We like to call it Applied Aikido. Use aikido to control the body, then *apply* your knee to the ball sack, your forehead to the bridge of the nose—whatever works best in the moment. You'll study pressure points, nerve clusters. You'll learn how to knock a man unconscious with an open-handed slap. How to dislocate joints, incapacitate limbs. How to kill with either hand. When we're done with you, you won't walk into a room and see chairs, lamps, telephones, books; you'll see improvised weapons. Why hit with your hand when you can hit with something harder and save your hand from injury at the same time?" He handed the facecloth to Daniel. "Press on it, it's still bleeding."

Daniel pressed the freezing wet cloth against his nostrils.

"It's not busted. But it will be. You can expect at least a half-dozen trips to the infirmary over the coming months. You'll play connect-the-dots with your bruises and your new best friend will go by the name of Epsom salts. But you will learn. And you will be a skilled street fighter by the time you limp out of here." Raoul pointed at Daniel's face. "Left nostril's stopped, focus on the right."

Daniel folded the now-pink cloth, pressed the coldest part to the right side of his nose. "Look, Raoul, I don't want to be accused of jocularity, but you guys *really* need to work on your sales pitch."

Raoul caught his eye, held it. "I'm not selling, I'm telling. Not everyone is up for this life. No shame in saying it isn't the life for you. Doesn't matter if it's day one, day twenty, day sixty—you quit today, you still get the severance payout. I don't want you here unless you want to be here, fully knowing what that means."

Daniel pulled the wet cloth away from his face. The nosebleed was over. He tossed the cloth aside and squared his stance.

"Teach me."

6: ARE YOU READY (FOR THE FUTURE)?

It hasn't even been three full months," said Raoul. "I'm not sure he's ready."

"Well, *I* think I'm ready," said Daniel.

Carter Ames raised a hand. "Your opinion will be heard in full, Daniel. *After* we finish hearing the assessments." A sensible way to run the meeting, no doubt. But Daniel didn't particularly enjoy hearing himself discussed as if he weren't in the room.

Ames turned to Dave Christleib. Before coming to the Foundation fifteen years earlier, Christleib spent twenty years at the University of Chicago following in Mihaly Csikszentmihalyi's footsteps, deconstructing the psychology of optimal experience. He'd studied elite athletes, surgeons, chess masters, musicians, mystics—the full range of human endeavor. He was in charge of the Foundation's psychological training, which included meditation but went far beyond it. There was a training program for everything from stress management and critical thinking, to memory and perception, to telling and spotting lies.

Christleib didn't hesitate. "From my perspective, he's ready." To Raoul he added, "He's shown remarkable ability, aced every simulation."

"Simulations," said Raoul. "That's my point. We're talking about a high-risk undercover op. In the *real* world."

"He did forty-nine hours, no sleep, no food, minimal water, blazing strobe lights and 130 decibels of death metal around the clock. Remembered the details of his legend perfectly and never broke character under interrogation." It had been Daniel's least favorite part of the training program, and the memory of it put a chill through him, even now.

Raoul tapped his copy of the case file. "He breaks character in here, he won't have to worry about interrogation—they'll just put a bullet in his head." He shifted his focus to Daniel. "Red Ridge is a black ops facility, an off-book project of the Defense Intelligence Agency. It's an old coal mine in the middle of Nowhere, West Virginia. All below ground, only one way in or out. Once the door shuts behind you, you're on your own. You mess up in there, no way we can get you out alive."

From the other side of the table, Pat Wahlquist sucked air through his teeth, said, "I've worked with Daniel in the *real* world. Twice. I'm tellin' you, he came here ready. For Christ's sake, he killed Lucien-frickin-Drapeau."

Daniel knew Pat would be on his side, and he could see that the others gave the man's opinion significant weight. Although Pat had once been a Navy SEAL, he wasn't a *joiner* by nature and identified with no particular tribe, maybe because of his background. Part Cajun, part Irish, part African American, and part Choctaw, Pat was a tribe unto himself, and he had an independence of mind that people immediately sensed and respected.

"Raoul," said Carter Ames, "we can't very well connect the dots and get a picture of this game until we have more dots. The opportunity before us could yield information that the Council knows and is acting on, information at which we've been merely guessing thus far." He glanced at the same folder Raoul had been tapping, giving it an emphasis of his own. "This Major Blankenship may be experiencing Anomalous Information Transfer, and he may be gravely ill. Even if he doesn't die, we have no way of knowing when they might move him to a different facility. Daniel's experience makes him the right man to evaluate on-site, but I must defer to your judgment vis-à-vis training. If you have a *substantive* reason to believe he is not able to handle the assignment, now is the time to give it a name."

Raoul directed his answer at Daniel. "If I'm being a hard-ass, it's for your own good." He thought for a minute, came up with an idea. "All right, how about this: a simple challenge. Improvised pretexting, working solo. He passes it, I'm happy."

"What do you want me to do?" said Daniel.

"I want to see the front entrance of the Plaza Hotel shut down at exactly noon tomorrow." Raoul glanced at his watch. "Twenty-four hours from now. No calling in a bomb threat, nothing like that. I want to see hotel staff cheerfully shut the entrance and clear all pedestrians off the sidewalk in front. I want the place totally clear."

"Don't be a dick," said Pat. "What's that gonna—"

"Naw, it's cool," said Daniel. "I'll do it."

✢ ✢ ✢

It was just before one o'clock that afternoon when Daniel hopped out of the taxi on the west side of Central Park, in front of the elegant white facade of the Plaza Hotel, the wide sidewalk bustling with tourists and businesspeople. Uniformed valets took car keys and handed people claim chits and moved cars with Busby Berkeley precision. An almost constant stream of limousines and taxis pulled to the curb and away as bellmen assisted with luggage and doormen opened doors for guests coming and going.

The Plaza was a five-star hotel with five-star security, and now Daniel had to improvise a pretext that would convince them to shut down the main entrance and clear the sidewalk in the middle of the day, inconveniencing their five-star guests. It was mid-August with highs in the mid-nineties—guests would not love being ushered around the block to a side entrance, and the hotel would not love making their guests angry. And Daniel had to get them to do this *cheerfully*?

A simple challenge, Raoul had called it. Daniel smiled to himself. He'd grown to like Raoul, but the guy could be a bit of a bastard.

Better get to it. He strode through the doors and into the opulent lobby, crossed under the chandeliers to the far end, past the reservation desk, where an electronic board on the wall displayed the hotel's event listings.

The screen scrolled through the events for the following day. There was a pharmaceutical conference, a meeting of the International Broadcasters Association, a local Chamber of Commerce luncheon, a society wedding. None were of use to him. But then the screen scrolled over again.

Here was something: the annual banquet of the Tri-State Area Canadian Women's Clubs would take place the next day, cocktail reception at eleven thirty followed by lunch an hour later.

An idea began to form in Daniel's imagination. The seed of a plan.

It just might work.

Daniel left the hotel and cabbed it down to Macy's. Along the way, he used the web browser in his smartphone to read through the website of the Tri-State Area Canadian Women's Clubs. The New York, New Jersey, and Connecticut clubs each held separate monthly luncheons but tomorrow was when they all came together for a big, boozy brunch to plan joint events for the coming year. The website proclaimed it the premier event of the season. He navigated to the Bios page and studied the names and faces of their senior officers—president, vice president, secretary, and treasurer. All elegant ladies of a certain age and substantial means.

Yes, Daniel decided, this plan was tailor-made for them.

At Macy's, he bought an off-the-rack navy-blue single-breasted suit, a white shirt, a dark-blue tie with red and white diagonal stripes, a pair of shiny black leather shoes, and mirrored aviator sunglasses. He changed into his new clothes in a Starbucks men's room down the block, leaving his old clothes in the trash. At a souvenir shop on Sixth Avenue, he picked up two lapel pins, which he pinned on his right lapel. One was an American flag and the other featured the Great Seal of the United States with the spread-eagled eagle. He stopped at an electronics store to buy a Bluetooth earpiece. Then he had his hair cut very short at Mike's Barbershop on Thirty-Seventh Street. He cabbed it back uptown, arriving just before four o'clock. He had the driver drop him a block from the hotel, using the walk to prepare for his big bluff.

To run a pretext like this properly, Daniel really needed a team. All he had was a costume and a hip pocket full of attitude, so he'd have to focus on the basics. You don't sell the con, you sell your persona. If you start selling the con, the illusion falls apart. But sell the persona, and with a gentle nudge, the marks will sell themselves on the con.

Daniel took a few decompression breaths, straightening his posture to perfection, slipping into his new persona as he'd slipped into the new suit.

He decided on the name Mitchell as he crossed the street. He would be Mitchell. It had a solid sound, reliable. And it could be either a given name or a surname. So it was reliable, but also cagey.

With the earpiece in place and a copy of the *Washington Post* folded under his arm, Daniel crossed the lobby to the reception desk. "I need a suite for the next two nights," he said to the model-pretty Asian woman behind the desk as he pulled out his wallet. Her nametag said she was an assistant manager. Perfect.

"I'm sorry, sir, we're booked solid. We did have a cancellation— the Royal Terrace Suite. Three bedrooms, formal dining room, over twenty-five hundred square—"

"It'll suit us perfectly."

"All right. Two nights at twenty thousand dollars a night. How would you like to pay?"

Daniel put a black Visa card on the counter. It had no spending limit. The name on the card was UNEX Incorporated. As the young woman swiped his card, Daniel turned slightly away, pressed the button of his earpiece, and said, "Advance One to Base One: Accommodation for Celtic is confirmed."

The young woman tried to hide her curiosity. She handed his Visa back to him. "Would you like the room under a person's name, or . . ."

Daniel relaxed his posture a little, leaned forward on the counter. "We're traveling under the radar, Ms. Chen, so we need to keep this very low-key. I'm going to ask you not to share this with anyone who doesn't need to know."

"Of course."

"It's the vice president and his wife. They arrive, noon tomorrow. But no name on the reservation, okay?"

"Absolutely, of course. We're honored to have them stay with us. Anything you need, just let me know."

"We will," said Daniel, taking the key card.

On the way to the ballroom, Daniel checked the Canadian Women's Clubs website again, memorizing the names and faces of the senior officers. The day before the big event, it was a safe bet that at least one officer of the club would be on hand to supervise preparations, and it would be better if he didn't have to ask someone to point her out.

Just inside the ballroom, he spotted the club president, Mary Donovan. She was about sixty-five, an attractive woman—although clearly face-lifted—with frosted blond hair and perfect makeup, wearing a white Chanel suit over a pink silk blouse.

"Excuse me, Ms. Donovan?" he said.

"*Mrs.* Donovan," she said with a sly smile.

"Yes, ma'am. My name is Mitchell. I'm not sure if you've been made aware, the vice president and his wife will be visiting this hotel during your brunch tomorrow—"

"Surely you don't have security concerns about *our* group."

"Oh no, you misunderstand. The vice president was very pleased to learn that you'll be here. You see, his wife has extended family in Nova Scotia . . . Halifax. They both have great affection for Canada. I'm here to ask you if they might stop by to say hello during the cocktail hour before brunch."

Mary Donovan's eyes went wide. Botox kept the rest of her face from moving, but she was clearly thrilled. "Oh my, that would be lovely," she said.

"Just an informal visit, you understand. They'll stop in around noon, mingle a bit. The vice president may say a few words. And of course some of you ladies may wish to have pictures taken with them."

"Yes, that's terrific! We can hold off the meal until one o'clock, or they're welcome to stay and dine with us."

"I'm afraid that won't be possible. They really only have a brief hole in their itinerary—twenty minutes maximum—but they would love to see you and your group."

"And we will love to see them, Mr. Mitchell. Thank you so much!"

"Great. If you need to coordinate anything with the hotel, just speak with Miss Chen. She's the manager taking care of us." He started to turn away, stopped as if remembering something. "One other thing, Mrs. Donovan, and this is very important: The vice president and his wife are looking for a nice, quiet weekend as a couple in New York, away from the press corps. So please ask your members to use discretion. We'd hate to find a dozen news vans parked out front tomorrow."

"You can count on us," said Mary Donovan, beaming as much as her face would allow.

✦ ✦ ✦

The formal dining table in the Royal Terrace Suite could seat ten. Daniel sat at it alone, eating a room-service filet mignon with a mélange of root vegetables under a port reduction. There was a fully stocked bar in the suite, but he limited himself to one bottle of good red wine, and he quit with a third left in the bottle. He couldn't afford to be fuzzy in the morning.

His cell phone rang as he was rising from the table.

"Yup?"

"What the hell are you up to over there, Padre?" said Raoul.

"Just working on your challenge."

"You managed to spend over forty *thousand* dollars in the last six hours. What, are you trying to set a record?"

"You didn't stipulate a budget," said Daniel. "Anyway, we're set for tomorrow. Don't be late or you'll miss the show."

"You sound pretty confident."

"Like you said, it was a simple challenge."

"Oh really? Then how about a side wager? A thousand dollars says you don't make it happen."

"How about this," Daniel countered, "I lose, I pay you a thousand dollars. I win, you never call me Padre again."

Raoul laughed. "You're on, Padre."

"And that'll be the last time," said Daniel, ending the call.

✦ ✦ ✦

Daniel took breakfast in his room while scanning the newspaper for any mention of the vice president. There'd been no mention in the previous day's paper and he was relieved to find none this morning. He kept CNN on in the background and kept an ear open. A simple news item about the veep at some function anywhere in the world other than New York City would be enough to sink his plan if the wrong people saw it.

He checked his watch: eight forty-five. It would be better if the hotel approached him rather than the other way around, and he hoped it would happen soon. He'd asked both Chen and Donovan for discretion, but he was counting on human nature. He'd given

Chen implicit permission to discuss the visit with whomever she thought needed to know, and he'd flat-out instructed Donovan to tell the members of her club and ask them to use discretion. He'd also invited Donovan to discuss the matter with Chen. He figured by now 80 percent of the hotel staff and every well-heeled Canadian woman in the tri-state area had heard the news.

The knock on his door came at 9:01. He opened the door to a man in a charcoal-gray suit. The man wore no nametag, but Daniel knew him by sight, having found his LinkedIn and Facebook profiles on the Internet the night before. He was the Plaza's director of security. His name was Anthony Root, but his online conversations revealed that everyone who knew him called him Tony. He lived in Newark. He was a fan of the Giants and the Mets and the Devils. He was married with two kids and a golden retriever named Goldie. Daniel hadn't bothered to memorize the names of Tony's wife and kids, his date of birth and wedding anniversary, the name of his high school, or his favorite books, movies, music, and food. But it was all there online.

Before the man could speak, Daniel said, "Mr. Root, come in."

"Thank you. I understand we're having a very important visitor today and I thought we should coordinate, so we're ready for the, uh, the motorcade . . ." Root stammered to a stop as he took in the room. "There's usually a lot more of you guys. I—I don't understand . . ."

Daniel put a hand on Root's shoulder. "Listen, Tony. Sometimes even the most powerful people in the world just need to get out like regular people living a regular life. You can't imagine the pressure living in that fishbowl. So there'll be no motorcade, as such. Sometime between noon and 12:05, two unmarked limousines will pull up to your front entrance. Our VIPs will exit the second car with two of our men and will walk into your hotel like regular folks. Okay?"

"Um, sure."

"Now here's what we need from you: At exactly 11:55, have your security team shut the front entrance to pedestrian traffic and divert guests to alternate exits. And you need to clear the sidewalk in front. The entire block, no foot traffic on this side. That's it. Once inside the hotel, our VIPs will head straight for the ballroom to meet with the Canadian Women's Club. As soon as they've cleared the lobby, you reopen the entrance. Got it?"

"I'll see that it's done."

"Good. Remember, this is a low-key visit. If word leaks out to the media and it comes from anyone on your team . . . you're responsible."

✣✣✣

At exactly noon, Daniel stood on the sidewalk in front of the Plaza Hotel, suppressing a smile. Nobody came or went through the front doors, security staff waved taxis and limos around the corner to the side entrance and politely maneuvered pedestrians at either end of the block to the other side of the street.

Daniel stood and admired the view. Okay, it wasn't an Edward Hopper canvas, but he'd created the entire scene out of pixie dust. In its own way, it was a minor work of art. A little pride was justified.

The rear window of a stretch limo parked at the opposite curb rolled down, and Daniel could see Raoul and Pat sitting in back. He jogged across the street and climbed in to find Pat laughing, saying to Raoul, "Pay up, buddy." Raoul stuffed a wad of money into Pat's hand as the car pulled away from the curb.

"Nice goin', Dan," said Pat.

"Thanks."

"So what was the scam?"

"They're expecting the arrival of the vice president and his wife," said Daniel, "and I feel terribly guilty. I'm afraid the tri-state area Canadian women are in for a disappointment."

"Impersonating a secret service agent carries long jail time—" Raoul cut himself off before saying "Padre."

"I never actually told anyone I was a secret service agent. And I never said the veep's name. I could've been talking about the vice president of UNEX Incorporated and his wife. I just invited the right people to make the right assumptions. Nothing I couldn't talk my way out of with a good attorney by my side." Daniel smiled. "I can assume you guys have a few of those on call, right?"

Raoul eyed Daniel's secret service getup and shook his head, laughing through his nose. "You got some balls on ya, man. I'll give you that."

7: SYMPATHY FOR THE DEVIL

Red Ridge, West Virginia

*T*oday *is a good day to die. But I've decided to stay alive until tomorrow.*

The sergeant behind the desk went a little ashen when he read what came up on his computer screen.

"*Well?*" said Daniel.

The young man snapped to attention. "Uh, I'm very sorry for the inconvenience, Colonel Pomerance, sir. Someone at the Pentagon must've forgotten to forward your electronic pass."

"Don't shift blame," said Daniel as he brushed past, "it's unbecoming."

He put his right palm on the reader and waited for the green light. After ten excruciating seconds, the light came on. The door buzzed and the sentry pulled it open.

Daniel walked through. He tried to ignore the sharp metallic report that echoed through the hallway as the door locked behind him.

He failed to ignore it.

Raoul's words came back to him now: *Once the door shuts behind you, you're on your own. You mess up in there, no way we can get you out alive.*

Daniel took a deep centering breath, in through the nose and out through the mouth. His body stopped pumping adrenaline into his bloodstream. He strode toward the man struggling into a white doctor's coat while hurrying up the hallway to greet him.

"Sir, I apologize, they didn't tell me they were sending anyone."

"So I gathered," said Daniel. "Where is he?"

"On level 3. Elevator's down the hall." They began walking.

"Brief me along the way. I don't have a lot of time."

"Yes, we can stop at my office on 2 and pick up the file."

Daniel didn't break stride. "Was I not speaking English when I said I don't have a lot of time? Just tell me what you know and stick to the most salient points. Details can wait until I decide if this is worth my attention."

"Yes, sir. Patient is Major Shields Blankenship, of South Carolina."

"Christ, I know his name. Describe his condition."

"He arrived to us gravely ill, but with no accompanying report."

"You were not informed where he arrived from?"

"That's right, sir. Colonel Dillman did not offer that information when he checked Blankenship in." They stepped into an open elevator. There were twelve underground floors. The doctor pressed B3, and the door closed.

"Go on."

"The patient's condition worsened while we sent his blood for analysis. We put him on intravenous antibiotics and saline right away of course, but I'm afraid he came to us too late."

"He's dead?"

"Oh no, he's going to live—the antibiotics are doing their job—but I feel certain he suffered some brain damage from the very high fever before our intervention brought it down." They stepped off the elevator and continued down the hall.

"Cut to the chase, Doctor. Why. Am. I. Here."

"Well, sir, this is strange, but the patient came to believe that he was, um, possessed."

"Possessed."

"Yes. By Satan."

"You have got to be shitting me."

"No, sir. But that's not why I contacted the Pentagon. You see, while claiming to be Satan, Major Blankenship began talking about the plague outbreak in fourteenth-century Europe, particularly in Norway. Some of it was disjointed but there was a definite narrative to his story, about families ripped apart and towns wiped out by the Black Death. He kept mentioning a town called Mandal; he seems obsessed with the place. So I looked it up, and there is such a town in Norway, in a valley of the same name. And other details of his narrative—other place names and the timeline of the Black Death's spread across the country, for example—are also accurate. But the patient's ancestry all goes to England and Ireland. No Norway."

"So maybe he has a Norwegian history fetish."

"And then he started speaking fluent Norwegian," said the doctor, "and with an authentic Norwegian accent." He shrugged. "My father-in-law is from Norway and he has the same accent. So I called up Major Blankenship's personnel file and found nothing in his history to suggest he would know Norwegian. And I thought, *What if the man isn't who he claims to be?* The situation looked to me, sir, like a possible security threat. So I called it in. We're now recording him 24/7, catching everything he says."

"You were right to call it in," said Daniel. "Current status?"

"He became violent, so we've restrained him and started him on Valium. He's conscious and lucid, but no longer manic. His mind is somewhat"—he searched for the right word—"*dampened*, if you'll allow the lay term." The doctor came to a stop just outside an unmarked door.

Daniel glanced at his watch. Eighteen minutes had elapsed. If all was well, the Foundation would have possession of the computer network for another forty-two. "Now I need you to go directly to your office and upload all records on this case to my office at the Pentagon. Everything you've got." He reached for the door handle.

"Sir, I think you may want me with you for the patient interview, for a medical perspective—"

Daniel waved him off. "You've got your orders, Doctor. I'll be fine." With a sharp nod toward the elevator, he said, "Go. Do. Now."

The doctor scurried off to obey his orders.

Daniel stepped into the room, where a man lay on a slightly inclined hospital bed, his wrists and ankles bound to the gleaming chrome rails by padded leather cuffs. A wide leather belt secured his waist to the bed. The man was awake but silent. A large flat-screen television monitor was mounted on the wall behind his head. The screen was divided into four segments, displaying the facility's front entrance, reception room, elevator, and this very room. On the screen, Daniel saw himself from behind, the man in the bed facing the camera lens, but not looking into it. The man stared unblinking at a spot on the ceiling above the camera.

Daniel started the voice recorder on his smartphone and approached the bed.

The man continued to stare at the ceiling.

Daniel threw a glance at the spot where the man was looking. "I don't see anything fascinating up there, do you?"

The man didn't move. Daniel stepped to the edge of the bed, clanged his ring three times against the chrome rail just above the wrist restraint. "Anybody home?"

The man finally turned and looked Daniel in the eye. "Please don't bang on the rail."

"Wasn't sure you realized I was here."

"I expected someone like you to come along."

"This may be an odd question," said Daniel, "but am I speaking with Major Shields Blankenship right now?"

The man's smile bordered on impish. "No."

"Then what shall I call you?"

"You know who I am. And I know who you are, *Pater*."

Pater? It was the Norwegian word for "father." But how could the man possibly know? Daniel felt a little dizzy, but he maintained his composure, gave nothing away on the outside.

He said, "Prince of Darkness then, is it?"

"Just call me Lucifer. Major Blankenship has been placed on temporary hiatus. I need use of his vocal cords, so I've taken possession of his brain."

"What about his soul?" Daniel kept any sarcasm out of his tone.

"Don't be silly; I've had the boy's soul for years. And I'll have yours soon enough."

All of the man's physical cues indicated that he believed what he was saying. But physical cues were somewhat muted by Valium—in fact, people had long used the drug to beat polygraph tests—so these cues were of limited value. Daniel said, "And you need use of Major Blankenship's vocal cords so you can talk about a tiny village in Norway during the Black Death. Is that correct?" This time he didn't hide the sarcasm.

"I know what you're thinking," the man said, "but you didn't really expect me to spin the major's head around and make him spit pea soup, did you?"

"Actually, I'm thinking you've had a high fever, which has caused some damage to your brain."

The man continued as if Daniel hadn't said anything. "Then again, you don't strike me as much of a priest, so I suppose that makes us even."

"I'm not a priest."

"Liar. Your uniform fools men, it doesn't fool Lucifer."

Daniel glanced at his watch. "I have neither the time nor inclination to debunk your identity. Lucifer, not Lucifer—doesn't matter to me. I don't even believe in the devil."

"It was 1349," said the man. He blinked very slowly, lids like window shades drawn shut and raised again. *"Det skjedde før i Mandal, hvor det åpenbare var engang skjult og det skjulte vil åpenbares . . ."*

Daniel's eye was drawn by movement on the screen behind the bed. Three men had entered the reception room. Two were military men dressed, like the soldiers stationed here, in unmarked uniforms. The third was a tall blond man wearing the uniform of a Roman Catholic priest.

Conrad Winter.

And he was now talking to the sergeant at the desk.

Daniel's gut clenched as he stared at the screen, his mind racing.

Conrad Winter was in this facility . . . and would know Daniel on sight.

Mess up in there, no way we can get you out alive.

"Bad news then, is it?" said the man strapped to the bed, regaining his smile.

Daniel took a deep breath, slowing his mind. He raised his watch and clicked the button to stop the chronograph, zeroed it, started it again, all while watching the screen as Conrad Winter placed his palm on the reader and walked through the inner door. Then another deep breath while visualizing the floor plan from the case file. Anything less than perfect timing and their paths would surely cross, and that would be that.

He held position, focused on the empty elevator in the bottom-left of the screen. Another slow centering breath, as Conrad Winter and his two military escorts entered the elevator. Conrad pushed a button. The door slid closed.

Time to go.

As Daniel reached the door, the man in the bed called out, "*Til vi treffes igjen, 'Prest.*"

Daniel jogged down the hallway to the stairwell, then up the stairs, grateful they were keeping the man on B3 and not B12. Slowing enough to quiet his footfalls as he passed B2. The doctor had said his office was on 2 and it was possible that Conrad was headed there first.

Keeping his speed in check, Daniel entered the ground-floor hallway and strode back to the door to the reception room. He pushed on the bar, but nothing happened. He rapped on the steel door three times with his ring, glaring at the camera mounted to the wall.

The door buzzed and opened, held by the sentry.

Daniel addressed the sergeant at the desk. "Your paranoid doctor has just wasted a day of my life. Call the car around, I'm leaving." Without waiting for a reply, he crossed to the exterior door. The soldier with the rifle stepped aside and Daniel said, "The door, sergeant. Now." He pulled his mirrored aviators from his breast pocket and put them on.

The thick metal door buzzed. Daniel stepped out into hot West Virginia sunshine. He checked his watch—six minutes since Conrad's arrival. They'd let him walk out of the place, so it was a solid bet that Conrad didn't know of his presence before arriving. But how long would it take? Did he know of Daniel's presence by now? Two minutes from now? Two minutes ago? Daniel whipped out his cell phone, texted:

Blown—CW on-site—SOS.

A car pulled around the corner. The same black Lincoln Town Car stretch limo that had picked him up at the Greenbrier Hotel that morning. And the same young soldier stepped out to open the back door for him. Daniel let him.

"Back to the hotel," he said as the car rocked into motion, "and step on it. I have *real* work waiting."

"Yes, sir," said the soldier.

They cruised down the treelined two-lane highway for about twelve miles before everything went sideways. The soldier in front lifted a cell phone to his ear and said, "Mobile One. Yes, sir. Affirmative." A solid black divider began to rise, isolating Daniel in the backseat. Just before it closed, Daniel heard, "Please repeat that instruction, sir."

And then he was alone.

The car began to slow. Daniel's phone vibrated. The incoming text read:

Seatbelt.

The car slowed further, then swung into a U-turn as Daniel clicked his seatbelt and pulled down the center armrest and held it tight, bracing his head against the seatback.

Something hard blasted through the windows in the front of the car. The car shook, swerved, crashed into something, and bounced off it. Daniel whipped from right to left, smacking the side of his head against the window frame.

Then everything just stopped. Daniel's head hurt. His ears were ringing and the world was muffled but he heard the muted click of the door locks. The door beside him opened and Pat Wahlquist reached in with one hand and pulled him out. A grenade launcher hung from Pat's other hand.

"You might not wanna look in front," said Pat, "that guy's got no head." He pointed at a green Subaru idling empty across the road, front doors standing open. "Your chariot awaits."

Daniel heard all the words but they sounded far away, somewhere behind the ringing in his ears, which had grown into a wall of sound separating Daniel from the world around him.

"What?" he said.

Pat pulled him toward the getaway car. "Dude, we gotta motor. Snap to."

8: RAT RACE

Sometimes stopping for a coffee on the way to a meeting can change the world. Everyone does it, but nobody considers how that simple decision splits the arrow of time, creates a fork in the road, chooses one path over the other, thus cementing their fate until the next decision.

It had taken twenty minutes to get off the highway, load up on fast carbs and black coffee, and get back on the highway. Twenty minutes. Had they arrived twenty minutes earlier, Conrad Winter would've been able to intervene before Dr. Assclown uploaded the bloody file to the bloody *enemy*.

And the coffee wasn't even good.

Conrad dropped the computer cord he'd ripped—too late—from the wall. The doctor still sat at his computer, looking like he might have a stroke. Conrad turned to his DIA liaison, said, "Colonel Dillman, alert the driver. Return the intruder here, preferably alive and in great discomfort. And show me what we've got on tape."

* * *

Unbelievable. It was Daniel Byrne on the bloody tape. That little prick. Conrad had half expected Daniel would end up working for Carter Ames, but to encounter him in the field so soon? Was it even possible, could Daniel have been a Foundation asset before he left the Vatican? No, he'd shown no sign of it, and Conrad had kept a close eye. It was as it appeared; Trinity's case had brought them together.

So the Foundation had rushed Daniel into the field. Good.

On the tape, Daniel Byrne was standing facing Major Blankenship's bed. Blankenship was saying, *"Det skjedde før i Mandal, hvor det åpenbare var engang skjult og det skjulte vil åpenbares . . ."*

Conrad's cell phone vibrated and he checked the screen. Charles Carruthers, number-two man to Conrad's boss, the director of the Council for World Peace. *This day just keeps getting better and better.*

"Yes?"

"The director requires an in-person progress report, without delay," said Carruthers.

"I can't come to Singapore right—"

"We're not in Singapore, we're in Barbados."

"Even so. The situation's too fluid right now and I have to make a stop in Atlanta."

"The director has pressing issues of his own, Conrad. This will not sit well."

"Hang on," Conrad put the call on hold as Colonel Dillman waved for his attention.

Dillman patted his short gray mustache, said, "We've lost contact with the driver."

"What?"

"His cell's gone dead. We've dispatched an intercept team but they're nine minutes out."

There was no choice to be made. Conrad knew he had to draw a proverbial line in the sand—now was the time. The director had assigned this project to him; he'd just have to trust Conrad's judgment. He took the phone off hold. "Tell the director the Foundation knows about this one. They sent an operative and they have a copy of the medical records. I'll brief him by sat phone once I'm in the air"—a glance at his watch—"two hours from now. I'll get to Barbados as soon as I can but if I don't make that stop in Atlanta, this whole thing could blow up in our faces. Conrad out."

He ended the call, signaled to Dillman, and the two men stepped out into the hallway.

"We tie this off," said Conrad, "right now. You need to give the order."

Dillman simply nodded and led the way back into the office. He walked straight to the doctor, still slumped in his chair, and barked, "On your feet, captain."

The doctor stood, a little unsteadily. "Yes, sir?"

"You just sent top secret records to one of the most dangerous terrorist networks on the planet. The legal word for that is *treason*, and the penalty for treason is death."

"But—but . . . I didn't *know*," pleaded the doctor. "I made a mistake, sir. I'm not a terrorist."

"If I say you knew, you knew," said Dillman without pity. "And if I say you didn't, then the penalty is ten to twenty in the stockade followed by dishonorable discharge, your pension stripped, medical license revoked." He stood in place, boring holes into the doctor with his gaze, as the doctor's own eyes welled up with tears. Finally he said, "But I will give you one chance to prove yourself worthy of my effort to cover this mess up and keep you in your current position."

"Anything—anything," the doctor sputtered, "I'll do whatever it takes."

Dillman glanced at Conrad. Conrad gave him a nod. Dillman turned back to the doctor. "You will now take us downstairs, where you will prepare a syringe and send our brain-damaged major to a peaceful and merciful death."

The doctor's gaze hit the floor for a moment but quickly returned, carrying a mix of fear and guilt . . . and relief.

"Yes, sir," he said.

9: LAST DANCE

Washington, DC

Evan Sage returned the cell phone to his breast pocket and adjusted his tie as he approached the table. Vanessa gestured at his untouched salmon, room temperature by now. Her plate was two-thirds empty, as was the bottle of good French rosé on the table, the condensation like cold tears prisming the flickering candlelight.

She sipped her wine as he took his chair again. "Welcome back." A forced smile, aborted.

"I'm sorry," he said.

"Twenty-seven minutes. Long break between courses, Evan. I understand it's work, but I can't pretend to be happy about it."

"I know, sweetie, and I am sorry but it's about to get worse." He caught the waiter's eye across the dining room, signaled for the check. "There's a situation. I have to leave right now."

"Where?"

"Out of the city."

Vanessa's expression hardened at his evasion. "I don't suppose you're allowed to tell me for how long?"

"I don't know how long."

"Days? Weeks? Months? Years?"

"C'mon, don't be like that. A couple of days, maybe a few weeks."

Vanessa put her wineglass down, picked up her red leather clutch. "Well, happy anniversary of the day we fucking met."

They cabbed it back to their stylish Georgetown townhouse in heavy silence. When he tried to open conversation, Vanessa cut him off with a look that said: *Civilized people do not air their differences in front of others.*

✤ ✤ ✤

Vanessa's townhouse, really. She'd made him an equal partner in choosing the place, but she'd bought it with her own money. He could never afford a place like this on a government salary.

Evan had to give her credit: The money didn't matter to her. She found his choice of public service noble, and she even urged him not to chase the big bag of money regularly dangled in front of him by intelligence contractors in the private sector. Not that he needed urging, but it was her way of assuring him the money really didn't matter.

The Department of Homeland Security paid Evan $162,000 per year, which is not a terrible salary until you compare it. The private sector offered Evan a *starting* salary of between $650,000 and $780,000, plus bonuses, a luxury expense account, and the opportunity for rapid advancement.

But Evan was performing a public service, defending his *country*—god how he hated the word "homeland"; it sounded just one step shy of "fatherland"—and his fellow citizens. Working his ass off for less.

Evan found the word "noble" embarrassing whenever Vanessa said it, although he would go as far as "honorable." Truth was, he'd gotten into the field because his inner twelve-year-old thought it would be fun to catch Bad Guys.

Turns out, it was a lot of fun.

But it was getting harder all the time. Evan had graduated the Department of Homeland Security training program in a class of forty-three—along with twenty-seven other men and fifteen women. In the years since, the CIA had poached four men and three women, the NSA had poached six men and four women. The private sector intelligence corporations had hired away fourteen men and three women.

Leaving three men and five women from the class of forty-three. Which might have suggested that women were, in the aggregate, more motivated by public service than men, or more loyal, or less willing to compete in the private sector.

Or some combination of the three.

Anyway, there was a massive brain drain and the Intelligence and Analysis division of DHS had become the redheaded stepchild of the intelligence community. Morale was low, and the constant churn in the executive suites ensured it would stay low—the culture was unstable, shifting every time they installed someone new at the top.

Frankly, it sucked as a place to work.

But Evan really enjoyed catching Bad Guys.

* * *

Vanessa dropped her purse on the black granite kitchen counter. "I'll put coffee on."

"We can't let this come between us," Evan offered.

"Little late for that." Vanessa filled the coffeemaker's water reservoir, spooned grounds into the basket. "Honey, you're forty-two years old. When will it be enough?"

He wanted to say: *When terrorists stop trying to kill us.* He wanted to say: *When are you going to pull your head out of your privileged Harvard ass and wake up to what the world is?*

He judged neither would be helpful.

He said, "I stop dirty bombs from exploding in our subways. I stop airliners from falling out of the sky."

"And you get off on the action. Still gives you a boner."

"So? I get off on saving American lives. Sue me. My job is more important—"

"Than being a pension fund manager?" she snapped. "Looking after the life savings of Americans? Bravo—score a point for you."

"I was going to say, more important than anything else I can imagine myself doing. Not everything is about you."

"Actually, nothing is about me, or even about us." Vanessa shook her head. "Hasn't been, for a while. And I'm not asking you to stop saving lives, I'm asking what kind of life we're building together." Her left thumb began absently turning her engagement ring in circles around her slender finger as she spoke. An unconscious gesture that had become more frequent this year. Their engagement was now twenty-eight months long and they still hadn't set a wedding date. "I'm asking, when do you plan to stop playing James Bond and start playing M?"

"I never lied to you about my ambitions," Evan said. The silence lingered as they looked into each other's eyes, neither willing to budge. He tried to lighten the mood with "And I'm not a spy," but it fell flat.

Vanessa dug in her bag and lit a Benson & Hedges menthol on the gas range. "Shit, everyone's a spy nowadays. The world just keeps getting meaner." She blew out a long stream of smoke. "I know you think I'm being selfish—fine, maybe I am. Maybe it's hypocritical, but I want to live something that at least resembles a normal life. And I want to live it with you."

Nothing Evan could say would fix this. Tossing out the word "bioweapon" might make this particular trip less of a heat score, but he knew there would be blowback. If he said it, it would actually increase Vanessa's desire to see him riding a desk in DC. He stole a glance at the clock above the range. He poured a mug of coffee mid-brew, returning the carafe to the machine in time to avoid a flood. He added a little cold tap water to his mug so he didn't have to wait for it to cool, took a long sip, and chose his next words.

"Vanessa, I want to work this out but I have to meet my team at Joint Base Andrews in seventy-two minutes so I can go play superspy and save more lives. I'm sorry you have a problem with that. But I love you too much to mislead you. I have zero intention of becoming a desk jockey in the foreseeable future. At some point, yes, but . . . five years? I doubt it. Ten years? Maybe—probably. I just can't make that a promise. You need to decide if that makes this relationship untenable for you."

She shook her head. "Jesus. The way you talk about it, you sound like a goddamn lawyer negotiating a deal."

He drained the coffee mug in three swallows. "I have to pack." He stepped forward and wrapped his arms around her, leaning down for a kiss. She returned it, but it was a kiss laden with sadness.

A kiss good-bye.

"Okay," she said, stepping back from him, "let the record show, you never lied to me about your ambitions." She took another deep drag on her cigarette, blew it out. "But when you get back from your new adventure, you need to move out."

10: BIG SHOT

London, England

The immigration officer behind the counter at Heathrow swiped Daniel's passport and read what came up on the monitor, then turned his attention to the declaration card.

He said, "The nature of your business, Mr. Byrne?" His accent said Birmingham.

"Management consultancy," said Daniel.

"For who?"

Daniel handed over a UNEX Incorporated business card bearing his name. Title: Senior Analyst. He said, "We work for Fortune 500 companies, help them find efficiencies."

The officer gave Daniel a hard look. He flipped through the pages of immigration stamps in the passport. "You were in Nigeria six months ago. Was that business or personal?"

"We have clients in the petroleum industry."

"And how long do you intend to be in the United Kingdom on this visit?"

"Shouldn't be more than a week or two."

"Local place of residence?"

"Claridge's, just like I wrote on the card." Daniel allowed a little annoyance into his tone.

The officer stamped Daniel's passport, finally. "Best of luck with your *efficiencies*," he said, not even pretending to mean it.

✣ ✣ ✣

Daniel settled into the back of the big black cab for the ride to Mayfair. He loved visiting London, and you couldn't beat their taxi service. He'd always enjoyed the ride into the city, but this time he barely took in the view, his interaction with the immigration officer still nagging at him.

The management consultant role was now Daniel's official legend—his NOC, or non-official cover—the go-to cover story when dealing in his own name with the world outside the Foundation. He'd learned enough about the job to bluff his way through conversation, even with real management consultants. He could talk about maximizing externalities and the disintermediation of middlemen in the supply chain and the extraordinary profit potential of metacapitalism until he put himself to sleep. Even thinking about it made him wonder: *Who would choose to do that for a living?*

But as management consultants, Foundation operatives could plausibly live on the road, and that road could reach every country on the globe. They had cover for meeting with people in every major industry, government officials, academics . . . at a certain fiscal altitude, consultants were simply part of the landscape.

Although his legend might rankle people like the immigration officer, it connected Daniel to money and power, which made it useful because frontline civil servants have learned that messing with people connected to money and power is bad for the career. Everyone's got mouths to feed.

Maybe that's all it was: The officer was a working-class bloke, well aware that when a fancy consultant helps a company find efficiencies, working people get the sack.

Yes, probably that's all it was. Daniel pulled out his cell phone, texted:

Border agent showed keen interest. Possibly nothing.

Whenever a Foundation field operative crossed borders, a computer at headquarters monitored various digital networks across the intelligence community, so they'd know if an agent's entry had raised any red flags.

The answer to Daniel's text came back only a few seconds after he hit Send:

Your name hasn't popped. Will inform of any change.—A. O.

A. O. was Ayo Onatade, who, because of her expertise as lead analyst on the Foundation's AIT team, had been assigned to shepherd Daniel on this operation. Although now based in New York, Ayo had only lived in the United States for five years. Originally from Nigeria, she'd moved with her parents to England as a child. She'd attended the best schools, and after Cambridge she'd risen through the ranks of support staff in the judiciary, eventually becoming the right-hand woman of a superior court justice, helping grease the wheels of the old empire. She was plugged into Britain's political machine at the highest level, knew her way around the House of Lords and Number 10, but what she'd learned there had led her to join Carter Ames and the Fleur-de-Lis Foundation.

Ayo was beautiful, full figured and mahogany skinned, with ferocity behind her eyes and a sharp, dry wit. For Daniel, the attraction had been immediate but he'd decided pursuing it to find out if the attraction went both ways was a bad idea, regardless of the Foundation's pro-fraternization policy. She was his first point of contact at headquarters when he was in the field, and that wasn't something he wanted to complicate.

✢ ✢ ✢

"What did you make of the man?" Ayo had asked the previous day when Daniel and Pat had returned to New York from West Virginia. Daniel's ears were no longer ringing, but voices still sounded far away so he leaned in to hear. She smelled lovely. "You've seen the real thing before. Is it AIT?"

"It *might* be," said Daniel. "He spoke Norwegian but that's not akin to speaking backwards, is it? Anyone can learn a foreign language. He might've learned it as part of a secret DIA assignment that was kept out of his personnel file. Or I suppose, as the doctor suspected, he might not be Major Blankenship at all—he could be a plant, an impostor. Exceedingly less likely than the first scenario, but not impossible."

"He called you *father*," Raoul said, flipping to a page in a file folder. "Look, he spoke two sentences in Norwegian during your interview. The first translates to: *It happened before in Mandal, where the revealed was once concealed and the concealed shall be revealed*. And the second: *Until we meet again, Priest*. But there's no way he could've known you were a priest—and don't start with the 'I'm not a priest' thing. You know what I mean."

"No, I get it," said Daniel. "It threw me at first, too. But then Conrad Winter showed up. See, Blankenship didn't know I was a priest, he was *expecting* a priest. And a priest did show up. Maybe he overheard the doctor telling someone a priest was coming, or maybe he'd requested a priest. Again, either is a more plausible explanation."

"But—"

"I'm not saying it isn't AIT. It probably is, given Conrad's presence there. I'm simply saying I didn't see enough for us to independently draw that conclusion. I also didn't see evidence of trickery. We just don't have enough information."

"Actually, we have a *lot* of information," said Ayo, "from the medical file."

Raoul shot Daniel with his finger, "Nice play with the doctor, by the way, getting him to send all this."

"Told you he was ready," said Pat from his place of repose, leaning back in his chair, alligator boots on the table, a bottle of root beer in one hand, bendy straw between his teeth. He shot Raoul with a finger of his own, then raised the finger and blew on it.

"A little focus, boys," said Ayo, opening the file folder in front of her. "Our Major Blankenship—who is not an impostor—was suffering from a strain of the bubonic plague, which we hoped would lead us to wherever he'd been before being shipped back home. He'd contracted the plague and he was talking about the plague, so it's reasonable to suspect he knew the disease was present wherever he got sick. We scanned recent World Health Organization reports of outbreaks." She shook her head. "There have been some isolated incidents, which we're looking into, but nothing of significance since Madagascar last December."

Daniel remembered reading the report on "physiological triggers" in his training material. The percentage of people experiencing AIT who were also suffering from certain maladies was, while small, disproportionate to the general population. Brain tumors and traumatic brain injuries, epilepsy, meningitis, schizophrenia, people who'd been pulled back from the very edge of death after flatlining, people who'd been hit by lightning . . .

Then he remembered the AIT prehistory brief. He said, "None of the modern strains of the plague are triggers, but it was once a trigger, a long time ago . . . is this a resurrection of an ancient strain?"

Carter Ames said, "More likely a new strain. Bacteria mutate, evolve. It's how they survive." He folded his hands on the table. "The man has the plague and he has AIT. Correlation does not imply causation, but we have to consider the possibility."

Ayo said, "For now, we operate on the assumption that this plague may indeed be a trigger."

Raoul said to Daniel, "You're on the red-eye to England, leaving in three hours. Bags are already packed."

Pat took his feet off the table, slurped the remaining root beer from the bottle. "Don't suppose I get to visit Her Majesty with Dan."

"Afraid not," said Ayo. "The files also tell us that Major Blankenship worked in DIA directly under a Colonel Michael Dillman. Dillman was one of the soldiers who signed in with Conrad Winter at Red Ridge."

"And Colonel Dillman is one spooky-as-hell spook," said Raoul. "There's almost nothing on this guy in the last twenty years, since he transferred from Air Force Intelligence to DIA. I mean, Dillman is so *shadow* he makes our fictional Colonel Walter Pomerance look like an open book. Your task is to find him and track him."

"Why do I always get the easy jobs?" said Pat.

But Daniel wasn't paying attention, thinking, *Leaving in three hours? Bags already packed?* After the day he'd just had, one night to decompress with some single malt did not seem an unreasonable expectation.

Unless . . .

"Wait, how bad is this new strain?" he asked.

"We don't yet know," said Carter Ames.

"Blankenship was responding to large dosages of Cipro," said Ayo, "so we know it can be treated. But this new iteration of the bug looks different, and more robust. We've forwarded the medical records to an ally—leading microbiologist, based in London. She'll brief you on what she learns. If we can find out what the hell we're dealing with, we might have some actual dots to connect for once."

11: THE DEVIL WENT DOWN TO GEORGIA

Little Five Points—Atlanta, Georgia

Conrad Winter sat alone at the bar, drinking a bottle of Chimay and eating an excellent cheeseburger and thinking about the bartender's bowling shirt. The shirt had the name *Chuck* embroidered on the front pocket and a big Piggly Wiggly logo across the back. Wild cartoon eyes on the happy pink face of a clearly overweight pig—a pig dressed up as a butcher.

A pig butcher happily butchering pigs for humans.

Humans, thought Conrad, *are an odd species.*

Conrad wore black jeans and a dark green T-shirt. He'd been out of his clerical uniform in public a lot in the past six months, and he was still getting used to it. Until and including the Tim Trinity assignment, Conrad's Council work had intersected with his job with the Vatican's Office of World Outreach, so he'd stayed in uniform most of the time and had felt it his duty as a priest to do so whenever possible.

Because Conrad's work for the Vatican wasn't just a cover for his work on behalf of the Council. No, he loved the Church and considered his work there and his work for the Council complementary to each other. He'd always told himself that he wasn't serving two masters, but serving God. Still, the Council had always come first, and each time he stepped out of uniform he missed it a little less.

* * *

Both the Vatican and the Council had wanted Tim Trinity silenced. The Vatican dispatched Daniel to debunk the man, but Daniel fell down on the job—walked away from the job, actually—and became Trinity's protector. So the Council sent Conrad and he got the job done. Once the preacher had been dispatched, Conrad was summoned to Singapore for a debriefing and lunch with the director.

If the director of the Council for World Peace was not an easy man to get along with, he was an impossible man to make small talk with. He managed a brief and awkward congratulations for a job well done over pre-lunch martinis, and after that they passed some time discussing the menu in excruciating detail.

The lunch took place at the elegant Si Chuan Dou Hua, on the sixtieth floor of UOB Plaza One, seven floors below the director's office. The food was outstanding and they forced some talk about their favorite restaurants in different cities, usually disagreeing, Conrad more politely than the director. And that got them through to coffee and brandy.

Clearing his throat for far too long, as old men do, the director signaled the end of their small-talk purgatory. "I've spoken with Cardinal Allodi and the Vatican has put you on indefinite leave from your duties at World Outreach."

"I'm being punished?" Conrad put his coffee down. "What for?"

"On the contrary, Conrad, you're being promoted. I'm putting you in charge of the Anomalous Information Transfer project."

It took a couple seconds to sink in. "Oh. Thank you, sir."

"You earned it." But it sounded like an accusation, entirely without warmth. "You'll still use your position at the Vatican as cover whenever needed—Allodi's office will back you up. Officially, you're on an extended research trip, the subject of which is confidential." The director sipped his brandy. "This is a significant step for you. I just hope you don't make a mess of it."

Conrad didn't rise to that. "What happened to Swan? I thought he was running the team."

"Swan wasn't strong enough. He thought he was, but as things moved forward he stopped looking at the target and started looking at the view. He got too soft. He couldn't carry the weight." The director finished the coffee in his cup. "You're not too soft, are you, Conrad?"

After what I did for you in Bangalore? Abuja? New Orleans? Are you seriously asking me that question? But he kept it all inside. He pushed the anger down into the dark pit from which it had sprung, hating himself for how easily he allowed the director to push his buttons.

"When do I start?" he said.

✠ ✠ ✠

When Colonel Michael Dillman entered the Vortex Bar and Grill with Dr. Hasting, Conrad left his spot at the bar and took a seat at a table near the back of the room. They followed. Dillman was also out of uniform, wearing chinos and a golf shirt. Hasting was a leading microbiologist at the Centers for Disease Control—thankfully,

CDC doctors didn't tend to wear their white lab coats or yellow biohazard containment suits outside of work.

As the new arrivals took their seats, Conrad said, "There's been a leak. They've gotten hold of a copy of the major's blood work."

"It didn't come from me." Hasting's tone and body language backed him up, declaring with absolute certainty that he was speaking the truth.

"We know," said Conrad. "Anyway, that's barn doors and horses, we need to focus on"—he almost said, "removing our fingerprints," but that was inelegant—"minimizing our footprint."

"The blood work is in the system. I can't just make it disappear down a memory hole." Hasting was silent for a moment, thinking it through. "What I can do . . . I'll run a flawed simulation on the computer tonight, get back anemic results in the morning. Then I can downplay the preliminary findings, shuffle the study to the bottom of a very long to-do list. It'll buy you six months, if . . ."

"Yes?"

"If Klukoff doesn't notice." Sasha Klukoff was the Foundation's most senior ally at the CDC, residing a rung above the Council's top man in the CDC hierarchy. "Sooner or later, the Foundation will realize what they've got and Klukoff will become a problem. He's got the clearance to look wherever he wants whenever he wants. Nothing I can do about that." Hasting's left hand flittered upward and adjusted the tie he wasn't wearing, his eyes ping-ponging between Conrad and Dillman. "I know you don't need my advice on tactics, but I really think you should take him out of the game."

Yes, Klukoff was a Foundation ally, but he was also one of the top four or five microbiologists in the world, possessed of a mind that would be of incalculable value as the planet struggled with the devastation that was coming, and Conrad understood the weight of the choice before him. He would let Klukoff live, as long as the man didn't get curious.

Conrad nodded at Colonel Dillman, who dug into a pocket and handed Hasting a micro USB stick smaller than a thumbnail.

Dillman said, "You plug this stick into your computer. Thirty seconds later, you pull it out. The stick commits suicide after uploading its package, so you can just toss it in the trash."

Conrad said, "If Sasha Klukoff tries to access the case file from anywhere in the system, he'll be blocked and we'll be alerted. Just play your part, bury the whole thing as best you can. We'll take it from there."

12: ARMAGIDEON TIME

London, England

Daniel's breast pocket vibrated three times in quick succession. He stopped walking and pulled out the phone. The screen showed three texts in a row:

She's cranky.

She's got good reason to be.

Stay charming.

He crossed Du Cane Road to the imposing Hammersmith Hospital, all orange bricks and tall windows, white trim and Edwardian importance, its green copper clock tower towering above. The grandest building on campus, it was now home to the molecular immunology department of Imperial College London. The *she* referenced in Ayo's texts was Dr. Descia Milinkovic, chief microbiologist.

She pronounced it *DAY-sha* as she introduced herself, and she held her tongue long enough to get through polite how-do-you-dos, waving Daniel into a visitor's chair across the paper-strewn desk, but her piercing blue eyes said the crankiness Ayo warned about was on its way.

As soon as Daniel was seated, it came.

"You can tell Carter he's got some cheek, dropping this into my lap without advance warning," she said. "I had that handsome bastard from Five here yesterday evening, Mike Stotter. Came by for one of his menacing little chats not two hours after this bombshell landed in my inbox, and he's intensely interested. And after you, I've got some Homeland Security Yank stopping in for a friendly cuppa. Instead of supervising my team in the lab, I'm spending my time explaining what little we know to a bunch of bloody spooks."

Descia's department worked with some of the deadliest pathogens in the world; hers was a Level 5 biolab. If they had a security breach, a terrorist could waltz out with a bioweapon capable of wiping out entire cities. To help forestall such a breach, MI5 computers kept constant watch over the department's computer network, including e-mail.

The Foundation computer geeks saw an opportunity to point the intelligence community toward the Council's operation. Blankenship's medical file was sent with an electronic breadcrumb trail leading back to a coffeehouse with public Wi-Fi in Wheeling, West Virginia. The one-paragraph e-mail message came from a Dr. Astor—they used the name of the doctor at Red Ridge—introducing himself vaguely as a "US military doctor" and suggesting that the lab look at the attached blood work, which seemed to indicate a previously unknown strain of *Yersinia pestis*. And since the message appeared to come from West Virginia, it was not unreasonable to suspect that Stotter, the MI5 man, might alert a contact at US Homeland Security. It seemed he had.

"What did you tell Stotter?" asked Daniel.

"The truth, after a fashion. That I've never heard of Dr. Astor but doctors around the world red-flag blood work to us all the time.

And that I replied to Astor's e-mail, asking if he had a live sample of the bug, but he hasn't yet replied to my reply." Her eyes locked onto Daniel's. "Please tell me we do have a live culture."

"We don't."

"Then we'd better get one, because we've definitely got a new strain of the plague on our hands and, if you'll forgive the medical jargon, it's a scary little bugger."

"But Astor told me it's susceptible to antibiotics."

Descia made no effort to hide her frustration at Daniel's ignorance. "Okay then, allow me to back up a bit. Each strain of *Y. pestis* is a different iteration, or version, of the plague bacterium. Each strain a separate population of little bugs, but all with the same goal. Their goal is simply to consume as much as possible and reproduce as fast as possible. That's it—mindless consumption and reproduction. Unchecked, they just keep at it until they become top predator and take over the world. Then after taking out the human population, they'd work their way through the rest of the mammals and so on down the food chain until there was nothing left to eat, at which time the little buggers would starve en masse, having consumed all the earth's resources available to them." Her smile was grim. "Remind you of any other predator species we know and allegedly love?"

"Sadly, it does," said Daniel.

"The human race is quite literally fighting for its existence against *Y. pestis* and *Escherichia coli* and *Staphylococcus aureus* and *Bacillus anthracis* and dozens of other deadly pathogens. That's just bacteria, I haven't even mentioned the viruses. And you know what? We're going to lose. That's not hyperbole. In the end, we are going to lose. The microscopic little bastards shall inherit the earth."

"We survived the Black Death in the Middle Ages," said Daniel.

"We didn't travel the world as far or as quickly as we do now, didn't have the population density we do now. Look, there's no debate among microbiologists—a pandemic is coming. Sooner or later one of these bugs is going to be stronger and faster than we are, and the way we continue to misuse antibiotics, it'll be sooner. Whenever it happens, my more optimistic colleagues estimate a global depopulation of between 20 and 30 percent. That's between 1.5 and 2.2 billion dead at today's population level. But the optimists are wrong, as are the pessimists who predict the total extinction scenario I painted for you earlier. We won't *all* die, probably. The realists—and it will not surprise you to learn that I count myself in this category—estimate a die-off of 50 to 65 percent, globally. Between 3.6 and 4.7 billion dead. Try to imagine what that will do to the world. The whole house of cards we call *civilization* will come crashing down, and life for those who survive will be abject misery for quite some time."

"Not the best news I've heard today," said Daniel.

"I imagine not," said Descia. "And truthfully, when microbiologists talk amongst ourselves, off the record after a few glasses of wine, the optimists admit their optimism is more wishful thinking than science."

"What do the pessimists do?"

"The pessimists just keep drinking until they pass out."

"And did you tell all this to Stotter?"

"Stotter already knows all this. I told him what I'm telling you—I need live bacteria to study. Look, there are three major categories of *Y. pestis*. Bubonic plague is by far the most common. Between one and two thousand cases a year are reported to the World Health Organization, and that's probably about a third of the total. Without intervention, it kills about 60 percent of those infected, but antibiotics knock it out. On the other end of the scale is septicemic plague, which is always fatal and kills within a day, so unless you're already hopped up on massive doses of antibiotics when you contract it, you're a goner. Thankfully, septicemic plague is very rare."

"Thankfully," agreed Daniel.

"Without a live culture to study, I can't be definitive, but I strongly suspect our new strain falls between these two extremes, in the third category known as pneumonic plague. As the name implies, it is not just insect-borne, but can pass directly from human to human. It takes up residence in the lungs, and as the sick cough up blood, it gets aerosolized and breathed into the lungs of those nearby, so it can spread very quickly indeed. In the case of a pandemic, quickly enough to infect more people than we have antibiotics to treat. In fact, it could exhaust the world's supply of antibiotics in a matter of months. And without antibiotic intervention, pneumonic plague has a mortality rate of about 95 percent." She rapped on the arm of her chair with a knuckle. "Are you hearing me, Daniel?"

"Every word."

"But they didn't send you here to help with my silly little war to save the human race, they sent you to find out why the Council for Puppies and Rainbows is interested in this pathogen. They sent you because they suspect it may be a trigger that turns a few people into Tim Trinitys. Lord knows that's more important than saving humanity. Right? Please, correct me if I'm mistaken."

Stay charming . . .

"Honestly, Descia, I think the two goals are connected," Daniel caught her gaze, held it. "I think you're an incredible woman and I'm grateful for your service to humanity, just as I'm sure you're grateful for the hundred-million-dollar trust we set up to help fund your work. Right?"

Descia acknowledged it with a nod. "Very grateful indeed," she said. "But it should've been a billion. You people really need to pull your heads out of the sand."

"Your objections have not fallen on deaf ears, believe me," said Daniel. "If I come across a live sample of this little monster, I promise I will get it to you."

"It would be much appreciated." Descia Milinkovic glanced at her watch, pushed back her chair, and stood up. "Here's the second part of my message to Carter Ames: I have no way of knowing if this new plague bacteria could trigger AIT, and frankly, I don't care. I think the Foundation has lost its way, chasing after soothsayers and hocus-pocus, while the government boys are busy warring against members of our own species. Meanwhile, we're losing the real war, and we need to fight a hell of a lot harder." She arched an eyebrow at Daniel. "Do pass that message along to Carter, won't you, dear?"

13: MIND CONTROL

Hey stranger." Julia Rothman spread her arms for a big hug, and gave Daniel's bicep a playful squeeze through his suit. "Someone's been workin' out."

"You know I do my best thinking while beatin' the crap out of the heavy bag," said Daniel. "You look great." He gestured toward the red-velvet booth.

Julia laughed as she sat. "No, I don't, but thanks for saying so. I look like a weary traveler and I smell like an airport. Got your e-mail after landing in Glasgow just after noon, turned right 'round and flew back."

"I thought you were in London. You didn't have to come back."

Julia winked at him. She did look great. "I had my own selfish reasons. Need to pick your brain."

The waitress delivered two Sazeracs to the table. He'd ordered them when Julia had texted to announce her imminent arrival at Claridge's. Daniel and Julia had a long history with the cocktail and he'd been unsure about the choice, didn't want her to read too much into it. This whole transitioning into friendship with an ex-girlfriend thing was new to him, after all.

It was Julia who'd broken the Tim Trinity story, writing for the New Orleans *Times-Picayune* and contributing to CNN's coverage. It made her a star, turned her from respected investigative reporter into celebrity journalist. She was pretty, but not like the plastic pretty people who increasingly play the role of journalists on our television and computer screens. She was real. And people loved that sexy New Orleans accent. As television news executives would (and did) say: The camera loved her.

Naturally, television came a-courtin'. But Julia wasn't in it for the celebrity, her heart was in digging up and reporting stories that mattered. Instead of jumping to television, she engaged a New York literary agent and landed a seven-figure book deal. Her publisher promptly promised that hers would be the definitive investigation of the Trinity Phenomenon.

Daniel and Julia stayed in touch mostly by e-mail, mostly chatting about Julia's research adventures, always promising to meet for lunch next time they found themselves in the same city at the same time. But she'd been jetting around the globe on a mission to solve the Trinity Phenomenon, and Daniel had been ensconced at the Foundation, and lunch hadn't happened.

Julia clinked her glass against his, and they sipped their drinks. "Nice," she said. "Tastes like home." He was pleased she'd taken it as intended. She put her drink down, patted Daniel's hand. "Now before we get to me, I want to hear all about your new job."

He'd already decided not to lie to her. She knew him too well, she'd see right through it. He suspected that telling the truth would make him sound like a bit of a dick, but it was the right thing to do.

"I really can't discuss my job without violating the confidentiality clause in my employment contract," he said. Thinking: *Yep, you sound like a dick.*

Julia let out a reflexive laugh. "Wait, what?"

"Sorry."

"You didn't join up with that mercenary friend of yours, did you?"

Daniel sipped his drink, said nothing.

"You're serious . . . you're really not going to tell me."

"I'm really not going to tell you." He made an apologetic face. "That's just the way it has to be right now." *Right now* implying *maybe later.*

Julia shook her head. "Okay, Danny. Fine. Weird, but fine. You tell me when you're ready, I guess."

"Thanks." Glad to clear that hurdle, however awkwardly. "You can still pick my brain about *your* job, so how goes the search for"—he was careful not to say AIT—"the Trinity Phenomenon? What've you found?"

Julia stopped just shy of rolling her eyes. "What I've found is a world full of crazy people. Whatever the hell happened to Tim, every crackpot on the planet feels legitimized by it. I tell you, I'm living on Cloud Cuckooland these days." She pulled a notebook from her messenger bag. "I mean, it's God, it's Satan, it's the Illuminati, the Bilderbergers, the Masons . . . and here's my favorite: It's telepathic communication from aliens in preparation for earth colonization."

"Ooh, I like that one," said Daniel.

"I know, right? I'm telling you, when it comes to the Trinity Phenomenon, no matter how crazy the conspiracy, there's a lunatic fringe out there promoting it."

Daniel shrugged. "Understandable though. Everybody's concept of reality took a hit because of Tim. Until we know what the phenomenon was, we can't know what it means—and people hate existential uncertainty. They're gonna freak out a bit."

"That's the problem," said Julia, "unless whatever happened to Tim happens again, we'll never know what the phenomenon was. Tim's death leaves nothing for science to study, and that void leaves room for the con artists and crazies to set up shop. People are freaking out a lot more than a bit."

She was right. The world had changed since Tim Trinity. Daniel found it unnerving that so many people now incorporated his dead uncle into their religious convictions, some in such a significant role as to alter their metaphysics. To some he was a saint or a prophet, to others he was the very messiah returned.

Differences of degree notwithstanding, well over three hundred million humans believed that Tim Trinity was some kind of supernaturally powered manifestation of the divine, and that number was continuing to grow. There were Tim Trinity cults within virtually every sect of Christianity, and most major non-Christian religions as well. There was even a breakaway splinter group of Jews for Jesus called Jews for Tim Trinity's Jesus (Tim would've found it hilarious). And then there were the myriad New Agers, occultists, druids, hippies, Discordians, and potheads with no other stated affiliation. The media had dubbed all these people "Trinity Pilgrims," after the multitudes who'd flocked to see Tim in Atlanta and followed him to New Orleans, and the term stuck.

Americans in particular were drawn to Tim Trinity worship. It seemed many felt it entirely appropriate that Jesus would return as an American. After all, to them God was American. There were Tim Trinity churches in urban storefronts and country chapels from sea to shining sea. There was even a Tim Trinity edition of the Bible, complete with royal-blue cover and pages edged in silver, just like the Bible Trinity had brandished on television.

The mainstream churches were hemorrhaging customers, church leaders stunned, caught flat-footed, unable to shift with the rapidly changing world. Some tried to incorporate Trinity as a saved sinner gifted by God with a message, but Trinity believers judged it an insufficient status for their new idol, and mainstream collection plates got lighter every month as flocks continued to disperse.

The televangelists were smart—they simply wrote off the Trinity Pilgrims and got busy scaring the hell out of people, declaring Trinity a tool of the devil, either demon or antichrist, embracing an apocalyptic Christianity and preaching the arrival of the End Times and the coming rapture. Their business thrived.

Julia opened her notebook. "The group I want to talk to you about, they're convinced the government is beaming voices into their heads using microwaves, what they call voice-to-skull technology, or V2K. But these people have been around for years—they're not a response to Trinity. And thanks to the Internet, they've found one another. Turns out there are millions of them. Over 380,000 in the US, 100,000 in the UK, significant numbers all across Western and Eastern Europe, Japan, China, Korea, Indonesia, Australia . . . pretty much every developed country. They've got online forums where they share their experiences, organize petitions and protests. There's a chapter in DC that meets on the mall, handing out pamphlets and collecting signatures—they want Congress to pass a law making it illegal for anyone, including the government, to beam voices into people's heads. They're actually registered as a non-profit political action committee. Other chapters are lobbying for similar laws in over a dozen countries."

"Sounds like a lot of paranoid schizophrenics uniting under a shared delusion, trying to wrestle the mental chaos into some kind of order." Daniel's mind went back to the schizophrenia page of the AIT Physiological Trigger report. He remembered the chill he felt when he read Ayo's handwritten note in the margin.

Was schizophrenia the trigger for AIT, or did the voices brought on by AIT simply drive these people mad?

Maybe some of the people who most cross the street to avoid— the gap-toothed old woman wearing garbage bags and a football helmet, pushing a squeaky-wheeled shopping cart full of jetsam, yelling at passersby . . . the yellow-bearded man with wild, greasy hair, mumbling gibberish at a brick wall—maybe some of these people aren't schizophrenic at all but simply unable to cope with the flood of real information invading their minds from the outside.

Julia was saying, " . . . and I've spent a lot of time with these people. It's obvious that a great number of them are mentally ill, but there's a minority—I don't know, maybe 5 percent?—anyway, a minority who don't present any symptoms of paranoid schizophrenia or any other mental illness."

"They think the government is beaming voices into their heads, Julia. That's a symptom right there."

"But for this minority, it's the *only* one. They're not generally paranoid. They don't distrust their coworkers or spouses, they don't think their neighbors are spying on them, they don't think bad guys are hiding in restaurant kitchens to poison their food. They do their jobs well, and until they started insisting the government was beaming voices into their heads, they enjoyed perfectly normal relationships with the people in their lives. The ones I've met are incredibly rational, aside from that one thing. They just don't seem ill at all."

"So, what do they seem?"

"They seem like people who are under great stress because someone is beaming voices into their heads."

Daniel couldn't hold back a snicker. "Nice one. But—"

"Wait, I buried the lede," said Julia with a mischievous grin. "Here's the kicker: Their American lobbying group, Sovereign Minds, filed a Freedom of Information request with the federal government. You'll never guess what came back." She plucked a file folder from her bag, put it on the table. "The Pentagon actually has a weapon that beams voices into people's heads."

"You're kidding."

"Incredible, right?" She pushed the folder across to Daniel. "Check it out."

Daniel flipped through the pages. It was a copy of a copy of a typed report, readable but somewhat blurry. And heavily redacted, over 80 percent blacked out by military censors.

Julia said, "It was developed for the Pentagon by Air Force Intelligence as an offshoot of their advanced microwave R & D. In those days, the military was into all kinds of exotic shit. Psychic warfare, remote viewing, all that *Men Who Stare at Goats* stuff— those programs were real. Of course most of it never worked. At the time, the Soviets and the Americans were constantly feeding each other disinformation about exotic weapons programs. We heard the Russians had developed what they called Directed Auditory Hallucination Technology, so we had to give it a try as well. Turns out the Russian program was pure fiction, a disinformation op designed to make us waste military manpower and money, but the US Air Force actually figured out how to do it."

She pulled out another file. "By 1984, they had a working prototype up and running successfully. The next year, they were granted a patent for"—she read from the top sheet in the folder—"*a portable electronic device that directs scripted auditory hallucinations directly into a subject's mind from a distance.*"

She handed the file over. Sure enough, it was a copy of the approval notice from the US Patent Office. Daniel paged through the document, which also contained mostly thick black lines laid down by government censors. How the device worked, how and of what it was made, details of the tests on live subjects, adverse side effects—all redacted from both documents. But what remained was enough to confirm exactly what Julia had said.

The weapon was real, and it worked.

"What kind of sick puppy dreams up such a weapon?" said Julia. "And what kind of government thinks it should *have* such a weapon? Hijacking people's minds, directing their thoughts, to me that's worse than simply killing them."

"You'll get no argument from me," said Daniel, "but even if it exists, it couldn't account for the Trinity Phenomenon. It doesn't explain the backwards tongues, and it certainly can't explain predicting the future. You were there when that billboard came down—you saw. Our very presence there caused the accident—setting up in the median, the dead battery, Shooter running across the highway. There was simply no possible way for Tim to have predicted it. None. And yet he did."

"Absolutely. This isn't what happened to Tim, but it proves that auditory hallucinations can have an outside source. It's worth at least a few chapters in my book." Julia sipped her drink. "I need to profile one or two sufferers from the seemingly rational minority, and so far my best candidate is here in London. I've spent the last week with her and she seems perfect for it. If you would meet with her, listen to her story, with your experience debunking—"

"I'd love to help," Daniel cut in, "but I've got a pretty full plate right now." It sounded lame, but *I'm a little busy chasing down a plague* was not an option. He needed to add something else. "And

I gotta admit I don't love the idea of spending a day listening to the sad fantasies of a crazy person. It feels, I don't know, exploitative."

Oops. Exactly the wrong thing to say. But he couldn't *unsay* it.

"The woman feels she's being victimized," said Julia, not amused. "She wants to tell her story and she's got a hell of a story to tell. She trusts me to tell it fairly, and you know I will. It is *not* exploitative, and I'm not asking for a day, just an hour." With a little effort, her face brightened. "Tell you what: I've found this awesome pizza joint in London—"

"London pizza? *Please*, I've spent the last three months in New York."

"The guy who owns it is originally from Brooklyn and he actually shipped his pizza oven across the Atlantic when he came—it's like a million years old. I guarantee his pie ranks with the best. You do this for me, and I'll take you there and prove it. What do you say, Danny?"

With Tim Trinity gone, Julia was the only person left who called Daniel "Danny," and although he hadn't thought of himself as "Danny" since he was a teen, it was nice to hear it from her.

"Have you approached the Pentagon for a comment?" he asked, hoping she'd go with the change of subject.

"Too early. But I know what they're gonna say. The official line is laid out clearly in the project report. The conclusion says after patenting the weapon, the Pentagon decided that putting it into use was unethical and a possible violation of the Geneva Conventions. So the entire thing was mothballed, and was never shared with any branch of the military or intelligence community." She smirked. "And if you believe that, I've got some primo swampland for sale at a bargain."

"You really think they're using this thing?"

"I have no idea. But I know boys love to play with their toys. It wouldn't surprise me to learn that someone, somewhere, is using one."

Daniel flipped through the project report as Julia spoke, still having trouble accepting the existence of this terrible weapon, this high-tech gaslighting device. He came to the final page, his eye immediately drawn to the name of the officer who authored the report. His heart skipped a beat.

Major Michael Dillman.

Colonel Michael Dillman, the DIA spook who'd transferred from Air Force Intelligence as a major, had been in charge of developing this weapon in the 1980s. And who was now working with Conrad Winter on the Council's AIT program.

Were they planning to use the weapon to fake AIT? And if so, to what end? No way to know, still not enough dots to connect.

But then a stranger idea hit Daniel. What were the chances that Julia's research would lead her to this fringe group with no real connection to the Trinity Phenomenon, which would lead her to Colonel Dillman's Air Force project from thirty years ago and to a woman in London she would want Daniel to vet for her book just as he was visiting London, leading him to see Dillman's name in the file?

An incredible string of coincidences, or . . . ? The questions were making him dizzy. Daniel put the file folder down and signaled the waitress for another round of drinks, as Julia slipped out to the ladies room.

While she was gone, he photographed the cover sheet of the Patent Office document, the cover sheet of the Air Force project report, and the page bearing Michael Dillman's name. He texted the photos to Ayo in New York, returning the phone to his pocket just as Julia returned to the booth.

"So?" she said.

"You're on for pizza," said Daniel. "Tell me about this woman you want me to debunk."

14: FINGERPRINT FILE

Daniel went through his morning routine—meditation, katas, yoga, shower, and wet shave. He selected the green-gray suit, blue mandarin-collared shirt, and suede Mephisto wingtips. The day-off uniform of a top-shelf business consultant.

In a brief video chat, Ayo told him Conrad Winter and Michael Dillman had melted into the ether without leaving a trail, so Pat had gone home to Louisiana to hang out with his coonhound until his services were next required. Daniel then gave Ayo a condensed version of the story Julia had told him the night before about Dillman's thirty-year-old invention that could beam voices into people's heads, and about the woman he was about to meet.

Kara Singh, forty-two, US citizen. Both parents deceased, both naturalized US citizens born in India, mother was a history professor at Stanford, father a prominent orthopedic surgeon. Kara followed in her father's footsteps and became a trauma surgeon in the California Bay Area, married John Watts, a Silicon Valley geek considered a rock star by the venture capitalists. Fifteen years ago, the couple had become a family when they'd brought a daughter into the world.

Eight years ago, they'd moved to London when Watts and his backers had bought into a small-but-rising tech company there. Relocated in England, Kara had worked for the National Health Service as an on-call ER surgeon. She was well respected and well liked by her peers. Kara and John had a robust social life with colleagues from work, friends he brought in from the golf club, and hers from the gardening club. Their daughter made friends easily and thrived in the academic world of UK private education, showing a talent for the sciences, looking more like her mother every day. Life was good.

Until six years ago, when Kara started hearing voices. She came to believe that they were not being conjured by her own mind but were coming from outside. Researching online, she found that she was far from alone. She learned from the Freedom of Information releases of the Pentagon's strange weapon. She tried to raise hell about it, going public in an attempt to pressure them to cease and desist.

The British tabloid press savaged her on the front pages with headlines like *Dr. 'Kara-zy claims CIA mind control!* and *NHS allows lunatic doc to operate on our kids!*

In the end, she lost everything. Her job, social status, friends, and finally even her family, when her husband had her declared by the courts an unfit parent and moved with their daughter back to California. Alone for the last three years with nothing to do, she'd filled journal after journal with handwritten transcriptions of the voices in her head. And she continued to vociferate about it to a world that wouldn't listen to the vociferations of a crazy woman.

"God," said Ayo, "it's tragic."

"Yeah it is. According to Julia, Dr. Singh is now self-medicating with alcohol." He wasn't very much looking forward to spending the afternoon with this woman. "Anyway, she isn't likely to be a productive lead—Julia read some of the journals, didn't see anything Dr. Singh's malfunctioning mind couldn't have supplied without outside help. I'll keep an eye out for a Dillman connection, but the odds on that are somewhere between slim and none, I'm guessing."

✤ ✤ ✤

The morning news mentioned a protest growing in front of the US Embassy, so Daniel avoided Grosvenor Square by walking north to Oxford Street, which was a more interesting route for people-watching anyway. The day was mild and blue-skied with enough clouds to make it interesting, like the classic Thames Television logo come to life.

He turned south at the eastern edge of Hyde Park, slowing to a stroll as he passed Speakers' Corner.

He loved the idea of Speakers' Corner—a designated place in the city where members of the public could climb up on their proverbial soapboxes and give voice to their beliefs, ideas, and grievances about the world. London's finest had officers on hand to enforce basic rules against excessive profanity and blatantly offensive speech, but beyond that it was pretty much anything goes.

Spectators gathered around the various speakers, egging them on with noises of agreement or ridicule, sometimes engaging the speakers in free-form debate. Daniel strolled past a hairy man in a green kilt calling—with an American accent—for Scottish independence; a skinny pink-haired punk girl issuing dire warnings about the worldwide collapse of the honeybee population; a UFO cover-up conspiracy hipster; a gray-haired Orwell enthusiast upset about perpetual war; and an even number of pro- and anti-Tim Trinity preachers, three on each side of the issue.

Dr. Kara Singh lived in Knightsbridge, a leafy district of high-end shops and even higher-end residences. Singh's husband had left her with more money than she could spend in a lifetime so she'd taken a ninety-eight-year lease on a large flat in the quiet neighborhood.

Daniel took the Underground to Knightsbridge. Across the street from Harrods, he stopped for lunch at Cafe Rouge. He sat facing the door, ate *moules marinières*, and drank lemon barley water.

The man who approached was in his early forties, powerfully built, close-cropped sandy hair, blue poplin suit. He pulled out the chair across from Daniel and sat.

"Evan Sage, fellow American."

Daniel shook the offered hand. "Daniel Byrne."

"Good to know you, Daniel," said Sage. "Here on business?"

"Yep."

"Work keep you on the road a lot?"

"Sure," said Daniel.

"Me, too. Man, it's brutal. This trip here? Cost me my fiancée."

"Maybe you should travel less," said Daniel.

"Not really an option in my line of work."

"That's too bad."

Evan Sage grinned on one side of his mouth. "See, a normal person would say, 'What line of work are you in?'"

"I enjoy dining alone," said Daniel. "Nothing personal, I'm just not looking for conversation."

"Aw, don't be like that." Sage plucked a roll from the bread-basket, tore a chunk off with his teeth, and chewed, making it clear he wasn't going anywhere.

Daniel figured Evan Sage might be the Homeland Security Yank Descia Milinkovic had mentioned the previous day. Whoever he was, he wasn't here by accident, and Daniel had not made himself easy to track.

Paranoia might leave you loveless and alone, Raoul once said, *but it'll keep you alive. Paranoia is your best friend.*

So Daniel had followed the protocol he'd learned in training. During the walk to Speakers' Corner he'd checked his rear using shop windows and other reflective surfaces, had crossed the street regularly, stopped into stores, reversed direction a few times, always looking for faces and clothing and cars and bicycles that he'd cataloged earlier in his walk.

After entering the Underground at Marble Arch, he'd taken the Jubilee line one stop to Bond Street, gotten off the train, and waited on the platform for the next one. Then he'd overshot Green Park by one station, crossed platforms, and returned. He'd let a few trains pass through Green Park in all directions before switching to the Piccadilly line, finally riding the two stops to Knightsbridge.

He'd employed all the standard maneuvers, but no surveillance had revealed itself. Which meant a surveillance team of at least eight, or none at all. He knew that London had the most extensive network of surveillance cameras of any city in the world, but there was nothing he could do about that.

Whoever Evan Sage was, either he had the power to plug into that camera network or he commanded a large team.

Bad news either way.

Daniel said, "Okay, Mr. Sage, I'll bite. What line of work are you in?"

"Evan, please. I work for a little outfit called the United States Department of Homeland Security. You may have heard of us." He produced a badge wallet and extracted a business card, slid it across the table. "Let's trade." Daniel didn't pick up Sage's card, but he did slide one of his own across in return. Sage looked down at it. "Right, Descia Milinkovic said you were some kind of money guy."

Daniel nodded. "One of our clients is a charitable trust that funds some of her work. They sent me to see that their money's being wisely allocated."

"Uh-huh." Sage tore off another chunk of bread, chewed it for a while before speaking again. "Thing is, I wouldn't be very good at my job without a functioning bullshit detector. Descia is a nice lady but she set my spidey senses tingling, so I made a few calls, got a few answers. *Nobody* goes from spooky Vatican investigator to jet-set business consultant in five months. Just doesn't happen."

"I'm a quick study," shrugged Daniel. Sage stopped chewing. "What can I tell you, Evan? Sometimes people are exactly who they appear to be."

Evan Sage dropped the half-eaten roll back into the bread-basket, wiped his fingers together to knock off the crumbs. He picked up Daniel's business card and sniffed it. "Smells like a front, my friend. The good doctor gets wind from the States of what could be the makings of a new bioweapon, and you just happen to show up from the States the very next day?"

"I have absolutely not a clue what you're talking about," said Daniel. He watched Sage's face for any reaction, saw none.

"Whose interests do you represent?" said Sage as he slipped Daniel's card into a pocket. "Who's behind the front?"

"Seriously," said Daniel, "you might as well be speaking Urdu."

Sage now put his face into an expression of concern. "You seem like a nice enough guy and I'm not sure you fully realize what you've gotten yourself involved in. But you are swimming in the deep end now, and you will soon need a friend. I am trying to be that friend."

Daniel said nothing.

"Pick it up." Evan Sage nodded as Daniel picked up his card. "You're just on a long leash, Daniel Byrne. I'll be keeping an eye on you." He stood. "In the meantime, if it gets hard to tell who your friends are, you've got my number."

15: WELCOME TO MY NIGHTMARE

If Kara Singh was drinking as heavily as Julia implied, Daniel wanted to catch her before she dipped her bill too deep. After running around in circles to spot a tail, and the unexpected visit by Evan Sage, he arrived significantly later than intended.

But as she shook his hand and ushered him into her living room, he caught no whiff of booze or anything used to mask it, and she seemed perfectly sober.

"Please sit. Coffee's brewing, I'll just get it."

"Thank you."

She paused in the doorway and as she glanced back her smile faltered. She quickly got it back in place, but now it looked more nervous than before. "Be right back," she said, retreating down the hallway to the kitchen.

Daniel closed his eyes, conjured her in his mind's eye just as Dave Christleib had taught him. We actually notice a lot more than we realize about people in the first few seconds after meeting them, but because we're busy dealing with each successive moment, we only consciously recognize a fraction of what we've seen. The trick is to stop and take stock in the first few minutes, before we forget.

He saw her now as she had appeared in the doorway, a hand on one hip. She stood about five foot six. Trim but not skinny, she'd given up neither exercise nor eating as her life came crashing down. She wore designer blue jeans and a raw silk blouse, untucked.

Thin-strapped leather sandals, long feet, toenails unpainted. Her hair was long and black, the inch and a half at the roots and temples showing some silver. Short upper lip. When she closed her mouth, he could just catch a sliver of teeth glistening behind full lips. A long, sharp nose and green eyes, almond shaped, almost hooded— beautiful windows into a badly damaged soul.

Daniel heard the coffeemaker beep from the kitchen. He opened his eyes and turned his attention to the room, dark woods and colorful silks, antique wool rugs covering the hardwood floor. The decor a mash-up of Arts and Crafts Americana and India, and it somehow went together perfectly.

She returned with a tray and placed it on the coffee table.

"You have a beautiful home," he said.

"Thanks." She poured the coffee into two mugs and handed one across to him. "I never saw India until after med school. My mother came to America as a toddler. Her accent was as California as mine—she even spoke Hindi with an American accent. My father was grown, already a doctor when he emigrated, and her accent always amused him."

"Julia said your father's name is Singh."

"Yes."

"Why didn't you end up Kara Kaur? I thought all Sikh women were given the name Kaur."

Kara Singh raised her coffee in a toasting gesture. "I'm impressed."

"I used to study religions a little," he said.

"Yes, my father was a Sikh, but I guess you'd call him a secular Sikh. He believed in the values of Sikhism while rejecting all theology. The common surname was an attempt by Sikhism to break the caste system, a proclamation that all are equal. But my father saw a contradiction: While Sikhs also claim to believe gender dif-ferences are transitory and see women as equal to men, they give their boys the name Singh, which means lion, and their girls the name Kaur, which means princess. My dad said he wanted me to be a lioness, not a princess. So I got to be a Singh. And he insisted on Kara—my mom's surname—as a testament to her equality. The way he saw it, he wasn't rejecting the values of Sikhism but follow-ing them more truly."

"Sounds like a remarkable man."

"He was. But he was also an angry man, angry about everything back home, the caste system, the low status of women, the political corruption, police brutality. He raised money from the California Sikh community, added some of his own, and sent it to people in India trying to achieve political reform, but he vowed not to return until things changed. And he never did."

"Was he upset with you for going?"

"No, he understood my need to see the place that had made him so angry, see it for myself. Shortly after I became a surgeon I did some pro bono work in Kolkata, and I fell in love with the place. India is deeply troubled in many ways, but also a country of such exquisite beauty and culture. So many wonderful people enduring so much hardship." She sipped her coffee and leaned back into the couch. "Like many places in the world, I guess. Anyway, I went back about once a year . . . until, you know. Until they took my medical license away."

"You sound appropriately bitter about it."

"Of course I'm bitter about it. Who wouldn't be?" She caught herself, blew out a breath, and combed slender fingers through her hair. "Okay, sorry. I just, I don't know how this is supposed to go. I've been diagnosed by my former peers as—well, they can't agree, since I'm clearly not schizophrenic and don't fit any other profiles. So they just say I'm borderline bipolar or depressive or delusional." She looked at Daniel squarely. "But I'm not." Her gaze dropped to her feet as she crossed her ankles. When she looked back, the intensity of her expression was a little unsettling. "I'm not. Not yet. But I know I'm headed in that direction, and I feel like Julia's book is my last chance to stop them."

"You mean the CIA."

"I don't know if it's the CIA," she said. "When I went public, I suggested it *might* be the CIA or the military or some group connected to them, maybe a private contractor, but the press just went with CIA because it sounds sensational and that's all anyone remembers I said. Whoever it is, they've been trying to drive me insane for the last six years and if I don't stop them, they'll eventually succeed . . ."

The speed of her speech increased the longer she talked. Not quite manic, Daniel decided, but well beyond simply agitated.

" . . . and now Julia says I have to talk to you before she'll agree to tell my story, but it's a catch-22 because if I tell you the truth, you'll just think I'm crazy."

"Wait, slow down," said Daniel. "Kara, I understand that telling your story has only brought you more grief, but here's the thing: I bring a different perspective. Tim Trinity was my uncle."

She arched her left eyebrow at him. "Really?"

"Really. I was with him for the last month of his life, and I saw things—"

"I'm sorry if he was your uncle, but Trinity was a con artist."

"Without doubt," said Daniel, "and one of the best. But what happened to him at the end was real."

Kara sighed, "I hope you didn't come here to tell me God put the voices in my head. If that's the case, you can just pack up your *Watchtowers* or whatever and leave."

"Not at all." Daniel smiled. "Look, you'll just have to take a leap of faith that I'm one of the good guys. Do you trust Julia?"

"I think so, yes."

"Then trust that she didn't send me here to hurt you."

Kara thought for a second, decided. "What the hell, I guess it's *once more unto the breach* then."

She left for the kitchen, returned with a bottle of Cutty Sark, and poured about three ounces into her coffee, then put the bottle on the table between them. "I'd feel better talking about this if you'd drink with me," she said, looking at the table, her voice very small.

Daniel poured a little scotch into his own coffee. "Sure."

She sipped hers. "You think they could've been using that weapon on your uncle?"

"Not a chance," Daniel said. "Tim predicted the future. Last time I checked, the CIA had a pretty crappy track record in that regard. Seriously, he knew things that were impossible to know."

"Well, I don't believe it." She smiled at the irony. "I know, crazy lady thinks CIA is beaming voices into her head, you'd expect her to believe anything. But I'm a medical doctor, I believe in science. You need to understand, that is how I approached my own condition. I didn't just jump at the idea that people were transmitting the voices into my head. I had every conceivable medical diagnostic test done, I allowed myself to be dissected by an army of psychiatrists, even submitted to their hypnosis quackery. Bottom line: I have no physical or neurological disease. And the shrinks can't find a convenient label to pin on me, either." She sipped some more coffee. "The most logically consistent explanation that fits the evidence is simply that someone is using that V2K weapon to torture me into madness."

Julia was right, this woman did seem incredibly rational. Almost hyper-rational.

"Okay," said Daniel, "I understand the weapon exists and it's physically possible for someone to do what you're saying. But why would they?"

She shook her head. "I have no idea. It makes no sense, and that's the only factor pointing toward mental illness. I simply cannot imagine a rational motivation for anyone to do this to me—but then again, I can't imagine a rational motivation for doing this to *anybody*. And yet the Pentagon built the hideous thing, so obviously there was a motivation."

"Fair point," said Daniel.

"I can only guess that maybe I'm an involuntary subject in some kind of experiment. They leave me alone when I've had too much to drink, so maybe they're simply experimenting to find how long it takes for this weapon to drive a sober, intelligent woman insane." She drank some more boozy coffee. "I know I'm grasping at straws, but again, based on the empirical evidence, it really is the most logical explanation. Of course, it's more comfortable for people to say I'm nuts than it is for them to face the fact that their governments build weapons like this."

"It would be an uncomfortable fact to face," said Daniel.

"Not *would be*," Kara said. "*Is*."

"Granted," he said, because what else could he say? "But let's focus for a minute on the experience itself. Tell me about the voices."

"There are three distinct voices, all men with American accents. But it's only one at a time, as if they're taking shifts."

"How often?"

"Four days a week on average, but it varies. A few times a year they leave me alone for a whole week, but there are also stretches when they harass me every day for as long as three weeks at a time. Usually starts in the late afternoon or evening, but sometimes they come in the morning. Once they start transmitting, they usually stay at it for three or four hours, but they also just pop in for a minute or two, no discernible timing pattern to those little visits. One thing is constant no matter the time or duration of their transmissions: Every time the voices come, my mouth fills with the taste of cinnamon. Not sweet like gum or candy, but almost astringent, like if you put a spoonful of powdered cinnamon on your tongue. It's the weirdest thing, like when they start transmission it inadvertently triggers some taste receptors in my brain. And it's always cinnamon."

"What sort of things do they say?"

"Sometimes they call me by name, like, 'Kara, pay attention,' and then they start talking. It's as if they're reading books to me, excerpts from novels, history books, travel books, memoirs. It's all over the place. I've Googled passages from my transcription journals, but I never get a match to anything online."

She drained the rest of her mug and rose from the couch. "Come. Let me show you." Daniel followed her down the hallway to a door on the left. A small plaque on the door read:

ROOM

101

Kara said, "I have to try and find humor in it where I can." Her face darkened. "It gets pretty bleak sometimes." She pushed the door open and forced the smile back into place as she swept the room with her arm. "Welcome to my nightmare."

It had been a small guest bedroom or home office. Now there was a daybed with a lap desk and beside it a small table with a digital voice recorder. "When I get too tired to write, I just dictate it here and write it out later over there." There was a desk in the corner, and on it he saw a stained-glass lamp, a laptop computer, a pencil cup crammed with pencils, a pencil sharpener, and a Clairfontaine journal.

And then Daniel noticed the bookshelves along the wall. Row upon row of notebooks just like the one on the desk.

Over a hundred of them.

It gets pretty bleak sometimes . . .

"Somehow," said Kara, taking a step toward the bookshelves, "my life has come to this." Not self-pity, but an honest reflection of the reality she was living.

Daniel faced her. "Jesus, Kara. I'm . . . I feel like I'm intruding on something very personal here."

Her jaw tightened. "You don't understand. They took my daughter from me—*my own child*—and . . . three years, they won't even allow me to petition for supervised visits until I prove to a judge I'm on antipsychotic drugs—drugs that turn me into a bloody zombie—and I will not go through life with a pharmacological lobotomy." She let out a long breath. "And my parents both died believing their daughter had lost her mind." Anger spent, she looked again at the bookshelves filled with identical journals, silently radiating pain and loss and despair.

This woman had run out of tears a long time ago.

Daniel said, "What's your daughter's name?"

"No." Kara shook her head. "Sometimes . . . you know, once in a while, I wake up in the morning, and for a few seconds I just lie there and let myself believe the last six years were only a nightmare, that she's in the kitchen eating cereal or packing her book bag for school . . . and for those few seconds life is almost tolerable. But then I have to lose her all over again. I should never do it, it isn't worth the pain, but sometimes I'm weak. And I pay for it. So I won't tell you her name. I just can't go through that right now."

"I'm sorry."

"They stripped my entire life away, Daniel. And you think you're intruding on something personal? I've got nothing *personal* left." She gestured toward the bookshelves. "So go ahead, read my mind. I'm going to get a drink." She walked out of the room, leaving the door open behind her.

Daniel stepped forward. There was a label on each notebook's spine indicating when it was written. He pulled one off the middle shelf, let it fall open in his hands. Kara's handwriting was strong but, unlike most doctors', legible. A feminine script, but written in a hurry, not filigreed. A word halfway down the page caught Daniel's eye.

Mandal. The town in Norway. He read the sentence surrounding it: *It happened before in Mandal, where the revealed was once concealed, and the concealed shall be revealed.*

The same words a plague-infected soldier had said to Daniel in West Virginia just three days earlier. *Exactly* the same. And Daniel had landed on this particular page, in this particular journal, completely at random.

He felt the floor drop out from under his feet, and a violent shudder ran through his body.

Like the dream of falling that jerks you back from the edge of sleep.

16: EVERYTHING YOU CAN THINK

In the video chat window on Daniel's laptop screen, Ayo Onatade scrunched up her face. "Back up just a second. Yesterday you thought she was crazy, now you think she's got AIT?"

"Both could be true," said Daniel. "They're not mutually exclusive. Anyway, now that I've spoken with her, I don't think she's crazy. Regardless, there's no denying what I saw in Kara's journal—the voice in her head said exactly what Blankenship told me in West Virginia. I mean verbatim to the translation in the case file."

"You've got my attention. Extrapolate."

"Okay, if we try to explain it with the Pentagon's mind-control gizmo—and we don't even know if that thing is actually in use anywhere—then sure, they could've transmitted the same sentence to both her and Blankenship on two different continents. But that means two teams in the field, a lot of manpower. And while Blankenship is a plausible target—he worked for Dillman—why some random doctor in London? Also, Kara really is self-medicating with alcohol, the voices don't come when she's drunk. They'd have to maintain constant close surveillance to know when she's drinking—a huge allocation of resources."

"When you put it that way," Ayo conceded, "AIT starts to look more likely."

"It does. For a while, my uncle kept the voices at bay with cocaine. Maybe for Kara alcohol has a similar effect. And finally, there's just the weirdness quotient."

"Do tell."

He recited the long coincidence chain that had led him to Claridge's Fumoir Bar, with Julia, looking at Dillman's name in a heavily redacted Pentagon project file from 1985. "And then last night I picked one of a hundred journals off the shelf at random, let it fall open in my hands, and it opened right to the page with the very sentence Blankenship said."

Ayo said, "I'll admit, that would qualify as weird."

"I know coincidences happen billions of times a day and people are hardwired to read meaning into them, but this is a hell of a long chain."

Like the universe is trying to tell us something.

"Okay," said Ayo, "but she is not to be read in."

"She'll have questions."

"So tell her a story. You're just a business consultant trying to solve the Trinity Phenomenon in his spare time. Tim was family, so you're driven—it's a personal quest. You can sell that easily enough. For God's sake, Daniel, we had you on radar for five years, actively scouting you eight months before we even learned your uncle had AIT."

"Your point is?"

"My point, darling, is that you're a chip off the old grifter's block. There's a lot of Tim Trinity in you, you just don't see it. Lying is what we do in this business. We lie so we don't have to kill as often and so we don't get killed as often, so just be glad you're good at it."

"How often to you expect me to get killed?" said Daniel.

"Smartass," said Ayo. "Now go use that silver tongue Trinity bequeathed you."

"Yes, ma'am."

"And please remember, Dr. Singh is a potential asset, not a potential paramour." Daniel started to speak, but she cut him off. "Don't bother. There's a tone in your voice every time you say her name."

"A tone?"

"A definite tone." Ayo pushed her glasses up her nose. "I'm serious, the woman is a train wreck. Don't get emotionally entangled."

"You're imagining things," said Daniel. "Singh's story is sad and I feel for her, but there's nothing to worry about here, I'm fine."

"Like I said, be glad you're good at it. I almost believed you."

17: DOWNPRESSOR MAN

Barbados

Conrad Winter sat back in the blue leather lounge of the air-conditioned stretch limousine, watching the palm trees outside. North of Grantley Adams Airport, where fields of sugarcane once swayed in the salty breeze, fields of houses now stood—some painted bright shades of pink, blue, yellow, green, others still under construction, gray cinder-block structures with plastic sheets billowing where windows would soon reflect the Caribbean sun. But the new development fit in well enough, and the character of the island seemed essentially unchanged.

As they left the parish of Christ Church and climbed into the hills of St. Michael, the scenery became more familiar. Older wooden chattel houses nestled beside rum shops painted red with signs advertising Banks beer and Cockspur rum, open-air fruit stands bustling with activity . . . Four older men playing dominoes at a folding card table by the side of the road, their cabs parked at the taxi stand nearby . . . Neatly uniformed children squealing and chattering as they dashed out of school . . . An enterprising Rasta calling to passing cars from beside a wooden cart loaded with coconuts . . . A Chefette restaurant where business was booming.

And music. Music everywhere, reggae and dancehall and soca spilling from rum shops and cars and the open windows of chattel houses, flashy young men selling CDs out of Suzuki hatchbacks with blackened windows.

It had been almost twenty-five years since Conrad had set foot on the Rock, so why did this insist on feeling like a homecoming?

The director could've called this meeting anywhere. Heartless son of a bitch.

Barbados had been Conrad's home from the age of three to the age of twelve, when he was sent to live at Eton. It was not a typical childhood, whatever that might be. Children of billionaires don't have typical childhoods. Although Barbados boasted one of the best public education systems in the world, Conrad was chauffeur driven to a private school with the children of other rich white bankers from London and Zurich and Toronto. And although Barbados boasted one of the lowest crime rates in the world, there was a ten-foot wall surrounding their property with an electric gate at the bottom of the drive, and a team of six live-in manservants who practiced martial arts before breakfast on the back lawn beyond the pool. These hard men had come with them from London. To the island's elite, Conrad's father was simply a rich, important, and very security-conscious banker. But even as a child Conrad sensed there was something much bigger going on.

The limo was well up the hill now, houses imposing and properties immaculately groomed. They passed the prime minister's residence, Ilaro Court, on the right. Named after a town in Nigeria where Sir Gilbert Carter had been governor before His Majesty promoted him here.

They were all coming back now, all the dusty memories Conrad never willingly took out of storage. Playing lawn darts on the grounds of Ilaro Court under tamarind and breadfruit trees . . . Playing Marco Polo in the prime minister's swimming pool with the children of other bankers and captains of industry while the statue of Neptune stood watch, trident held aloft . . . Drinking lime squash served by kindly Bajan ladies on the pool deck while parents drank planter's punch in the elegant living room, talking of things that do not interest children . . .

The limousine turned left and continued to higher ground, the road steepening, then another left and they pulled to a stop. The driver pressed a button on the dash, and the electric gate swung open.

On either side of the gate, on concrete pedestals, stood two *tong shi*—bronze Chinese guardian lions. Conrad's mother had named them Antony and Cleopatra. And it was here, standing next to Antony, that Conrad had seen his mother for the last time. He was ten years old.

She howled like a wounded animal, spit flying from her mouth, tears glistening on her cheeks in the moonlight, red nails on ringed fingers clawing at the widening space between them as Morris pulled her toward an idling Range Rover. Father standing in the headlights' glare, watching with no expression at all.

Ten years old. And that was Conrad's last image of his mother.

⁂

She awakened him in his room, making a shushing gesture with an index finger pressed to her painted lips.

She smelled of flowery perfume. And gin. She'd been drinking a lot more gin lately.

"Connie," she said, "sit up." She was pretending to be happy, but she wasn't happy. She was scared. "We're going to have a little adventure, you and I."

She said they were going to play a joke on Father and sneak away to Miami for a few days to buy him a present as a surprise. But Father was a man who never laughed and made Conrad earn every smile. He did not like surprises, and he was not the sort of man people played jokes on.

She rushed the boy into his clothes, assuring him that everything was fine and this was going to be a grand adventure and Father will be so pleased with his surprise.

She paused at his bedroom door. "Now we mustn't be seen, or it'll ruin everything. Connie, dear, take Mum's hand." Her hand was cold and her grip too firm. She led him along the dim corridor and down the servants' staircase into the kitchen, then quietly through the mudroom, picking up a BWIA carry-on bag and slinging it over her shoulder. But Mum never went anywhere for even a few days with less than a full-sized suitcase plus a carry-on plus a purse.

They stepped out through the side door and she closed it silently behind them. Tree frogs and crickets filled the night air with frantic singing—louder, it seemed to the boy, than he'd ever heard them before. He stopped walking at the edge of the gravel drive, trying to make sense of things.

She tugged at his hand. "Please, sweetie, be cooperative. You don't want to spoil the surprise, do you?"

Conrad held his ground. "We're running away," he said, "aren't we?"

"Don't be silly. Of course not." She was lying again.

"I don't want to go without Lucy," said Conrad.

"Oh, for God's sake. You'll survive three days without your nanny." Another false smile. "We'll be back before you know it."

He jerked his hand free from hers. "Why aren't you telling me the truth?"

"*Lower your voice,*" she whispered louder than he had spoken, reaching forward and snatching his wrist, nails digging in. "Stop asking questions and do as you're told, right this instant." She drew a flashlight from her bag and aimed the beam down the curving hibiscus-lined drive. Started walking, pulling him along by the wrist. "I promise I'll explain everything later. All you need to know right now is I'm a mother protecting her son."

A chill ran down Conrad's arms and his scalp tingled. "Protect me from what?" He was careful to keep his voice quiet. The iron gate at the bottom of the drive was now within range of the flash-light's beam.

"From the life your father is planning for you." She slowed and looked back at the boy. Her eyes were wet. "I'm sorry, Connie, but this is real grown-up stuff and it's going to be a while before you can understand it completely. Please trust me, I'm doing this for you."

To Conrad's ten-year-old mind it was like the point in a jigsaw puzzle where you add one more piece and now you can see what the finished puzzle will look like. So many secret meetings and private phone calls . . . so many never-to-be-discussed subjects . . . so many men with guns.

His father was some kind of Bad Guy.

"You can let go, Mum," he said. "I'm coming with you."

She let go of his wrist and approached the gate, pulling a key on a silver chain from under her shirt. She turned the key in the electric box and the gate began to hum open. They slipped through as soon as the opening was large enough. Conrad heard something nearby in the darkness to their right.

A car.

The Range Rover's headlights came on, flooding the boy's eyes with blinding light.

18: IRON SHARPENING IRON

Nice of you to join us, Conrad."

Conrad stepped past Carruthers into the airy entrance hall. "Don't start, Charles. Where is he?"

The deputy director pointed to the louvered French doors. "Back patio. You know the way." His mouth tightened. "He wishes to see you alone."

The director sat out beyond the wet bar and covered patio in the full sun, his back to the house, facing the swimming pool. Beside him on the pool deck a second wicker chair waited for Conrad. Sometime in the last four months, the director had accepted impending baldness and shaved the dome completely. Conrad marched up behind him, thinking: *Ignore the venue, focus on the meeting. He's an asshole. Stay professional.*

Or not.

"Hi, *Dad*," he said.

The old man sat very still, didn't turn around. "Son."

Conrad sat in the empty chair and faced his father.

Mother of God . . .

The old man hadn't shaved his head at all—his hair had fallen out. He'd lost about twenty pounds, the mirrored sunglasses like bug eyes on his gaunt face. And he was wearing a cardigan in the tropical sun.

"Inoperable," the old man said. He gestured to the small table between the chairs. "Pour yourself a drink. I'm on strict rations, don't get my next dram until after supper."

Conrad uncorked the bottle of Mount Gay Extra Old, poured the amber spirit into a tulip snifter. "How long have you got?"

"Six months to a year, they say." The director cleared his throat for a full half minute. "You and I are never going to be friends, Conrad. I didn't raise a friend. I raised a successor. Nothing in your life has happened by accident. Cancer forces me to bring the schedule forward five years, but you were always meant to inherit my role in the game. Make no mistake about that."

✤✤✤

The boy stopped in the darkened entrance hall and spun to challenge his father. "Where's Mum? Where did Morris take her?"

"Do not address me in that tone of voice," barked his father. "Get ahold of yourself."

Conrad couldn't match the challenge, his gaze dropping—against his will—to the floor between them. "Yes, sir."

"I'm going out back for a cigarette. You stay here, take a moment to collect yourself. When you're ready to discuss this calmly, come out and see me."

It felt like a test. Conrad didn't wait behind but followed right on his father's heels, out through the French doors.

Thinking: *You can do this.*

His father stepped over to the patio bar, pulled a small bottle of Coca-Cola from the fridge, and pried off the cap. "Bring a chair," he said, turning his back and walking into the moonlight.

Conrad dragged a wicker chair behind his father out to the pool deck, the bleep-bleeping of tree frogs now a wall of sound hollering from everywhere at once, as if coming from inside his own head.

His father pointed at the chair and Conrad sat. He stood over the boy, handed him the bottle. "Have a Coca-Cola."

Keep it together . . . "Thank you, sir. But I don't want Coca-Cola. I want to know where Mum is."

His father seemed to search the canopy of stars above for the right words, then he simply shrugged. "Here is the bottom line: Your mother could have chosen to stay here with you. She was also free to leave by herself. But *nobody* takes what's—nobody takes my son away. I'm sorry to tell you this, but in the end she chose to go and leave you behind. She didn't love you enough to stay. She loved leaving more than she loved you."

Do not cry . . . do . . . not . . . The boy could feel his eyes stinging, his bottom lip trembling.

"Stop that right now," said his father. "Be a man."

"I'm TEN!" Conrad shouted. The tears came, he couldn't stop them, but he found he could still control his voice, and all at once he knew that he would not sob. He could feel anger push despair out the window. That gave him strength. He grew steadier as his father took the time to light a cigarette and blow a long, blue stream of smoke.

Conrad's father looked at him now with something like grudging tolerance. "I acknowledge this is a very difficult time for you, and there will be an adjustment period. And you may cry in your room. There's no shame in crying alone, but a man does not cry in front of others."

"I'm not a man yet," Conrad insisted, somehow managing to say it with no quaver or whine in his voice.

"I'm afraid you're going to have to be. And the blame for that falls squarely at the feet of your absent bitch of a mother. But we will manage this difficulty as best we can. In fact, it will strengthen you, so you'll grow up to be more than just a man. You'll do world-changing things. You'll be among the authors of history. What I mean to say is, everything will work out fine, son." Father cleared his throat. "Now drink your soda."

✣✣✣

The old man drank some water. "Five more years would've been optimal. I probably should've promoted you out of the Vatican a few years ago . . . but that's barn doors and horses now."

He looked out at the pool. "On the day I become too ill to run this organization, the board of advisers will appoint either you or Charles to the director's chair. The other will serve as deputy. Charles is of course beside himself that they might leapfrog you over him—he feels he's earned it. And he has."

"So why not give it to him?" Two other Conrads stared back at Conrad from his father's mirrored lenses, but just the angle of the old man's head made clear his displeasure at the question.

"Because he isn't half the man I raised you to be. I've always been hard on you. Iron sharpening iron, to make you ready. Now it's up to you. If you want the director's chair, you have to take it. You have to claim it and own it."

"Yes, sir."

"You'll take the reins—if you can take them—at a major turning point in history. The next director will change the course of human affairs in ways I both dreaded and dreamed of. The very earth will wobble as we transition out of the dying empire and into the empire to come, but it is necessary and it cannot be stopped. And time grows short. There will be sacrifices, but we must preserve our essential culture, our essential structures. If we don't manage this shift, the so-called *people* will, and they'll make beasts of us all. When the ranchers do battle, fences fall and the livestock begin to wander about, begin to consider independence. But livestock can't run the ranch. Well, the livestock are becoming restless, they can feel the tides shifting. We'll have to risk a little heating-up of the game."

"I'll do what's necessary," said Conrad. "You know that."

"Yes. The question is whether or not you'll do what's necessary well enough."

Dying of cancer, still an asshole.

The old man dug into the pocket of his cardigan, pulled out a set of keys, and smiled for the first time since Conrad's arrival. "Keys to the kingdom. *Need to know* is no longer a restriction for you. For there to be a level playing field, you need access to the same operating intelligence your rival has." He reached forward a once-strong hand, now bony and covered in liver spots, passing the keys to Conrad. The gold fob said *Fountaine Pajot*. "She's a sixty-foot motor cat, sitting at anchor just off Speightstown. I assume you still have a fondness for the sea?"

"I do."

"Then consider the boat a graduation present in advance. I hope you earn it. The computer on board contains the files I've deemed crucial. Read all you can."

Conrad pocketed the keys. "I'd better get at it."

The old man held up a hand. "One more thing. You've just promoted Michael Dillman to your second-in-command for the next phase of the AIT project."

"I have?"

The director nodded. "Let him think it came from you. Dillman's been a Council ally since you were a boy in short pants, and he's loyal to me. He'll be loyal to my son." He looked out at the pool again, a field of diamonds dancing above cold blue tiles. "And my son cannot afford to fail with this project."

19: GAMMA RAY

London, England

"Oh," said Kara. She opened the door wide and gestured Daniel inside. Her eyes were a little glassy. "You came back."

"I came back." Daniel followed her into the living room. A half-full bottle of red wine stood on the coffee table, wineglass beside it empty but still wet. It was eleven thirty in the morning.

"I'll get you a glass." She was back in less than a minute. They sat and she poured. "You report back to Julia?" The effort to smile looked exhausting. "Don't spare my feelings. Did I pass or fail?"

Go easy . . .

"I haven't spoken to Julia yet, but I'm almost certain I'll recommend she include you in the book."

"Almost?"

"Yes. But Julia's chasing down another bongo-playing theoretical physicist with another mathematically sound but currently untestable hypothesis about the Trinity Phenomenon. She'll be tied up a couple weeks maybe." He drank some wine. "Meanwhile, I have a proposition for you."

He laid out the line, selling himself as a nephew on a personal quest. Then he baited the line with a pitch he'd thought up in the bathtub. A pitch framed as logic, designed to appeal to her hyper-rationality.

"First of all," he said, "I suspect you're right. The voices are coming from somewhere other than your own mind."

An inch of tension dropped from Kara's shoulders and her smile was genuine. "You have no idea how long I've waited to hear those words." She let out a breath. "I can hear it whenever I want from fellow sufferers on the forums, but . . ."

"But a lot of them are crazy," said Daniel.

"Not all," she said, "but yes, a lot of them—most of them—are . . . crazy. Anyway, thank you."

"Just calling it as I see it. Which brings me to this: While it's possible that your working hypothesis—the Pentagon weapon—is the source of the voices, I suspect the truth is something different."

"Please don't tell me you think I'm another Tim Trinity."

"Just hear me out for a minute. You're a scientist, consider it as you would any competing hypothesis."

"Okay . . ."

"*It happened before in Mandal, where the revealed was once concealed, and the concealed shall be revealed.* I read that in your journal last night."

"I haven't got them memorized. I'm not *that* crazy."

"It's there. I can show you. And four days ago in West Virginia, a man said those exact same words to me."

"I don't understand."

"See, my uncle thought God was speaking to him, and I figured if what happened to Tim was happening to other people, I should look for people with similar notions. And I found this man who thinks he's possessed by Satan."

"And people say *I'm* crazy."

"Think of it this way: Information is coming into your head from the outside, manifesting as disembodied voices, auditory hallucinations. If you're my uncle, you interpret it as the voice of God. If you're this other man, you think it's the devil's voice. And if you're you . . ."

"I'd give it a technological interpretation, because I don't believe in God or Satan."

Daniel nodded. "The Pentagon weapon explains your experience in a way that supports your hard-core materialist world view—maybe that's why you're so committed to it. Because from where I'm standing, you sound more like a believer than a scientist, and your working hypothesis is at risk of hardening into dogma."

Kara looked at him for a long moment, evaluating. "For a man with a proposition, you're distinctly lacking in tact. But you do have an interesting mind." She sipped some wine. "Go on, I'm listening."

"Okay, so we've got the exact same phrase spoken into two different minds a continent apart. At a stretch, this could be explained by your Pentagon weapon, but some of the man's other symptoms cannot."

"What symptoms?"

"Mandal is a town in Norway, and the man has started speaking fluent Norwegian, a language he has never even been exposed to, complete with a real accent."

"That's not possible."

"Kara, listen to yourself. How many times have people heard your story and said *that's not possible*? I'm not asking you to believe in the supernatural. I honestly don't know what's causing the Trinity Phenomenon, but I do know it's happening. And whatever its cause, it describes your experience perhaps better than secret government mind-control gamma ray guns." He held up a hand.

"Sorry, I don't mean to sound sarcastic . . . it just seems to me the rational thing to do is to test your working hypothesis against this competing one. And if you're resisting that idea, then I think you need to honestly ask yourself which is more important: Preserving your working hypothesis, or finding the truth?"

"*Merde.* You're right."

"Excellent." Daniel made a toasting gesture, sipped some wine. "This *Mandal* phrase is our only lead, so I propose we follow it to the actual town, see what we find in Norway. I bet you could use a change of scenery and I'm covering expenses, first-class travel."

"Wait . . . is this some kind of elaborate come-on?"

Daniel smiled. "My come-ons are not so elaborate. Scout's honor, separate bedrooms all the way. Guess I probably should've opened with that."

Kara sipped some wine. "Huh. I guess I'm both reassured and a wee bit disappointed all at once." Her long neck flushed as she said it. She thought for a moment, nodded to herself. "I'll come," she said. "Definitely separate bedrooms, though."

20: FLYING NORTH

R eady for pizza?" said Julia.

Daniel switched the cell phone to his other ear as Heathrow's public address system announced a flight to Amsterdam. He could see Kara through the glass wall of the Duty Free shop, selecting a bottle of booze. The PA system echoed through the airport again, announcing a flight to Frankfurt.

"Pizza's gonna have to wait a week or two," said Daniel. "I have to leave town for a bit."

"You get a chance to visit Dr. Singh?"

"I saw her. She's interesting."

"I already know she's interesting, that's why I sent you to meet her. How crazy is she?"

She's a little unhinged, but she's not crazy. He didn't say it out loud.

He said, "Too early to say. I'll spend some more time with her but I've also got my own work to look after. Why don't you chase down that Glasgow physicist you were telling me about, and I'll call you when I've got a better handle on her condition?"

"Thanks," said Julia. "Any chance she's experiencing the Trinity Phenomenon . . . or someone's actually beaming voices into her head?"

"I don't know," said Daniel, "but don't get your hopes up. For now let's just stick with *interesting*. Listen, I gotta skedaddle."

"Why does it feel like there's something you're not telling me?" said Julia.

She did know him too well. And he had to admit, he wanted to tell her.

During Daniel's indoctrination, Raoul had said, *A million ways you can mess up in the field that can be forgiven, but reading people in against orders is the one that'll get you thrown out on your ass. We simply do not share our business—or even our existence—with outsiders. This is the life we choose.*

Daniel said, "Uh, I don't know why it feels that way."

"Daniel, what's up?"

His training clicked in, planted firmly in his gray matter by hundreds of role-playing sessions with Dave Christleib.

Startle and redirect . . . be rude.

"Whatever, Julia."

"Whatever?"

"You don't want my help on this thing, I've got other things to do with my time."

"Why are you being so weird all of a sudden?"

Double down on it . . .

"I'm just saying I'm happy to help you with your research, but I have to work it around my schedule and I don't have time to stop and share my every passing speculation about what might or might not be causing Dr. Singh's auditory hallucinations. So just back off a little. Give me room to breathe, for God's sake. When I have something, I'll let you know."

"Okay, fine . . . *weirdo.*" Julia hung up. A mild parting shot, her restraint belying her quite justifiable pique.

As Daniel pocketed the phone, he caught his reflection in the glass wall. He needed Julia to lose interest in Kara, needed her to shift her attention to another chapter of her book for a while, long enough for him to make this trip. It was that simple. He didn't love acting like an ass, but it got the job done.

Ayo was right about there being a lot of Tim Trinity in him, but she was wrong about Daniel not seeing it. He'd been raised with grifters, raised by the very best of them. Among con artists, Tim was a first ballot hall of famer—and Daniel had learned the skills as a child, by osmosis.

Valuable skills in a world of secrets and spies. But he'd just manipulated and lied to a woman he'd been in love with for a long time and still considered a loved friend.

This is the life you chose.

21: RADIO SILENCE

Highway E18—south of Oslo, Norway

A decade investigating miracle claims for the Vatican had taken Daniel to over half the countries on the planet, but he'd never been to Norway. Not surprising, really. Shaped by five centuries of Lutheranism, the culture here discouraged people from even feeling special—miraculous was completely unacceptable.

Highway E18 was smooth enough to star in a skateboarder's dreams, its crisp yellow lines flowing beneath a cloudless blue canopy, stretching through green pastures, gracefully curving around rocky granite hills, occasionally tunneling right through, sometimes spanning rivers on gleaming steel bridges of striking modern design and engineering.

Daniel had no idea what he might find at the end of this journey, but he liked being here, on this road, at this moment . . . with this woman.

He glanced over at Kara, now sleeping in the partially reclined passenger seat, sunlight landing softly on her face, the stress gone from her brow, her mouth turned up slightly at the corners in what struck Daniel as an intimate smile.

Her expression in sleep had an openness that contrasted sharply with her nervous and guarded state when they'd first met.

And why wouldn't she be nervous and guarded, with all she'd been through? Six years. It was actually astonishing how well she'd held things together. Daniel doubted he'd have the same strength, were their roles reversed.

And she still had the will to chase after the truth.

It was a close call, though. Could've gone either way.

✥ ✥ ✥

As soon as Kara opened the door to her Knightsbridge flat that morning, Daniel had known the trip was in jeopardy.

"You all right?"

"I don't know if I can go. I'm operating on one hour of sleep and about a gallon of coffee. My head is pounding."

"What happened?"

"I didn't drink before bed last night. I wanted to look present-able for today."

Now he noticed she'd had her hair cut shorter, about an inch above the shoulders, and the silver at the roots was gone. An urge flickered, to tell her she was more than presentable, she was beauti-ful, and she was also beautiful with silver in her hair . . .

Kara was saying, ". . . no voices came and I went to bed sober. About an hour later I had this horrible dream. It was in Norway, and I have no idea how I knew that, I just did, the way you know things in dreams sometimes. A rural village, not even a hamlet, really . . . it was a very long time ago, preindustrial, everything was filthy and everyone had bad teeth. The people in this place were all walking around the village, just wandering, not going anywhere, not doing anything, just smiling at each other with their bad teeth . . . and then all at once everyone was just—just falling down dead, all dying at the same time." Her hand reached forward, then withdrew. "And I just stood there and watched them collapse like dropped marionettes. I didn't even try to help them."

"Sounds awful." She could've been dreaming about the Black Death. Or not. She hadn't described the people as appearing sick before they dropped dead . . .

"The worst part, it didn't feel like a dream. It was more intense . . . like a vision. Like they were transmitting it into my head while I slept. They've never done that before, but my mouth tasted like cinnamon when I woke, the same sensation that accompanies the voices, so maybe they were."

The Foundation's research said eighteen percent of confirmed AIT sufferers experienced these vision-dreams, but Daniel couldn't tell her that.

He said, "At one point, my uncle started having hyper-real dreams he called visions." They'd started a couple weeks before Tim Trinity's death, but Kara didn't need to hear that. She also didn't need to know that Daniel had been there when one of Tim's vision-dreams came true. Not yet.

He put his hand on her shoulder. "One thing's for sure: Staying here isn't helping you. Either your tormenters are pointing you toward Norway, or the universe is. Let's just take this trip and find out which. I'll be right beside you the whole way."

✢ ✢ ✢

Kara had slept through the two-hour flight and now the four-hour drive from Oslo to the southern tip of the country. She woke as they approached the outskirts of Mandal, pressed a button to raise her seat upright, brushed a few strands of hair out of her face.

"Oh, it's lovely," she said, blinking the sleep from her eyes.

And it was. A picture postcard of a harbor town with a big trade in summer tourism. White wooden houses with red roofs dotted the lush green hillside, becoming more concentrated lower down, with larger buildings by the water. A marina full of pleasure crafts, another with beautifully maintained fishing boats. To one side of town, a wide, sandy beach almost a kilometer in length.

They checked into a three-bedroom luxury waterfront rental cottage, unpacked in their separate bedrooms, then Daniel went back downstairs to the open kitchen and made a pot of coffee.

Kara descended the floating staircase, wrapped in a pale blue microfiber robe with navy trim. It looked soft. "Thank you for the quiet drive," she said.

"You needed it. Coffee?"

"I'll freshen up first," she said. "Feels like a new day."

"Sure. Take your time." His phone vibrated on the counter, rattling against the car keys. He glanced at the screen, shrugged. "Office. 'Vacation days' is a bit of a misnomer in my racket."

"Business consulting," said Kara. Nothing to read in her tone.

Daniel nodded, reaching for the phone as it vibrated for the third time. "Just be a few minutes."

Kara smiled. "I'll hop in the shower then." She turned and walked up the stairs with a little more hip sway than he'd seen from her before.

He caught the call before it hit voice-mail. "Yep?"

Raoul Aharon said, "You never call, you never write . . . it's enough to make a mother sick with worry."

Daniel stepped out onto the balcony and closed the door behind him. "Yeah, sorry for the radio silence, but I can't exactly call you without blowing my cover, *Mom*."

"She's buying your story?"

"I think so."

"You *think* so?"

"She's a very smart woman with a scientist's skeptical mind. So yeah, I *think* she's buying my story. So far." He leaned against the balcony railing. The five o'clock sun bathed the harbor in warm light, reflecting off the aluminum masts of sailboats. The same harbor had welcomed trade and sailors and rats and fleas and *Yersinia pestis* in 1349, leading to the death of a third of the country's population within a single year. "Was gonna e-mail a sitrep tonight, but there ain't much *situation* to *report*. Just conversation and travel."

"Right," said Raoul. "Ayo thinks you've got a hard-on for Dr. Crazy."

"Ayo said that?"

"'Course not—she said 'smitten.'"

"Not that it's any of your business," said Daniel.

"Of course it's my business. I've seen a dozen field operatives destroy themselves this way, some of them veterans." Raoul chuckled. "Fair warning: I will kick your ass on the mats if you fall into this trap."

"Thanks for your concern," said Daniel. "I'd feel a whole lot better if you and Ayo gave as much mindshare to this mission as you do to fantasizing about my sex life, or lack thereof."

"I'm just saying: you wanna get your dick wet, no skin off my nose. But *smitten* worries the hell out of me. *Smitten* overrides judgment."

"Fine. Busted. There's chemistry."

"Oh, *chemistry*. So she wants to do you, too. Wonderful, have fun. But play her as an asset, period. She's nuts—you can't rely on her."

"The woman's had voices in her head for six years, had her entire life stripped away, and the world thinks she's insane. She's coping a hell of a lot better than I would." Daniel remembered Julia's assessment. "She seems like a woman under great stress because someone is beaming voices into her head. She's misidentified the source, but she's thinking clearly. Someone—some*thing*, the universe, God, whatever—*is* beaming voices into her head. She's not nuts. And the booze is just self-medicating to keep the voices quiet."

"Regardless, you are not cleared to read her in."

"Ayo already said that," said Daniel. "And I didn't."

"Yet," said Raoul. "Soon as you consummate this bad idea, you'll have a strong desire to share with her. Not because of the sex, per se. Because, *smitten*."

"I heard you the first three times," said Daniel. "Moving on to actual business, tell me you've learned more about my buddy from Homeland."

"Evan Sage is as he appears, no allegiance to any parties beyond his employer. His team's specialty is clandestine work, infiltrating Bad Guy networks, a lot of the heavy lifting abandoned by CIA after the silent coup that turned the Company into a de facto branch of the Pentagon. Sage is serious business, he could write his ticket anywhere in the intel community, but he's got some kind of Captain America thing going on. Definitely got skills, but he's not in the larger game, so I wouldn't worry. After your meeting he ran a full background check on you, and last night—end of business in New

York—he called UNEX Inc. and spoke at length with your boss, Dave Christleib. All as expected. Your NOC is intact."

"Hope so," said Daniel. "He promised to keep an eye on me."

"And we're keeping an eye on him keeping an eye on you, so don't sweat it. Sage used his Amex to pay for lunch three hours ago at a pub two blocks from Thames House. If we had to, we could hack into London's eye in the sky, but my guess is he took Mike Stotter to lunch. Probably asked if you were on Five's radar, which you were not previous to the question being asked. I promise, if either of these guys travels to Norway, you'll know it before they land."

22: A MILLION VACATIONS

Mandal seemed smaller than its population of fifteen thousand, and Daniel figured some of the tourists were actually new locals—wealthy retirees cramming a million Mandal vacations into their remaining years. Aside from looking both Indian and too young for retirement, Kara fit right in with the Norwegian sailing set, in capri pants, a Liberty print shirt, and a zippered cable-knit cardigan.

As they strolled down a cobbled shopping street, Kara stopped to read the menu posted in a restaurant window. She turned away from the window and shook her head. "The benefits of travel are lost on anyone who eats pizza on a trip to Norway."

"There's a Chinese joint a few blocks up that's got good online reviews," Daniel deadpanned.

Kara made a face. "I'm holding out for local fishy delicacies."

They crossed a pedestrian bridge spanning a large salmon river that ran through the center of town—which explained the three fish on the coat of arms displayed all over town. On the other side of the bridge stood a large modern building with expansive glass walls and a gently arching white roof partly covered in green turf, providing a smooth aesthetic transition from the ultramodern building to the traditional hillside town behind it.

Inside the building, they stopped at an art gallery featuring a local history exhibit—pen-and-ink renderings of important events through the centuries, a plaque beside each giving a thumbnail accounting of the event and any historically significant people involved.

Daniel slowed as they hit the Black Death section. He'd been careful to make this seem like a casual stroll, but he'd read about the exhibit while researching the town online and he'd brought Kara here to see her reaction to this. He hadn't told her about the soldier's fixation with the sweep of the plague that had killed just about everyone living in Mandal. He didn't want that information to influence her, either.

The plaques described the plague's decimation of the region, but also the local legend that gave the place its name.

Mandal meant Man Dale, or Man Valley. But many among the older generation translated the name to One Man Valley, adding another layer of meaning. The local legend said that after the Black Death claimed victory, there was but one man left alive in this entire valley. In another valley there was but one woman left alive, and the town there was called Kvinesdal, or One Woman Valley.

At a plaque titled a romantic legend, Daniel read the story a few old-timers still believed: The One Woman came here after the plague and married the One Man, and they became the Adam and Eve of this valley, the original ancestors common to almost everyone who'd been born here since.

"It's a myth, of course," said Kara. "To populate this entire valley from just two people, especially considering infant mortality rates in the Middle Ages, brothers and sisters, fathers and daughters, mothers and sons would all have to breed together. The bloodline would've committed suicide long ago."

"The legend sounds somewhat less romantic as you describe it," said Daniel.

They moved on to a photography exhibit, beautiful rural landscapes printed on canvases as large as six feet across, fjords and forests and farms and valleys. In front of each photo, a page from a topographical atlas was mounted on a pedestal, a red dot showing where the photographer had stood when capturing the photos.

Daniel was almost at the seascape photos when he realized Kara was no longer beside him. He turned to see her, frozen, staring at a canvas.

"Kara? What is it?" She didn't answer. He touched her shoulder but she didn't seem to notice. He followed her gaze to a landscape photograph of an empty green valley.

Kara's voice sounded far away as she said, "That's impossible." Her hand went up to cover her open mouth.

"What is?"

She kept staring at the photo, her expression growing more haunted as she took in the details. "That's where my dream took place. The hillside—the ridgeline in the background—I mean it's identical. In the dream, the little hamlet was in the foreground where that field of wild grass is, but it's the same place. I'm positive."

Daniel pulled out his phone, photographed the page from the atlas and the landscape photo. He examined the topographical map. It was a rural part of the valley about a hundred clicks north of the town of Mandal. "We'll drive there in the morning," he said. "I'm hungry, let's go find some fish balls."

"But Daniel . . ."

"What?"

"There's no way they could've transmitted this into my head. Even if they sat with this photo and described it in detail, they couldn't have put the *exact* picture in my mind."

"I know," said Daniel. "Let's eat."

23: RIDDLE ME

Berlin, Germany

The problem was, eight microbiologists had to die in the next ten days. It wasn't a logistical problem . . . a few hours in the data stream to determine who among the eight had a heart condition, who drove drunk, who drove tired, who was having an affair, who was drowning in debt, who was secretly gay, who was secretly depressed. Match each problem to a plausible cause of death, and the wet teams could be dispatched within a day.

In fact, the process was already in motion.

Logistics was the easy part. The problem was that these weren't just any microbiologists, but eight of the world's preeminent molecular immunology specialists at leading research labs—WHO in Geneva, CDC in Atlanta, ECDC in Stockholm, Institut Pasteur in Paris, University of Illinois in Chicago, National Institutes of Health in Bethesda. Even if the deaths were spread out over ten months, people would notice. But ten days? God just doesn't make coincidences that big. It was so statistically unlikely, it would be impossible *not* to see it. It was sure to blow up the blogosphere and social media, and once that happened, even an establishment journalist or two might notice.

Regardless, it had to be done. Conrad had read the final report from Africa—complete success with phase one—and the old man had been explicit about accelerating the timeline.

Bottom line: The timing of these deaths would be noticed, so Conrad's computer geeks would play it up. They'd plant the seeds in online forums and blogs, leading the conspiracy-minded down the rabbit hole to a cornucopia of competing theories ranging from plausible to truly insane. The lunatic fringe would take sides and argue violently over minutia, discrediting both themselves and the idea of conspiracy in general, leading reasonable people to conclude that the issue had been looked into and the timing was really just a coincidence—strange but nothing nefarious.

That's how it would play out—you could bet grandma's pension on it. Reasonable people always shrug these things off and get on with their lives, reassuring each other that all those other folks are paranoid, spouting bromides like *three can keep a secret if two are dead.*

They were as reliable in their way as the paranoid were in theirs.

Michael Dillman said, "Big Pharma is an obvious choice, they subsidize almost every major research lab to one degree or another, plenty of overlap, plenty of dots to connect. I'm also thinking we should put a nation state in the mix. Russia, or—"

"Not Russia," said Conrad, "we're active there right now on other projects. Let's say North Korea. Call it a preemptive strike against world pressure to open their bioweapons program for international inspections."

"Great, done."

"We still need some red meat for the fringe," said Conrad.

Dillman nodded. "I was thinking a large-scale eugenics-slash-depopulation scheme, pointing to the usual suspects both real and imagined—Club of Rome, Bilderberg Group, Illuminati. New World Order stuff, UN black helicopters . . . just go full-on crazy with it. Too much?"

"No, it's good. Those'll be our Big Three. You fill out the rest, say another half dozen or so. We need this up and ready when our scientists start dropping tomorrow."

"On it." Dillman picked up the target files and left the room, the soundproofed door whispering shut behind him.

Asshole or not, the director was an excellent judge of people to whom he was not related, and Colonel Dillman was proving to be a perfect choice as Conrad's first mate.

Asshole or not, the director wanted to die knowing he was leaving the Council in the hands of his son.

That had to count for something.

Claim it and own it, the old man said. Now Conrad would.

Having read the files left for him on the boat, Conrad understood the director's insistence that this project could only succeed if no fingerprints were left behind.

"This isn't Iran-Contra or the Kennedy boys," the director warned in their final meeting before Conrad left Barbados. "This is a huge gamble. As we move to the next phase, we must give it solid cover. We've got the new Middle East offensive almost ready to go—the next front will be Yemen. You cloak AIT into the Yemeni project, make them serve each other. But AIT is the top game, the one to protect. It can never be known. If we lose this game, we could very well spark an unsponsored revolution. We cannot afford that outcome."

"But if we win," Conrad said, "the entire game board is ours. We write the future unopposed."

The old man smiled for the second time during their meeting. "You need to keep that thought if you're going to win the director's chair. Charles is playing to *not lose*. You play to win."

Claim it and own it.

Conrad had always known this day would come—his father had laid out the long-range career plan when installing Conrad at the Vatican after university. And Conrad had worked tirelessly for it, had done unspeakable things to get here.

Now he was just one step away from proving himself.

It was everything he ever wanted, but it also meant closing the door on the church that had given him so much for so many years. The church had become his home, had given him structure and camaraderie and the closest thing to love he would ever feel, and had shielded him from the treachery of women.

Conrad would always have God, but he would no longer have God's grace. That was the price to be paid.

24: NUE

"Man, Norwegian is easy." Daniel put his menu aside. "Fish balls? *Fiskeboller*. Fish soup? *Fiskesuppe*. Fish burger? *Fiskeburger*."

"What?" Kara's mind was still back at the photo gallery.

"Guess how to say, 'Shall we go pick blueberries?' in Norwegian. Go ahead, give it a try."

"I've no idea."

"*Skal vi gå plukke blåbær.* Seriously, I read it in the phrase book. I mean, how easy is that? Speak English with a Norwegian accent and you're practically speaking Norwegian." He sipped his wine. "Why the phrase book thought I'd need to invite a Norwegian blueberry picking is, however, perplexing."

Kara brought her hand down hard enough to rattle the cutlery. "Daniel, stop. I know what you're trying to do, but please stop it."

"You've had a bit of a shock," said Daniel. "I was just—"

"I haven't had a bit of a shock, I've found out that what I've been going through for the last six years, everything I learned about it—my *working hypothesis* as you so cavalierly put it—is dead wrong." She shook her head. "I mean, how is this possible? Why are my dreams leading me to a photography exhibit in Norway? Doesn't make any sense."

Carter Ames had once said to Daniel: *Walk the path and you'll learn the truth.* Daniel now said, "We're looking for the same thing,

Kara. And we're finding it . . . or it's finding us. Either way, we're on the right path." She broke eye contact and stared at her wineglass but didn't reach for it. "I know letting go of what you thought you knew is hard," he said, "but were things really better when you thought government thugs were beaming voices into your head?"

Kara smiled despite herself. "No, of course not. It was just . . . something solid."

With her working hypothesis now shattered, Kara wanted to hear all the details of Daniel's experience with Tim Trinity. He told her all he could without mentioning the Foundation or the Council, focusing on Trinity's voices and vision-dreams and predictions, holding back on all of the Foundation's research on AIT.

"So there's me, your uncle, and the man you told me about who said the thing about Mandal. How many other people have you found?"

"I don't know. Just take some comfort in the fact that you're not alone."

"Don't be ridiculous, you know exactly how many others you've found." She stiffened. "What else aren't you telling me?"

"Actually, I don't know means *I don't know*. Most of the cases have turned out to be mental illness," Daniel lied. He could've sealed the deal with *Don't be so paranoid*, but he couldn't bring himself to strike at her soft spot. Not because he was smitten, he told himself, but because she deserved to know what was happening to her and not telling her was bad enough.

He continued the riff. "Other than my uncle, I haven't had as much time with the other cases as I have with yours. Of those I've seen so far, maybe a half dozen will be the real thing, maybe more."

Maybe about ten thousand more . . .

⁂

Alone by the flickering orange light of the living room's gas fireplace, Daniel sent the photo of the topographical map to Ayo with a message:

Need GPS to location of red dot ~100k n/nw Mandal.

That done, he plugged his phone into the speaker dock and put Nils Frahm's *Wintermusik* on and returned to the couch where he sat with his coffee and his music, not trusting himself to climb the stairs and walk past Kara's bedroom door without knocking and asking if she needed a glass of water . . . or anything.

⁂

He fired up his laptop, opened the e-mail application. There was an e-mail from Julia. He clicked on the message to open it.

> *Danny: Sorry I called you weirdo. You've been a huge help with my research and I appreciate it more than I can (or do) say. I didn't mean to put pressure on—I'm sure you'll get back to Dr. Singh as soon as you can make time. I guess I'm having a little trouble accepting that you won't tell me about the new job that's keeping you so busy. And this isn't some ex-girlfriend thing—this is a friend thing. Friends talk to each other about their lives, keep each other grounded, and I want us to be friends forever, no matter what else. I'm worried about you, Danny. You seemed different when I saw you in London . . . harder. You've been through a lot in the last year, and that's when people lose their way. I hope you're not isolating yourself. And I hope you haven't joined Pat Wahlquist's world. Pat's*

charming and I know you love him, but the man is a mercenary. His world scares me. It isn't the world for the Daniel Byrne I know. Love, Julia.

Awesome.

Daniel sat back and sipped his coffee. He didn't bother to pretend he was going to hit Reply. He knew he wasn't. Because what could he say? He'd already lied to her and poached her interview subject, and capped that off by manipulating her so that *she* was now apologizing to *him*.

What a guy.

"Being a spy means being an asshole to pretty much everyone in your life," Raoul had said during training. "It's part of the price this job demands of you, a price paid not only by you but also by anyone foolish enough to love you. That's why dating citizens is a bad idea." Training had included coping techniques, which mostly meant knowing how to draw boundaries and sell lies.

There would be a reckoning with Julia once he and Kara returned to London. It would be ugly, and Daniel would have to figure out how to fit it in with his cover story. He'd sheepishly admit to Julia that solving the Trinity Phenomenon had become a personal obsession, he'd cop to poaching Kara, but he'd mitigate that by offering whatever he and Kara learned here. And when the Foundation had enough to begin to understand AIT, Daniel would bring it all to Julia and she would bring it to the world. It would be the journalistic scoop of all time.

But would that undo the damage he was now doing to their friendship?

The worst part, Raoul had warned, was that no one outside the game would every really know you. Daniel could feel the distance growing between the man Julia had known and the man he was becoming. He realized now that he was playing the role of his earlier self whenever he spoke with her, and as time went on that role would only recede further from reality, and she would continue to know him less until she didn't really know him at all.

And this too was the life he'd chosen.

He opened a new message, to Ayo and Raoul, cc'd to Carter Ames. He told them about Kara's vision-dream and the matching landscape photo they'd found.

It is becoming increasingly clear, Daniel concluded, *that Dr. Kara Singh is suffering from Anomalous Information Transfer. To keep her on board, we will need to tell her more about her condition. She deserves to know.*

He held down the backspace key, erasing the last sentence before hitting Send. Singh was a chess piece to them, as he knew she should be to him. What one woman *deserves to know* doesn't much matter when you're playing the big game, fighting for the future.

But with this woman, it did matter. Raoul would call this a case of smitten overriding judgment. Maybe he'd be right.

Daniel heard a door close upstairs. He put his laptop away as Kara came down the staircase carrying the bottle of Laphroaig she'd picked up at Duty Free.

"Too wired to sleep," Kara held up the bottle, "thought you might like to help me crack this." She was wearing the soft blue robe again, over purple silk pajamas. She was wearing a little lipstick and eyeliner, too.

Daniel stood. "I'll get glasses."

"Sit, I'm closer." She walked into the open kitchen. "I was already a single malt drinker before moving to the UK and, like a typical American, thought people who put water in their whisky were doing great violence to it, thought true *aficionados* drank it neat." She opened the fridge, poured some water from a filter pitcher into a small milk pitcher, put it beside the bottle on a tray. "And I went around London proudly ordering my single malts neat and collecting some strange looks from the Brits, especially the Scots." She put a couple rocks glasses on the tray and carried it to the living room. "Imagine my embarrassment when I went on a distillery tour of Scotland."

She sat next to Daniel on the couch. He could feel the tension in her body, a living energy field reaching him from two feet away. And she was wearing perfume. Smelled like honey.

"I learned the truth at the first distillery on the tour," she said. "The master distiller was a very kind man, he didn't make me feel foolish at all when I expressed astonishment that people were adding water." She handed the bottle to Daniel. "Pour, and don't be stingy."

He stripped the foil and pulled the wooden cap. Kara jumped a little when the cork came out with a louder-than-expected pop. As he poured, she continued her story. "The distiller asked me about my favorite single malts and complimented my choices, and told me that many people, not just Americans, make the mistake of taking it neat. He explained how scotch is made, saying, 'Fer heaven's sake, we add bloody water to it with great violence before we put it in the bloody bottle.' He explained how adding a splash of water opens the spirit up, unfolding layers of complexity on the tongue."

Kara lifted the little pitcher of water, poured a splash into the amber spirit in her glass. She hovered the pitcher over Daniel's glass, cocked an eyebrow at him.

"I'll take a little water, thank you," he said. He could feel the pulse throbbing in his neck.

"Thought so," she said, splashing a little water in his glass. She sat back, lifted hers in a toasting gesture. "Hey Mr. Phrasebook, how does one say *cheers*?"

"*Skal*," said Daniel, clinking his glass against hers.

"*Skal*," she said.

They sipped the smoky, peaty scotch. Daniel said, "And the moral of the Master Distiller story is . . . instead of feeling embarrassed for not knowing, you should feel proud for wanting to learn. Or is there a twist coming?"

Stop flirting, you idiot. This will only end in tears . . .

"There's always a twist," she said, her green eyes reflecting the firelight, "and I'd like to face it without blinders on, if you don't mind."

"Meaning?"

"Meaning I know there's something you're not telling me, and if you want to continue to study my case, you are going to have to open up. You cannot feed me *just so much* of what you know." She sipped her drink. "But I propose we table that discussion until after our field trip. You asked me to trust you. I'll give you a day. When we get back here tomorrow night, you are going to tell me everything you know about my condition, or we are going to part ways. Sound reasonable?"

"Eminently," said Daniel with a grateful smile. "Thank you for the day."

Kara put her glass down. "Well, I'm glad we can both be such reasonable people."

And then she kissed him.

He tried to break the kiss, really he did. But this was a hell of a kiss, a kiss destined to be revisited in future fantasies, lips so soft, tongue so warm, need so naked.

He did break the kiss, finally. "Kara, I—"

"No, don't." She slid back a foot, picked up her drink. "I'm sorry, I know we shouldn't. It's just, ever since the tabloid press branded me Dr. Crazy . . . it's just been a very long time since a man looked at me the way you look at me."

"It's not that I don't want to . . ."

"That much is obvious," Kara smiled. "Has been for a while."

"Really? I thought I was being subtle."

She laughed, almost choking on fine whisky. "Oh, Daniel. Okay, I'm just going to say this so it's out in the open: Julia told me you two used to live together—"

"No—no, it's not that at all," said Daniel. "Julia and I are good friends. We tried to be a couple, twice, and it didn't work out. Neither one of us wants to try it a third time."

"So, is it the priest thing? Julia said you'd been a priest for . . ."

Daniel laughed. "Believe me, the best thing about leaving the priesthood was being released from the vow of celibacy."

"Okay. So we've got this mad chemistry going on—which by the way, you have been doing a terrible job of hiding on your end—but you won't, and it's not because of Julia or because you were a priest . . . Wait. Is it because I'm a *case study* to you? Is that it? Because if that is it, after the way you've led me on, I will slap you."

"No. God, no." Daniel took her hand in his. "Look, there's nothing I can say right now that's not lame. I just need you to trust me . . . like the other thing, let's just say we're tabling this for future discussion." He put his arm around her shoulders. "Because we can both be such reasonable people."

Kara sipped her drink. "Okay then," she said, "consider it tabled. But if you don't want me to kiss you, you have to stop flirting with me."

"Deal," he said.

She leaned against him, resting her head on his shoulder. "This last year especially, it's been . . . before today . . ." It came out like a self-conscious confession. "I haven't even left my neighborhood for the last eight months. And here I am chasing dreams in Norway with a mysterious man who knows something he's not telling me." She rested her palm on Daniel's chest and he stroked her hair.

After a minute, she said, "Is it okay if I just . . . stay here, for a bit?"

It was not okay at all. It was about as far from okay as Daniel was from New York.

"Of course it's okay," he said, and hugged her a little closer.

25: CINNAMON GIRL

The GPS led them over increasingly steep terrain, deeper into wilderness, and now the roads were packed gravel and Daniel felt better about renting the BMW SUV instead of the M5 sedan he'd have preferred on the highway.

They passed the time in relatively easy silence, listening to his iPod. The discovery that they shared a love of reggae pleased Daniel inordinately. A relief after the awkward start to the day, both Daniel and Kara a little too careful with their words, a little too aware of their body language.

At one point during breakfast, when they both reached for the salt and their hands met unintentionally, Daniel saw a chance to break the tension.

"That was *not* flirting," he said, "that was just a shared love of salt."

"Not to worry," said Kara, "I had a long think this morning, and I promise you are in no danger of being kissed again."

"What? You mean, ever?"

"See, now you're flirting."

"Mea culpa," said Daniel. "But I wasn't about the salt."

♣ ♣ ♣

The gravel road came to an end. Daniel stopped.

"Road ends," said the English-accented fembot voice of the GPS.

"Gee, thanks," said Daniel.

"Destination is north 853 meters, on the right," said the fembot.

Daniel looked down the rocky hill to the valley floor. He put the car in low gear. "A little bumpy, but it's doable."

"This is nothing," said Kara with a wide grin, "when I was a teenager I had a dirt bike."

Daniel tried not to think of Kara on a dirt bike. He failed miserably, of course—like telling yourself not to picture an elephant makes you picture an elephant. So he went ahead and pictured her on a dirt bike.

"Ready when you are," said Kara.

"Right." He lifted his foot off the brake.

It took a few minutes to cross the 853 meters but Daniel got it done without damaging the rental. He pulled the key from the ignition and got out. Kara put on her sunglasses, took a few steps, and came to a dead stop.

She stood silent for a few seconds, then said, "It's real. It's really real. I mean a photograph was weird enough, but this is . . ." She scanned the ridgeline along the northern horizon. "The ridgeline, the way the sun hits the trees . . . even the smell of the place . . . it's like walking right into my dream."

Daniel took stock of the immediate area. A half-dozen large bedrock outcrops to their left, almost a story in height. A hundred yards to the right, a small stream, flowing south. The rest of the area just a field of rocks and wild grasses, punctuated by bursts of little pink wildflowers. "Why don't you show me where things stood in your dream?" he said.

Kara turned and walked through the tall grass. "Over in this area, there were maybe ten or fifteen small buildings, not in a circle exactly, but with a common area in the middle." She continued walking. "There may have been a well in the center, I'm not sure . . ."

"Kara, watch your—" Kara pitched forward and fell, disappearing into the tall grass. "—step."

She was back on her feet before Daniel reached her. "I'm okay, I'm fine," she said. "Slightly bruised ego is all."

"Telemark landing," said Daniel. "Straight tens from the judges."

She laughed. "Not very Grace Kelly, I'm afraid."

"More Katherine Hepburn," said Daniel "Looks good on you."

"Hey—flirting," Kara warned, still smiling. She brushed dirt off her sleeves, then off her palms.

"Right, sorry." He reached out and wiped some dirt off her forehead. "This is not flirting, this is checking for a bump."

"I'm fine, I didn't hit my head. I just rested it on the ground in shame."

"Oh. Okay then." Daniel brushed the tall grass aside, pointed down. "See here? This raised line of stones? It goes straight out . . ." He followed the line a few yards, found the corner. "Then it turns ninety degrees. It's the foundation of a very old building."

Kara stopped. "Oh my god. The village was real."

"The village was real." Daniel walked a little farther, swishing the tall grass aside with his hand. "Look, there's another one over here."

Kara stepped over to him. "This is incredible . . ."

Daniel looked over the ancient stone foundations, picturing what the village might have looked like in 1349. "One Man Valley," he said. "Imagine it's 1349, and you're a man living a bare subsistence life with all your relatives. Your brother falls ill with a violence you've never seen before, black lesions on his skin, sores oozing puss, coughing up blood. And then your brother's wife. And then it spreads to your uncle and your cousins and there's no science in your world, so you think this is some punishment from God. Everyone does. Everyone prays. But pretty soon you and the dwindling members of your clan are burning the dead bodies of your wives and parents and children, trying to stop the spread of this unholy curse. And after weeks of unanswered prayer, there are no bodies left to burn. There's no one left but you. You've watched every human being you know die. You don't know a soul in the world, and you don't know if God has visited this curse across the entire world. It's enough to make you want to just sit down and die. But you don't. You hunt and gather and make fire and eat, and you leave this dead place behind. You forge into the unknown, searching for fellow survivors, for a way to survive together and rebuild."

Kara stepped in close. "Daniel, I—" She closed her eyes and pressed a palm against the side of her head. "I don't feel so well."

Daniel took hold of her elbow. "Let's find you a place to sit."

"No, I—" Her mouth opened and closed twice. "Cinnamon, I'm tasting cinnamon. Get the thing."

Daniel pulled out his phone and launched the voice recorder. "Recording. If the voices—"

"Shut up." She closed her eyes again. After a few seconds, she said, "Kara, listen: The work of men who strive to become gods . . . the work of men who strive to become gods . . ." She fell silent again, listening for more, then shook her head and opened her eyes. "They're gone, that's it . . . the taste is fading. That's all. You can put it away."

Daniel pocketed his phone. "The work of men who strive to become gods."

"Whatever the hell that means," said Kara.

A bird called out from the hillside, a shrill cry that carried across the valley floor. That's when Kara lost consciousness and dropped like a rag doll into Daniel's arms.

26: WHO BY FIRE

Kara's eyes flickered as Daniel lowered her gently to the ground. "What happened?" she said.

He helped her sit up. "You passed out for a few seconds. Happened to my uncle as well. I never witnessed it, but he told me about his fainting spells, said it only happened to him a few times."

"Fewer the better," she said, reaching for Daniel's water bottle. "Taste is back." She took a few gulps. "There was a dream but I can't . . ." Her expression darkened. "Wait. It was a . . . a child, screaming. A little boy, filthy blond hair, screaming into a fire."

"Sounds like your brain was just making a movie out of the story I was telling—"

"No, it was real. I know where it was." Kara stood up and marched off in the direction of the rocky outcrops. "Over there, c'mon."

Daniel caught up with her and kept pace, following her lead. "How is that coming to you?" he asked. "Voice? Image? I can't read your mind, you have to tell me what it looks and sounds like in there if we're gonna figure this out."

Kara stopped abruptly and looked at him. "Neither. It's more like an intuition but with absolute certainty, like how in dreams you know things without knowing how you know them." A new intensity crept into her voice. "And I know where this boy stood."

She thrust an accusing finger at the third rocky outcrop, about the size of a three-car garage. "He was over there, behind that one. There's a cave. I know it." She strode off and Daniel followed, walking to the end of the outcrop and turning right.

On this side, the bedrock sloped down from the height of about fifteen feet all the way to the valley floor. Long green vines hung down thickly from the top, obscuring the wall, but a few feet past the corner there was a blackness behind the vines that suggested an opening about five feet tall and four feet wide.

"See? Cave." She did not sound happy about it.

Daniel grabbed handfuls of the ropy vines and used his folding pocketknife to cut them back from the opening. He put the knife away and ducked through the entrance, into a cave nobody had seen for . . . maybe centuries.

The air inside was dry and dusty and smelled vaguely of charcoal.

Kara entered behind him, stirring more dust up into the light streaming through the hole in the vines. Daniel moved deeper into the cave, past the daylight, shining his phone's tiny flashlight ahead. The space was about twelve feet across, the blackened ceiling just a few inches above his head. He ran a finger against the ceiling. "Soot," he said. At the back wall of the cave, just visible in the flashlight's beam, was a large pile of white rocks.

Halfway into the cave, they found the charred fire pit, almost eight feet in diameter. "Too big for a cave of this size," he said stepping around the pit. He aimed his light at the back wall.

It wasn't a pile of white rocks. He was looking at a pile of human bones.

Kara grabbed his free hand. "My God, look how many there are."

Daniel stepped closer, counting skulls. "There's gotta be over a hundred."

He squatted down, sifting through the scattered bones of a hand and forearm. He picked up a small skull. "No charring. These bodies weren't burned. He glanced back at the fire pit. "They died of smoke inhalation—they were trapped by the fire, couldn't get out."

"Look at this." Kara held out a rock to him. "There are dozens of others in the pile just like it." One edge of the rock was deeply gouged and chipped. Kara pointed to deep scratches in the sooty wall. "They were trying to dig their way out through solid rock. A desperate final act, nowhere to go. Daniel, these people were murdered."

How must it have felt to have been trapped here, pressed back against the wall by the intense heat, unable to escape the flames, choking on smoke, finally to grab a rock and claw against the wall, knowing it would be your final act?

And Kara was right—somebody had done this to them. No one would build a cooking fire that large in so small a cave.

"The work of men who strive to become gods," said Daniel.

He looked from the charred fire pit back to the pile of bones. At the edge of the pile, slightly apart from the rest, lay the remains of three skeletons. One small, perhaps that of a six-year-old child, the other two adults—the largest bones on top, as if the man were trying to shield his wife and child from the heat. Or perhaps not shielding, but simply choosing not to die clawing impotently at solid rock, but rather in a final embrace with the people he loved.

A better choice.

"I need some air," said Kara, moving through the dusty cave toward the light.

"Right behind you." Daniel took flash photos of the wall and the rocks and the bones, paused on the way to the entrance to get shots of the fire pit and the charred ceiling. He brought the chipped rock Kara had given him.

Then he heard the sound of a car's engine outside, grabbed Kara's arm just before she stepped into daylight. "Stop." He listened as the engine died, followed a few seconds later by two heavy thunks—car doors closing. "Stay."

He ducked out into the bright sun, keeping his body tight against the wall, and crept to the corner of the outcrop in a crouch. He pulled a small mirror from his wallet, palmed it, and inched it out past the edge of the wall.

Reflected in the mirror, he saw a black Range Rover parked halfway between the outcrop and his BMW. There were two men, dressed like hunters.

But hunters don't carry Heckler & Koch MP5s, and these men had the hard look and cocky swagger of guns for hire. One of the men stood by the Range Rover scanning the valley through field glasses while the other began walking slowly toward the outcrops. Daniel dashed back to the cave and stepped inside.

"We've got bad guys with guns," he said.

"Maybe they're police," said Kara.

"Kara, listen to me: They are not police."

Kara's look turned to a glare. Her voice was cold steel. "What have you been keeping from me?"

"Lots," said Daniel, maneuvering them to the side, out of the streams of daylight. "And if we're going to have that conversation, I have to get us out of here alive." He opened his pocketknife and stuck it in her hand. "You're a surgeon," he said.

"Are you kidding me?"

"Look, I'm not going to let it come to that. Just stay behind me. But if I go down, slash for the eyes and throat, and block with your other arm." He held a finger to Kara's trembling lips. "*Shh*, everything'll be okay." He tucked the car keys into her front pocket, turned away, and moved closer to the entrance.

Footsteps now, just outside. Daniel held the rock aloft in his right hand, waited.

The big man ducked into the cave and Daniel brought the rock down hard against his skull, behind the right ear. The man grunted and pitched forward, hands at his sides, forehead slamming into the cave's rock floor, submachine gun clattering to one side.

Daniel dropped the rock and picked up the gun and made sure a round was chambered. He quickly rolled the man on his back, went through his pockets, found the nothing he expected. You don't carry identification on a kill mission.

He snapped a photo of the man's face, grabbed Kara's hand, and led her outside.

"I'm gonna draw the other guy's attention, then we take off the long way around. When I say go, you start running and don't stop until you get in the car. Stay low. Once you get past the Range Rover, keep it behind you for cover. Now wait here."

He crept back to the corner, used his mirror again to peer around. The man was still at his post, just on the other side of the Range Rover's engine compartment, standing profile. At this distance a hit with an MP5 was extremely unlikely, and the gun's report would send the man straight into battle mode.

"Hoy!" Daniel called out. As soon as the man turned and began walking, Daniel took off behind the outcrop, grabbing Kara's wrist, pulling her into a running crouch as the wall sloped down to meet the ground. He held their position for a few seconds, then pushed Kara ahead of him. "Go."

They ran straight for the Range Rover, and almost made it before the man started firing. Daniel spun and returned fire and the man took cover behind the outcrop.

Kara was on the other side of the Range Rover now, running low as he'd told her. Daniel spun again and both men fired at once, bullets pinging off rocks, the smell of gunpowder filling the air. He let off a second burst, forcing the man back behind cover.

Then he ran like hell, slowing just enough to shoot out the Range Rover's tires on the way to the rental.

27: SAFE AS HOUSES

First I have to get us safe, then we'll talk."

Kara nodded. "Do that."

Daniel swung the BMW onto the smooth blacktop, leaving the gravel road behind, and stepped on the gas. His phone vibrated with an incoming text:

Evan Sage just departed LHR for OSL

He texted back:

Got bigger problems—SOS

SOS was a priority extraction request—right now, Raoul Aharon would be addressing the control room back in New York, directing everyone's attention to a valley at the southern tip of Norway.

A reassuring thought, but Daniel wanted confirmation.

The next minute passed slowly.

Then another incoming text:

On it, my friend—Stay frosty. R. A.

Raoul was an experienced handler, he understood.

Kara watched the scenery fly by for a few minutes, then pulled the sun visor down and looked at herself in the mirror. Her hair was all over the place. She started to work it back into shape with her fingernails but stopped short, staring at her reflection for a long moment, then snapped the visor back up.

"You sure know how to show a girl a good time," she said, her eyes a bit wild.

"Just hang on. Stick with me. We'll talk soon."

"You know what?" she said. "I don't want to talk about it while you're driving anyway. I want you to look me right in the face when you tell your next lie. Business consultant, my ass."

"I deserve that," said Daniel.

"Damn right you do." She looked out the window at the road ahead. "I could use a drink."

Within a couple minutes, New York had taken over Daniel's phone, launching the GPS app. A bright blue line glowed right into Oslo. He followed the line, reconnecting with the main highway, and set the cruise control just below the speed limit. Then he sent the photo of the soldier he'd laid out in the cave to Raoul.

From the north end of the valley, it was about two hours to Oslo. The silence hung heavy between them at first, but Kara seemed brighter after she closed her eyes for a while. Daniel reached for her hand, and she let him take it.

"I won't lie to you again, Kara."

"We'll see." She put his hand back on the wheel.

The GPS lead them to Oslo's *sentralstasjon*, teeming with tourists and business travelers. As Daniel put the BMW in park, his phone buzzed. The text read:

Train 162 -> Copenhagen—Tickets @ will-call

Kara reached for the phone and Daniel showed her the text.

He said, "Okay, this part is easy: We're an American tourist couple, been in Norway a week, heading to the next stop on our vacation. Just follow my lead." He killed the engine. "Ready?"

"Daniel, we're a mess and you've got a scratch, we hardly look like tourists." She reached out and touched his left cheek. He hadn't been aware of it, but now he could feel the stinging.

"Here's the story: We went for a walk in the woods, um . . . looking for the place where Edvard Munch used to hang his canvases on trees."

"Edvard Munch used to hang his canvases in the woods?"

"Yeah, and people call *you* crazy." He gave her a reassuring smile. "Anyway we were in the woods and I slipped on some wet moss and did a face-plant into the root of a tree. I'm a klutz like that. You helped me up, we both got a bit dirty."

Kara nodded, reached for the door handle, stopped. "You're keeping things light for my benefit," she said. "But we're not safe yet, are we?"

"We will be."

They walked into the terminal hand in hand, passing beneath the massive electronic arrivals and departures board, straight to the ticket counter's will-call window. Daniel showed his passport and picked up the tickets waiting for them. Raoul hadn't missed the chance to poke Daniel, booking them a private sleeping berth. Daniel's heart sank a little at the knowledge that they'd never set foot on the train.

Another incoming text:

Avis—Mr. Rector—U R crane—GPS to safe house

Daniel showed the text to Kara.

She said, "We're not leaving?"

"Not just yet."

The blond man at the Avis rental counter smiled as they approached. His nametag said, *John Rector—Manager*. "Nice to see you again, Mr. Crane," he said.

Daniel nodded to him. "Mr. Rector. How's the family?" He put the tickets on the counter.

Rector deftly made the tickets disappear. "Never a dull moment with so many children to look after," he said. "Keys?"

Daniel fished the car keys from his pocket and handed them across. "Needs a wash," he said.

"No worries, it'll be spotless." He handed Daniel a small laptop bag and a new set of car keys. "This one certainly is. You'll find it in space number two, just through those doors over there. Welcome back to Norway."

As they left the train station, Daniel glanced back to see Rector handing the train tickets to a couple who didn't much look like Daniel and Kara but matched their general size and coloring. Decoys for the train.

Nice touch, Raoul.

A white Saab sat in space number two. A few years old but well maintained, perfect camouflage. Daniel plugged his phone into the lighter socket as he drove them out of the lot.

"So Mr. Rector wasn't really a car rental guy," said Kara.

"Not really, no."

The phone's GPS app launched again, showing a somewhat meandering route through downtown Oslo. Daniel followed the route, periodically circling the block with right turns, and he watched mirrors and cross streets closely, cataloguing surrounding traffic.

They were not being followed.

After flitting around Oslo for twenty-five minutes, they finally parked in front of a modern gray stone townhouse in the fashionable West End district.

The front door was steel, embossed with a woodgrain pattern and painted glossy black. A text arrived to Daniel's phone: *35289.*

Daniel punched the digits into a small keypad on the doorframe and the door buzzed open and they went inside.

Kara headed straight for the kitchen, opening and closing cupboard doors. "There's gotta be some hooch in this place." She opened the refrigerator, slammed it shut, and spun to face Daniel. "There's a gun in the refrigerator."

"Better to have a gun in the refrigerator and not need it than to need a gun in the refrigerator and not have it." Daniel shrugged. It was intended to lighten the mood. It didn't.

"Who the hell *are* you? Christ, it's like I'm meeting you for the first time." She turned and opened the freezer, reached in and drew out a frosty bottle of akvavit, and poured cold caraway-infused vodka into a couple of glasses from the cupboard. "Why didn't we leave on the train?"

"Trust me, the people I work for, there's an extraction protocol in place."

"An *extraction protocol?* Do you even hear the way that sounds?"

"Look. We're safe in this building. The fridge is stocked, not just with a gun. There'll be a change of clothes for us upstairs. As of right now, we're under satellite surveillance. If anyone starts casing this place, they'll be noticed. I promise we'll get you out of here deliberately and without incident. We're very good at what we do."

"Let's start there. Who are *we?* These people you work for. Specifically."

"That's not something I can tell you yet, specifically," said Daniel. He held up a hand. "Said I wouldn't lie to you, didn't say

I could tell you everything. Let's focus on what I can. I work with a group of people investigating the Trinity Phenomenon—we call it Anomalous Information Transfer, or AIT. My uncle was just one of many."

"How many?"

"Right now we have over nine thousand confirmed cases, but we've no idea how many there are in total. And it's not a new phenomenon. It's actually very old, something that waxes and wanes throughout history. Been practically dormant for a very long time, but now it's spreading again."

"And why isn't this news?"

"It will be," said Daniel, "if we succeed. As you saw today, there are people trying to stop us. But you didn't sign on for all this, and we'll get you out safely."

"That's it? You're giving me a lift home? 'Thanks for your help, lady, but here's where you get off'?" She drained her glass in one long swallow and put the glass down hard on the counter. She glared at Daniel. "What?"

"The men who came after us knew we were in that cave. We have to assume by now they know who you are. It won't be safe for you at home. You'll have to disappear for a while. We'll set you up with an alternate identity, pretty much wherever you want to live, assign a bodyguard to you."

"And then?"

"Believe me, there are a lot of people working on this thing. If we're successful, you might be able to return home." He drank some vodka. "But I've got to be honest: Your new identity might be permanent. These same people killed my uncle to keep AIT for themselves. If they learn you've got it and you're trying to go public, they will kill you, too."

Kara topped up his glass, replenished her own. "I thought some deranged religious fanatic killed Trinity."

"Religious fanatics are very useful to rich men who want bad things done," said Daniel.

"Who are these rich men?"

"Another thing I can't tell you—it would only put you in more danger." Daniel drank some vodka. "Listen, I'm sorry I got you into this—"

"You're an idiot. You think *that's* why I'm pissed at you? You could set me up at the Four Seasons in Bora Bora with Clive Owen as my bodyguard, I still wouldn't go. I'm in this thing, and you don't get to kick me out. You never would've even found that cave without me."

"I'm not discounting what you've done, Kara. I hate to point out the obvious, but I almost got you killed by bringing you here."

"No, *we* almost got me killed, and I'm not pissed at you for bringing me here, I'm pissed at you for not telling me what the hell is going on."

"Understood. I just don't want to keep putting your life in danger."

"That's not your choice to make. It's mine." Kara swallowed some vodka, anger simmering in her eyes. "Playing tourist with you in Mandal was a nice distraction and I do enjoy the way you look at me, but I don't *have* a life to put in danger. My life ended three years ago when they took my daughter. I'm a dead woman marking time. When you look at me, that's what you should see."

"I do," said Daniel. "But I also see there's more of you left alive than you're willing to admit to yourself. Because if you admit you want to live, you're admitting you want to live even without your daughter. And the guilt of that fact is crushing you."

Kara looked at Daniel for a long time before speaking.

"You're a bastard," she said.

"I know." Daniel reached forward and took her hand in his. "But I'm not wrong . . . and I'm not sorry. I said I wouldn't lie to you and I won't. I have a lot to tell you about your condition, but there are other things I can't discuss and I don't want to spend all my time apologizing and saying, 'I can't tell you that.' I'll tell you all I can."

"So what you're saying is, even though you lied to me from the start, you're still asking for my trust."

"I guess one could put it that way." He smiled. "You know, if one had to."

"You assume a lot, Daniel Byrne," Kara said, a smile forming on her lips. "I've no idea why I find it so hard to stay mad at you."

She stepped in close and he wrapped his arms around her, kissed the top of her head. "Hell of a day. Why don't you go get changed and I'll make dinner?"

28: CANARY IN A COAL MINE

Gulfstream G650
Thirty-three thousand feet above France

Conrad eased the hand-stitched beige leather recliner upright and swiveled to face the rear cabin wall as the large flat-screen monitor came to life. He sipped his Bloody Mary. "Give me good news, Colonel."

On the monitor, Michael Dillman stood in the Berlin control center, facing the camera. "Wish I could, sir. We had a satellite trained on the valley, as per your orders, and Daniel Byrne was there this morning. He found the cave."

"*Was* there? I told you to put a couple men on it."

Dillman's expression was grim. "I did. And this is what happened . . ."

A satellite photo of the valley in Norway took over the screen.

Conrad got to his feet and moved a little closer to the monitor.

The satellite photo went out of focus as it zoomed in, zoomed in closer, and then closer still. The image resolved to sharp focus, showing a section of the valley floor about thirty square meters. A BMW SUV was parked near the top of the screen, a Range Rover dead center, and a rocky outcrop on the left. One of Dillman's mercenaries stood beside the Range Rover, another just outside the mouth of the outcrop's cave. Both men carried weapons.

The video started to play. The man by the cave stepped inside. A minute later, Daniel Byrne stepped out carrying the man's gun, followed by a woman.

Conrad stood staring at the screen, Bloody Mary in his hand, questions swirling in his mind.

On the screen, Daniel drew the other merc away from the Range Rover and then took off with the woman, laying down covering fire as they made their escape. *Shit. He's good . . . he's very good.* He even had the presence of mind under fire to stop and blow out the merc's tires.

"Damn it all to hell!" Conrad flung his drink across the cabin, splatter-painting the fuselage red. He'd ordered surveillance on the valley *just in case*, because Daniel had heard the soldier's ramblings about Mandal. But it was a big valley—how the hell had he found that cave? And who the hell was this woman? A Foundation asset? And had Daniel uncovered the next link in the chain?

None of that matters. West Virginia should've been the canary in the coal mine, but Conrad had been distracted and he'd under-estimated Daniel. He would not do so again.

The video went away and Michael Dillman came back full-screen. "We were able to isolate an image of the woman, but the angle isn't ideal, it'll take some time to run through facial recognition. We have no idea how Byrne found—"

"Doesn't matter how," snapped Conrad. "The prick is right up in my business, we're way past *how*. He's climbing the chain, he'll find the next link. So cut the bloody chain. And Daniel Byrne with it."

"Understood. I can join the team there by morning. I'll supervise it personally."

"Just set it up fast and get out. I'll meet you stateside in forty-eight hours."

"Yes, sir."

"And put a fire under the wet teams. Get those scientists done and dusted," said Conrad. "Accelerate everything. We're going straight to phase two."

29: RIGHT PLACE WRONG TIME

They put the akvavit away and switched to wine for dinner, and Daniel kept his promise, telling Kara all he knew about Anomalous Information Transfer. And she focused her questions on the condition itself, ignoring for now how he came to know it.

Another thing tabled for future discussion.

When he told her about the possible physiological triggers of AIT, she put her fork down. "Now we're getting somewhere," she said. "So it's some kind of neurological or neurochemical abnormality."

"Maybe."

"We know I don't have a brain tumor or epilepsy, my hormone levels are normal, and despite popular opinion, I'm not schizophrenic. What else?"

"People who've been hit by lightning or survived some other powerful electrocution—"

"Nope."

"People who've dropped a lot of acid."

"Really? I should go back and read Timothy Leary again."

"I'll take that as a no," said Daniel.

Kara smiled. "Wanted to try it with my girlfriends in pre-med, but I'm a chicken, pretended I had the flu and backed out of the camping trip. Nothing stronger than ganja for this girl."

"I don't suppose you've ever flatlined," said Daniel.

"What?"

"Ever been brought back from death after your heart stopped."

"I *know* what it means." She stared at Daniel with her mouth slightly open as tears welled in her eyes. "I mean, yes. I flatlined when I was four years old."

"And you remember it."

"Vividly." Kara sipped some wine and took a very long, very deep breath. "I—I drowned, actually." She wiped her eyes with a sleeve. "We . . . had a swimming pool in the backyard. My big brother, Adeeb, was in the pool with his friends from down the block, playing water basketball with the net that floats around. My father had just lifted me out of the pool and helped me out of my water wings and wrapped me in a red terrycloth beach towel. It could go around me twice, it was so big. I wasn't allowed in the pool while the big kids played roughhousing games. My father put me down on the grass, away from the pool in the shade, and went back to reading his newspaper up on the porch."

"But you wanted to play with the big kids."

"Yes. I went back along the pool deck wrapped in my towel—I had to shuffle not to trip over it—and I stood at the edge of the deep end. I leaned forward to speak to Adeeb but he and his friends were splashing around and calling to each other and he didn't notice me. The ends of the towel hit the water and the towel acted like a sponge. It was suddenly very heavy, pulling me forward. I pulled back but I wasn't strong enough and I went headfirst into the water and the entire world became a swirl of red cotton and blue sky and white concrete and bubbles all around me, thousands of tiny bubbles coming from the towel and larger ones from my mouth as I sank deeper. I remember my back hitting the bottom. Then it goes black." She took another long breath and let it out slowly.

"What's the next thing you remember?"

Kara turned her wine glass by its stem and looked at the surface of the wine as she spoke. "I'm lying on the pool deck, heaving up water and gulping down air, and my chest hurts so badly. My father is holding my shoulders and patting my back and shouting something to me. When the water stops coming, I look up and there are all these faces. My father's right over me, and Adeeb and his friends behind him, and everyone is crying. My mother is right behind me, just screaming. A horrible sound. And then my father is hugging me and sobbing and stroking my hair and kissing my face. And that's when I started bawling." She swallowed some wine. "When I was older, I was told that my father had heard a kid scream and dived over the children and down to the bottom and dragged me up. But when they unwrapped me from the towel, I wasn't breathing and had no pulse. He performed CPR and brought me back."

"That's quite a memory," said Daniel.

Kara looked like she was trying to decide. Then decided. "It's much more than that. It's my very *first* memory. I don't remember anything before it." She was silent for a moment. "I could tell you stories of things that happened when I was two or three, but those aren't memories. They're fantasies, imaginings based on the *remember when* stories I heard from my parents and brother over the years. I sometimes visit them as if they were memories, but they're not. My first memory is of dying."

Kara reached forward across the table, and Daniel held her hand in his. She said, "And I've kept that secret all my life, I don't know why. You're the only other person who knows it."

In a parallel universe, Daniel swept the dishes off the table and pulled her into his arms and kissed her, opening the floodgates to what they'd both been holding back. But not in this universe. In this one, he gave her hand a squeeze and let go, thinking: *She couldn't be more vulnerable than she is right now. Right place, wrong time.*

He reached for the wine bottle to top up her glass, but she shook her head, saying, "After everything I've seen since yesterday, I've decided not to block the voices—this AIT, as you call it—with booze anymore. Whatever this thing is, it contains real information that can help us, and it's getting stronger. Voices have grown to feelings and dreams and fainting spells and . . . as freaky as it all is, we need it to happen in order to find the truth, right? So blocking it doesn't make much sense."

"You're a brave woman, Kara Singh."

Daniel made a pot of tea, and they moved to the living room, where he connected his iPod to the Bluetooth speaker and put on Dr. John. Kara sat on the couch. She raised an eyebrow when Daniel sat a safe distance away in a chair, but she didn't comment on it.

Instead she said, "So maybe my experience of dying changed something, rebooted my electrical system or altered my brain chemistry, which somehow caused AIT later in life?"

"Maybe," said Daniel again. "Which doesn't explain the phenomenon itself, how the information comes to you or where it's coming from. We still have no idea *what* AIT is, we only know *that* it is."

Kara said, "The same can be said of existence itself."

Daniel said, "I wish you'd stop saying things that make me want to kiss you." But not out loud. Out loud, he said nothing at all.

They drank tea and listened to the music in silence for a couple of minutes. Then Kara said, "Do you think he died, the man in the cave?"

Okay. So they were gonna talk about that.

"You're the doctor." Daniel sipped his wine. "You tell me."

"I've seen people succumb to lesser head traumas. Would it bother you if he died?"

"No. When he chose not to respect our right to live, he relinquished his own. Live by the sword . . ."

Kara leaned forward. "This isn't the first time you've killed a man, is it?"

How to answer that question? If the man in the cave died, he would be the fifth. The first three were corrupt soldiers storming a church basement in Honduras to kill a political reformer. There had been six on the hit squad. Pat Wahlquist had killed the other three. That was almost five years ago. The fourth was a professional assassin gunning for Tim Trinity.

"Not the first," said Daniel.

"How does it feel? To take a life, even in self-defense. Doesn't it keep you up nights? Don't you think about it later?"

"I'm not a moral relativist when it comes to self-defense," said Daniel. "So no, it doesn't keep me up nights. But it still feels . . . ugly. It's a weight you carry, and yes, you think about it later."

Kara shook her head slowly. "You walked into my life as this oddball business consultant. And then this morning"—a short bewildered laugh—"you transform right before my eyes into some kind of secret agent man."

"Oddball?" said Daniel.

"I like oddballs," said Kara. She held his eyes and patted the couch cushion beside her. "Come."

Ah, what the hell . . .

Daniel abandoned his tea and sat beside her on the couch. She raised her hands and he put his palms against hers, barely touching, feeling her heat merge with his and grow into something new and powerful. He leaned forward and so did she, her eyes closing, lips opening slightly.

He stopped when their mouths were barely a couple inches apart and whispered, "I read somewhere that a shared brush with death can cause an intense feeling of intimacy between two people."

"Uh-huh," she said.

"It can be a very difficult feeling to resist." He moved an inch closer.

"So are you going to kiss me?" she said.

"I might."

She moistened her lips with her tongue. "Soon?"

He brushed his lips against hers, ever so gently, and she made a small animal sound and her fingers interlaced with his, the strength of her grip astonishing.

He kissed her now, hard and deep, still keeping their bodies apart, Kara returning the kiss with pent-up passion, her body arching off the couch, straining closer, her hands squeezing so hard it was like she was trying to break his, so hard it hurt.

He broke the kiss and rested his forehead against hers, their breaths coming ragged and hot. He said, "The people back at the office are expecting me for a video conference. In fact, I was supposed to check in two hours ago. That's a serious dereliction of duty."

"Very serious," she said. She thought he was kidding.

"Those people back at the office are going to help me keep you alive, Kara. So we're gonna table this discussion again for later." He kissed her quickly, disengaged his hands, and headed for the stairs, tossing a grin over his shoulder. "Because we can both be such reasonable people."

"You really are a bastard," said Kara, trying not to smile.

"Blame John Rector. He gave me the laptop."

"Oh! I hate you."

Daniel started up the stairs. "I'll see you in my dreams," he said.

30: THESE DREAMS OF YOU

Daniel sat cross-legged on the bed, the laptop computer open on a pillow in front of him, Raoul and Ayo looking back from the screen. He gave a concise account of the events in the valley that morning—Kara leading them to the stone foundations and the cave with the fire pit and skeletal remains and scarred rocks. And then the arrival of bad guys with guns, the confrontation and escape.

Hard to believe it was still the same day.

"How's the good doctor holding up?" said Ayo.

"She insists on continuing forward with this, wherever it leads. She's incredibly brave, actually."

"She'll need to be," said Raoul. "We got a hit on facial recognition. Turns out the guy whose skull you caved in with a rock—he croaked by the way, nice work, Grasshopper—was a paramilitary contractor."

"As I reckoned," said Daniel.

"Don't break your arm patting yourself on the back," said Raoul, making up for his earlier compliment. "Here's where it gets interesting: The PMC your guy worked for is small and elite—all their mercs are former ranking military—and their team leaders all served at one time under Colonel Michael Dillman."

"That *is* interesting," said Daniel.

"Boys, we don't have time," said Ayo. "Dr. Alexander Klukoff—our highest-ranking ally in the field of microbiology—suffered a massive coronary last night, died in his sleep. This afternoon a colleague of his at the CDC named Hasting topped himself. The suicide note said he was distraught over the loss of his mentor. Only the men didn't actually get on that well. And *here's* where it gets interesting: It was Hasting who ran the blood analysis on the soldier with AIT. He was a Council ally."

"Oh shit," said Daniel. "If this was staged, then Conrad Winter sacrificed his own man to make it clean. He's tying off loose ends."

"Which means," said Ayo, "whatever they've been planning, they are now doing. And we still don't have enough dots to connect."

✤ ✤ ✤

Daniel woke to the turning of his bedroom doorknob. The nightstand clock glowed 3:00 a.m. The door opened and Kara stepped into the room, silhouetted by the hallway light. Daniel drew in a breath. She couldn't have been more beautiful.

Or more naked.

She leaned back against the open door, out of direct light, barely visible now. Daniel felt himself growing hard under the sheets. There was no way he would turn this woman down again.

Not after today.

And not after the stunt he'd pulled downstairs. Kara thought she was here by invitation, and Daniel couldn't honestly say she wasn't. This was going to happen, right now.

"Hey you," he said, "come on over here and let's continue that discussion."

Her voice sounded far away, her tone mournful. "The path you're walking will lead you into darkness. It's . . . so cruel, this place."

A chill ran through Daniel's core. "Kara, what's wrong?"

"So cruel, no escape. No mercy . . . and no relief."

Daniel tossed the sheets aside and jumped out of bed. Closer, he could now see the thousand-yard stare. Kara was sleepwalking, unaware of her nakedness, unaware of his presence.

"Dozens of them," she said, staring right through Daniel, "restrained, held somewhere between life and death, allowed neither to die nor to live . . . such unfathomable cruelty . . ." A single tear slid down her face.

Daniel put his hands on her shoulders as gently as he could and guided her into the hallway. "All right, Kara, you're okay, you're just dreaming and I'm taking you back to bed now. Everything's fine . . ." He steered her back into her room, got her into the bed, and pulled the covers over her. He sat on the edge of the bed and patted her head.

Her eyes closed as the dream evaporated.

31: DISSOLVED GIRL

London, England
2:35 a.m.

D escia, wake up. Descia. Wake up now."
    It sounded far away.

Descia felt a long way beneath the surface, and it took some effort to pry herself out of the dream she was having. In the dream, she was in her office talking to all the spooks at the same time. Mike Stotter, the handsome one from MI5, and Evan Sage, the tough Homeland Security man, and the Foundation's new man, Daniel Byrne. She was pacing the floor, warning them about the coming plague, but they weren't listening to her. They were sitting around her desk playing poker, ignoring her completely.

"Descia, time to sit up."

Descia opened her eyes. Everything was wavy. Someone was tugging at her arms—a man, the man who had spoken—and then she was sitting up. A man with an American accent. In her room. An American man. And why was everything so wavy? She knew the answer, she just couldn't locate it . . .

The American man was helping her to her feet . . .

Ambien. She'd taken an Ambien before bed. That's why, wavy. He was helping her walk . . .

Living room now. Couch. He sat her down on it, stood behind her. She tried to speak. Her tongue was thick in her mouth, and she couldn't make the words come out.

Soldier. The man was big and thick, like a soldier . . .

There was a second man, sitting in the wing chair. Hard like the other, but older—salt-and-pepper hair, close-cropped mustache . . .

She tried to speak again. "What're you sitting . . . Who? Are you?" Her voice sounded small to her, and slightly slurred.

The older one sitting in the chair looked at her pleasantly. "I'm Mike. The man behind you is Bobby."

Mike was also American.

Then Descia's muddled brain put the pieces together. Bobby and Mike were here to kill her. That's why they were here. The thought caused panic to balloon in her chest, but her body was becoming a foreign thing—she could barely even make it sit up. And everything was getting wavier . . .

She concentrated on making her mouth work. "You know, you don't have to . . ." She heard herself slurring from far away. "Just a research biologist . . . don't know anything . . . nothing at all, really."

Mike said, "You and I both know that's not true, Descia." He got up out of the chair and walked closer, but it was like she was looking through the wrong end of a telescope and he was very small, at the end of a long black tunnel.

She felt Bobby pressing his hands down on her shoulders from behind. Hands like heavy pillows . . .

Bobby said, "Rest assured, Doc, your reputation will be intact. You didn't commit suicide. You were just careless with your sleeping pills."

She let her head loll back against the couch, looked up at him. He was now small, too, at the end of the black tunnel. She opened her mouth, willing herself to speak again. When her voice came, it didn't sound like her. It sounded impossibly slow. "Only . . . took . . . one . . ."

"I came by earlier, switched your pills."

"But . . . I've . . . my deadbolt cost fifteen hundred pounds."

"You overpaid."

And then Mike again, standing very close now but still looking far away. Holding something in his right hand. A bottle. Two bottles. She squinted. No, just one bottle. A blue glass bottle. He lifted it higher . . .

She searched for the right words, made them with her mouth. "Mike, Bobby, please . . . I don't want to die."

Bobby said, "You took a sleeping pill, but you forgot and took a second. It happens. Then you were sleepwalking, went to the liquor cabinet . . ." He stuck something in her mouth, held it there. A tunnel . . . no . . . not tunnel . . . a tube . . . not tube . . . *funnel.*

Mike tipped the blue bottle, and Descia thought: *Oh. It's gin.*

Then the funnel was gone and someone lifted her legs and she was lying on her back on the couch, but the couch was dissolving into waves, and then everything was dissolving into waves, even the men standing over her.

The whole world, merely waves. Waves of light . . . waves of not-even-light . . . waves of almost nothing . . . waves of nothing but probability.

And then Descia herself dissolved into waves.

32: LAWYERS GUNS AND MONEY

Daniel had just finished sliding the carafe back into the coffeemaker when the doorbell buzzed "Shave and a Haircut." He pulled the Sig Sauer from the fridge, held it down by his side.

The electric lock buzzed the front door open. "Don't shoot, broheim." Pat Wahlquist's distinctive drawl—somewhere between Cajun country and Mid-City New Orleans—was like a letter from home. Pat hip-checked the door wide and stepped inside, a large black duffle bag dwarfed by his muscular frame. He winked at Daniel. "I'll be your escort home."

"Geez Louise, I must be important." Daniel put the cold gun on the counter. "Coffee?"

"Always." Pat dropped the duffle with a thud and bounded into the kitchen. He clasped a paw on Daniel's shoulder and took the steaming mug with a nod. "Nice to see you not full of holes."

"Nice to be not full of holes," said Daniel.

Kara rounded the corner and froze, letting out a startled cry.

"Hey, sleepyhead," said Daniel.

"Sorry," said Kara. "I just"—she nodded at Pat—"your friend looks like those men . . . yesterday."

"He is like them. But he's on our side. You can trust him."

"Y'all know I'm right here in the room, doncha?" said Pat. He pointed at his ear and stage-whispered, "I can hear you."

Kara laughed and stepped forward to shake Pat's hand. "Pleasure to meet you . . .?"

"Pat Wahlquist at your service, Miz Kara."

Daniel filled another mug and held it out to Kara.

"Thanks," she said. "I need it, feel like I barely slept. I had another episode. Even in my sleep, I could taste cinnamon."

"How much do you remember?"

"All of it—a short but nasty little nightmare. Somewhere in Africa, or maybe the Caribbean. I didn't know the location the way I did with the Norway dream, but the place looked tropical and everyone was black. A poor village, but in modern times. The buildings were behind me, I couldn't see them, but somehow I know it was a very small village. I stood by the side of a dirt road facing a huge freshly dug pit, like a giant trench. About fifty or sixty people stood side by side with their backs to the trench . . . men and women, old and young, even kids . . ." She sipped her coffee. "And then gunfire rang out—like the guns you and that man shot at each other yesterday, you know, rapid-fire, machine guns—and the people fell back into the trench. Everyone. The shots came from behind me but I didn't turn around, never saw the gunmen. I looked to my left and saw one of those big metal prefab buildings, you know, with an arched top?"

"A Quonset hut."

"Yes but huge, maybe an airplane hangar. Some of the people were still alive, their voices crying out from the pit, but I just turned away from them and started walking toward the giant Quonset hut as the gunmen finished the job behind me. That's when the dream ended."

"Nothing about people not being allowed to die?" said Daniel.

Kara gave him a strange look. "Should there be?"

"You talked in your sleep."

She raised the coffee mug to her lips, stopped short. "You could hear me down the hall through two closed doors?"

"You were sleepwalking. You came into my room."

"I was . . ." She looked away, suddenly shy.

"Yes," said Daniel, "you were. And incredibly beautiful."

"Wow, that was awkward," said Pat.

Daniel shot him a look, turned his attention back to Kara. "You stood in my room and described dozens of people restrained—held somewhere between life and death, you said—not allowed to live, not allowed to die."

"No, these people were definitely allowed to die," she said. "Must've been another dream. I don't remember it at all."

"Try," said Pat.

"I said I don't remember it, don't be a bully."

Pat grinned broadly at Daniel. "She's a pistol."

"I knew you two would hit it off," said Daniel. "Kara, put yourself back in the dream you do remember, see if you can notice any other details. Close your eyes."

She did. "I . . . oh. A river ran past the village. It was in front of me, beyond the trench. Um . . . I don't see—wait." Her eyes opened. "One of the men wore a dirty white T-shirt with a faded flag on the chest. Like the Stars and Stripes, but the blue square in the corner was smaller and it had just a single large white star in it. The bullet struck him right in the middle of that star."

Daniel grabbed his phone and launched the web browser. He ran an image search, handed her the phone. "Like this?"

"That's it."

"That's the flag of Liberia."

"Hot damn," said Pat, "you're the real deal, Doc." He shifted his focus to Daniel. "You and I need to have a little powwow."

"We can powwow right here," said Daniel. "Kara's working this case with me, she can't do it in the dark."

Pat shook his head. "Your mother's gonna be displeased."

"He's always displeased."

"A'right . . . she's your asset, long as you realize you'll catch hell for this later back at the office."

"I'll worry about later, later."

"*Excuse me?*" said Kara.

Uh-oh . . .

"I'm your *asset*, am I?"

Daniel turned to Pat. "Thanks, buddy. So glad you're here."

"Whatever," said Pat. "The mercs you did battle with yesterday—I'll give you one guess where they flew into Norway from." He pulled out his cell phone, speed-dialed. "Let's get the geeks in on this. Hey man," he said into the phone, "I need you to hack me into satellite imagery over Liberia. Yup, send it to my laptop." To Kara, "What direction does the river run?"

Kara shrugged.

Daniel said, "Close your eyes again, put yourself back in the dream, try to remember what it looked like." She closed her eyes. "Okay, what time of day is it? Can you tell?"

After a moment, Kara said, "Afternoon, I think." She kept her eyes closed. "Yes, late afternoon."

"Good. Now face the river and look for shadows—any trees you see, or shadows of the people standing in front of the trench. What direction do the shadows fall?"

Kara opened her eyes, looked at Pat. "They're parallel to the trench and the river," she said. "They fall from left to right."

Pat spoke into the phone. "We're looking for a small village with a large Quonset hut, hangar-sized, standing just south of an east-west river. Start near Monrovia and work your way out. Yup, thanks."

Pat brought his duffle bag to the dining table and pulled out a Toughbook computer, opened it. Within a minute, a window opened on the screen, a satellite photograph encompassing Liberia, along with parts of Sierra Leone, Guinea, Ivory Coast, and a blue slice of the Atlantic in the bottom-left. It zoomed in until Liberia filled the screen. "Could take a couple hours," Pat told Kara. "Don't feel obliged to stare at it."

"In that case," said Kara, "I'm going back to bed to stare at the inside of my eyelids. Wake me if something happens." She headed for the stairs.

Daniel said, "What's our timeline for getting outta here?"

Pat said, "Tonight. We drive to Denmark. Got dummy passports in the bag—you and Kara will have to memorize your legends before we hit the road. There'll be a private jet waiting for us in Copenhagen."

Daniel said, "We get a hit from the satellite, we could be in Monrovia for breakfast."

33: SECRET AGENT MAN

When an hour passed with no hit from the satellite feed, Daniel decided to change the channel in his head. He put in twenty minutes of zazen and went through his kata routine a few times, then changed into his running gear and a baseball cap.

"Call me if we get a hit," he told Pat on his way out the door.

He set an easy pace and kept his body loose, running along tree-lined residential streets, along boulevards with boutiques and bakeries and cafes, navigating prosperous Norwegians pedaling spotless bicycles or pushing designer baby strollers, and when his water bottle ran dry, he stopped and realized he'd been at it almost an hour.

The smell of roasting coffee beans drew Daniel another block to a place called Kaffebrenneriet. Decidedly underdressed in running shorts and a sweaty T-shirt, he took an outdoor table on the sidewalk patio in the sun and ate a smoked salmon sandwich on good rustic bread. His coffee came in an AeroPress and was refreshingly strong, and the lemonade was squeezed from actual lemons and not too sweet. He took his time with lunch and glanced at his phone only four or five times.

Impatient, he decided, but not worried. After everything he'd witnessed with Kara, he had no doubt that her latest AIT episode would pay off.

He dropped some money on the table for a tip and pushed back his chair.

"Don't get up," said Evan Sage, taking the seat across from Daniel.

Well, damn . . .

"Evan Sage," Daniel said, "this is a hell of a coincidence."

"Not even slightly."

"What are you doing in Norway?"

"Was gonna ask you the same thing." Serious, but not unfriendly.

"Had some vacation time, thought I'd come see the woods where Edvard Munch used to hang his canvases on trees."

Sage just looked at Daniel with a blank expression, giving him nothing, stretching out the silence until it became a palpable thing in the air, letting it linger and grow stale in the sun. Most people can't stand this kind of pregnant pause very long, so they jump in and start talking just to fill the air with words. And that's when they screw up.

Daniel said nothing.

Sage's gaze came to rest on the scratch on Daniel's left cheek. "Cut yourself shaving?"

"Clocked myself in the face getting my carry-on from the overhead bin." Daniel smiled. "Know how they always say, 'Items may shift during flight'? They ain't just whistlin' Dixie."

"I never put anything up there," said Sage. "And the woman you're traveling with, Kara Singh?"

Just keep dancing the dance . . .

"What about her?"

"She a fellow Edvard Munch enthusiast?"

"Not yet." Daniel put on a sheepish expression. "Okay, busted. We just started dating, and I thought a culture trip to Norway might impress her."

Evan Sage glanced over Daniel's shoulder and nodded to someone just so Daniel would know there was a man behind him. "Okay. Let me tell you a story: That bioweapon tip sent to Descia Milinkovic I told you about? It came from a military doctor in West Virginia named Astor. Yesterday afternoon, Dr. Astor bought the farm. Skidded his car off a perfectly paved dry road under a cloudless sky at exactly the spot where a gap in the guardrail allowed him to plummet two hundred feet into a gorge. And he wasn't wearing his seatbelt, not that it would've helped. He strike you as the kind of guy who doesn't wear a seatbelt?"

Daniel shook his head. "I don't know the man."

"No, of course you don't. I mean a doctor . . . you'd expect a doctor to wear his seatbelt, wouldn't you?"

"I don't know. Lot of doctors smoke."

"True enough. Anyway, Dr. Astor had a connection to a Colonel Michael Dillman at the Defense Intelligence Agency. Ever hear of *him*? Ever meet him?"

Daniel's training kicked in. When accessing a mental picture, the eyes unconsciously shift—slightly up and to the right for a remembered image, or up and left when constructing an imaginary picture. For an auditory memory, they shift straight to the right. It wasn't perfect but it was pretty reliable, and Daniel knew Evan would be trained to watch for it, so he shifted his eyes straight left—signaling not an auditory memory, but sounding out something unfamiliar in his mind's ear.

"Never heard the name," he said.

Sage dismissed it with a wave of his hand. "No reason why you should have. Colonel Dillman is a black ops guy—"

"Black ops. I've heard that in movies, but what does it really mean?"

"Secret projects, everything off the books, total deniability."

"Oh. Just like in the movies."

"Right. Dillman works with a lot of private military contractors—what used to be called mercenaries in pre-Orwellian times—and two of his favorites arrived in Norway day before yesterday. I came here to find them. Imagine my surprise when you popped up."

"I don't know what to tell you. I'm just a business consultant."

"I know you are, I've checked you out. Also know Tim Trinity was your uncle, and you've got some kind of hobby helping Julia Rothman try to solve the Trinity Phenomenon for her book. I know a lot about you. And I don't think you're involved in bioweapons. But perhaps someone else does. Like those two mercenaries who arrived in Norway shortly after you did."

Daniel assumed the role, looking aghast. "What are you saying? Am I in danger?"

"You could be. It's possible you may have stumbled upon something without knowing it, sometimes we know things we don't realize. Or maybe you don't know anything, but they *think* you do. These aren't the kind of men who take chances."

"Oh my god." Daniel put a slight tremor in his voice. "I can't believe this is happening. What happens if they catch up with me? I don't even know anything."

"We'll work this out, Daniel, don't panic." Sage pulled out his badge wallet and handed Daniel another of his business cards, then glanced at his watch. "Here's what you're gonna do: Go back to your hotel and stay there for a few hours. At four o'clock I want you and your girlfriend at the American embassy. Give my card to the reception desk. We're gonna sit down and have a long talk, find out what it is you might know, or what it is they might think you know. And then I'm gonna take these bastards down. And you can get on with your life."

"Thank you," said Daniel. "We'll be there." He stood up and so did Sage.

"Let's be very clear, Mr. Byrne: You and Kara Singh are both US citizens, and your government requires your assistance with a possible bioterror threat. Whether you think you know something or not, you are going to report to the embassy and answer my questions, or the Department of Homeland Security will have you both on terrorist watch lists you never even heard of. You won't be able to fly, rent a car, use your credit cards, access your bank accounts, or wipe your own ass until I say so."

"You needn't threaten, Mr. Sage," said Daniel. "You think I want mercenaries chasing me? I said we'd be there."

"Don't be late."

✤ ✤ ✤

"Got a hit," said Pat with a triumphant grin as Daniel came in the front door. "Couple hours' drive north of Monrovia, next to an offshoot of the Lofa River." He pointed at the laptop. "Check 'er out."

"We're blown," said Daniel. "We gotta go."

Pat immediately started packing his duffle bag. "What happened?"

Daniel bent over the laptop screen, looked at the satellite photo—most of the screen densely packed with green treetops, intersected horizontally by a thin, winding brown ribbon, a red-dirt clearing just south of the muddy river. "Evan Sage happened. Homeland Security guy." He clicked on the image, zooming in closer. Twelve small dwellings were scattered around the clearing, and the arched roof of a large Quonset hut appeared at the north-west edge of the clearing, close to the river. "Sage ordered me to the embassy at four o'clock, said to bring my girlfriend."

"Shit."

"I know. I played dumb, but . . ."

"What?"

Daniel looked up from the screen. "Just the way he was playing me. He's hard to read."

Pat unplugged the computer's power brick and coiled the cord and stuck it in the bag. "He put a tail on you?"

"'Course he did. I lost them."

"You sure?"

"Yes, Pat, I'm sure." He pointed at the screen. "This rectangle, next to the structure. Semi-trailer?"

"Yeah, converted into one big-ass diesel generator, and the roof is wall-to-wall solar panels. And those two smaller squares? Big-ass AC units. So, not an airplane hangar. Whatever they're doing inside draws a lot of juice, and they're keepin' the place cool."

Daniel closed the computer and handed it to Pat. "Let's go find out."

He headed upstairs and knocked on Kara's door. She opened it and put a hand on his forearm.

"You were gone a long time, I was worried," she said. "Did Pat tell you? We got a hit."

"He told me. Pack up, we're leaving in fifteen minutes. I'm just gonna jump in the shower, I'll meet you downstairs in ten. We gotta go. Now." He gave her a quick kiss. "I'll explain on the way."

34: DEMOLITION CITY

London, England
9:05 a.m.

Michael Dillman sat against the edge of the desk in Dr. Kara Singh's room of horrors and flipped back to the front page of the file folder for the third time.

She was one of *them*.

What're the chances?

He stood and speed-dialed Conrad Winter.

Conrad answered on the first ring. "Give me good news, Colonel."

"Roger: Stockholm is confirmed and I supervised London myself last night. That's five, and as expected, the Internet's lit up about it. Our seeds have sprouted—six of our theories are getting major play on the conspiracy forums—and the Illuminati theory has even started up without us. We'll keep watch and keep it fed as necessary. The final three bodies drop over the next forty-eight."

"Okay, now let's have the bad news."

Spoken just like his father, thought Dillman. He said, "We got a hit from facial on the woman with Daniel Byrne. Kara Singh, a medical doctor here in London. I'm standing in her apartment right now."

"And?"

"Sir, have you ever heard of Project Cassandra?"

"Saw a file on it once but . . . long time ago, wasn't it? Some failed AIT initiative?"

Didn't seem such a long time ago to Michael Dillman, but when you get to a certain age, nothing seems very long ago.

"About thirty years ago, my first project after joining the Council, actually. The Air Force thought I was developing a next-gen psyops weapon, a machine that could direct scripted auditory hallucinations into the mind from a distance. And in fact I was, and I did. But for the Council, Project Cassandra had much greater ambition. Because schizophrenics are disproportionately affected by AIT, the idea was that if the auditory hallucinations were the trigger, and we replicated those symptoms, perhaps we could trigger AIT artificially with this weapon. We had a prototype working by early eighty-four, shut the project down in early eighty-six. The weapon failed to trigger AIT."

"What does this have to do with the woman?"

"Sir, there's a large number of mentally ill people in the world who believe that various government or private entities are beaming voices into their heads using Cassandra. They're quite organized. They filed a lawsuit against the Pentagon after an FOI request revealed the existence of the weapon—some idiot DIA bureaucrat actually granted their request. Worse, he neglected to black out my name on *one* page of *one* document in the records dump."

"She knows about you."

"She's got multiple copies of the FOI records in her office. She was a co-complainant in the lawsuit. Sir, since joining the Council, I've managed a near-invisible career in DIA. The public disclosure of my connection to Cassandra is the one major point of"—he quickly rejected the word "vulnerability"—"visibility."

"Delineate your level of exposure, exactly."

"Just that I ran a successful project for Air Force Intelligence developing voice-to-skull remote auditory hallucination technology in the 1980s. That's all, nothing relating to AIT or the Council. They don't even know the name of the project."

"But the woman traveling with Daniel Byrne knows of your existence and your connection to auditory hallucinations. And she has voices in her head."

"Yes."

"That's how Daniel's been climbing the chain. Blankenship pointed him to Mandal, but *she* led him to the cave. Mike, the woman has AIT."

"Yes, I suspect she does."

Conrad sighed into Dillman's ear. "All right. Do what you have to do. But I need you stateside tomorrow."

11:00 a.m.

Michael Dillman stood in Dr. Kara Singh's living room, drinking her scotch and looking out through her bay window as a blue British Gas service van parked in front of the building.

Two men in blue coveralls, reflective yellow vests, and white hardhats got out of the van. One man opened the back doors and started placing orange traffic cones to prevent anyone from parking in front, while the other confirmed the address on his clipboard with the number on the building. Together the men lifted a large packing crate out of the van and carried it to the front door.

Dillman buzzed them in and opened the apartment door, and they came in and put the crate down in the living room and removed their hardhats.

Bobby had brought George Richards, a demolitions expert from Blackpool. Former SAS. Reliable man, if a little too in love with his job.

"Welcome aboard, George," said Dillman, extending his hand. "Let's try not to bring down the whole building, shall we?"

George grinned broadly, flashing a gold tooth, and shook Dillman's hand firmly. "Wouldn't dream of it, sir." He opened the crate, pulled out a scuba tank with a hose attached, and placed it near the apartment door.

Bobby removed another British Gas uniform from the crate, along with a hardhat and tool belt. Dillman slipped into the uniform while the others loaded the crate with Kara Singh's notebooks, computer, and files.

George opened the apartment door wide and turned the valve on the scuba tank. The hose began hissing out into the hallway. Then he and Bobby closed the clasps on the packing crate and carried it out to the van. They returned, and Bobby checked the clipboard.

"One upstairs neighbor, a Mrs. Gertrude Browne. Widow, lives alone. I'll go get her out before George toasts the place." Bobby turned to go.

"Hold up." Dillman gestured to the scuba tank. "George, how long until you can smell that upstairs?"

"Two minutes, sir."

"Wait three minutes, Bobby. We want her to smell gas as soon as she opens the door."

35: BABYLON SYSTEM

Monrovia, Liberia

Dawn was breaking, sky bruising in waves of purple and orange to the east as they flew in low over the Atlantic and touched down at James Spriggs Payne Airfield, runway lights switched on for their arrival, the airport itself still dark. They taxied straight past the building, directly to an open gate in the chain-link fence at the end of the airstrip, where two men stood waiting.

The pilot lowered the aluminum stairs, and Daniel disembarked ahead of Pat and Kara, stepping into the equatorial sea air, hot and wet on the skin, heavy with salt. Like being embraced by a living thing. He breathed deep, enjoying the smell of jet fuel as he'd enjoyed the smell of diesel when he was a boy living in a motor home with his uncle.

The taller man walked forward to greet them. He looked in his middle forties, skinny but strong, with sinewy arms and a way of moving that suggested a tightly coiled spring.

"I am Jacob," the man said. "You are Daniel." Not a question.

Daniel shook Jacob's hand and introduced Pat and Kara by their first names.

The man at the gate was evidently a customs officer Jacob had dragged out of bed for this, his uniform shirt still half-unbuttoned over a white undershirt. He looked at the three arrivals with no expression whatsoever, then turned to Jacob and held up five fingers.

Daniel handed a bank envelope to Jacob and Jacob passed it to the customs man. The man tucked the bribe in his belt and stamped their passports on the hood of a vintage Toyota Land Cruiser, scarcely even looking at them. He handed the passports back and resecured the gate and climbed into a little Daihatsu hatchback and drove away into the early morning light.

Without a word.

Jacob gestured to the Land Cruiser's mottled paint job—once green, now more primer than paint. "No beauty queen but when I say go, she go, and when I say stop, she stop." He opened the tailgate, revealing four five-gallon jugs of water, a large blue Coleman cooler, three dirty gas cans, and a red blanket bearing the logo of the Arsenal football club. "Plenty, plenty food in the cooler. Flashlight, binocular, and DEET—*bathe* in it. And sat phone, no cell coverage out there." He pulled the blanket aside. Two Browning Hi Power pistols and a Mossberg tactical shotgun, and enough boxes of ammunition to start a small war. "I think this enough. Yes?"

"Plenty, plenty," said Pat.

Daniel said, "It really is just reconnaissance, Jacob. Don't worry."

"I ain't worried," said Jacob, replacing the blanket. "I live here. This shithole is my home." He reached deeper, pulled out a medical kit—a heavy white metal box with a red cross painted on it. He opened it and removed a pill bottle, rattled the pills, and handed it to Daniel.

"Antimalarial, take one a day. If you plan to stay for any length of time you also need injection for yellow fever, hep B, typhoid, diphtheria, polio booster, and God knows what more." He tossed the keys to Daniel. "Map is in front. Best to double-clutch, it stick a little sometime."

"Wait, you're not coming?" said Pat. "I thought you were supposed to be our local fixer."

Jacob sucked air through his teeth. "Man, I ain't your anything." He fought a silent battle with himself for a few seconds before deciding to speak his mind, then jutted his chin at Pat. "I say you the muscle"—turned his head to Daniel—"and you the boss." He looked at Kara. "The hell are you?"

"Deeply involved citizen," said Daniel.

"You should not bring the woman on this mission. It's wrong." Jacob's look dared Daniel to break eye contact. He didn't.

Kara said, "I thank you for your concern, Jacob, but *the woman* is here by her own choice."

Jacob faced her. "The woman don't know what the hell she get involved in." Back to Daniel. "You chasin' some of the most dangerous men I ever see. And I see"—a glance at Pat—"plenty, plenty. The same thing ever since: moneymen from London and Zurich and New York, Paris and Berlin, Moscow, Beijing. Everybody come Liberia, do they dirty deals, run they dirty shipments under Liberia flag, steal African wealth out the ground. Oil, diamond, gold, uranium, timber—every damn thing." He sucked air through his teeth again. "Monrovia the *real* Wild West now—everybody come here do things they don't want nobody know about. And where moneymen go, spooks go. CIA, SVR, MSS, *everybody* pass through—and bring they tin soldier. Liberia *awash* in mercs, they in our bar and hotel and whorehouse, get drunk and wave they gun around, do what they like, always brag loud and flex bicep. Like peacock. Mercs everywhere, like rats. Always, always, it never change, even since the revolution everything just get worse—" Jacob caught himself, stopped talking with a sharp nod of his head.

He stood silent for a minute, refocusing. "But the guys you after, they a different breed. These guys nail down. Don't flash they gun, don't get drunk, keep to theyself, import they own pussy. *Real* discipline."

"Any idea what they're doing here?"

"Everybody guess, nobody know. Six month back, they fly that big metal structure upriver in pieces. Sikorsky helicopter: back and forth, back and forth. They take over a village, about three hundred people live. Isolated place, only one road in, you gotta turn around and come back the same way. They use the Sikorsky because large trucks can't get there, the road is just dirt and tight to the trees in many place."

"Nobody went up to check it out?"

"Put enough money in enough pockets, nobody want to know. And they bring in new clothing and cook pan for the people live up there, toy for they kids, Angus beef for they table. But no visitor allowed. Then a reporter come, Englishman, white, writing some book or 'nother about private militaries and secret wars. He ask me about them. I rent him a car and he go up see what he can see. He don't come back. So no, I ain't gonna carry you up there, do your dirty business."

"Fine, I get it," said Daniel, "but we're not the same as them. You just got done telling us how bad these guys are. You really think they came here to give teddy bears and Angus beef to poor villagers? They look like Oxfam to you?"

"So what?"

"So you know they're playing the devil's game up that river, doing wrong. And I mean to stop them."

Jacob shook his head. "I wish you luck. But it won't change nothing. World is run by the people who live far from the equator, and your luxury is paid for by the people who live near it. That's the bottom line, never change."

Jacob walked to the fence and straddled a Kawasaki dirt bike parked there. "I work with you because you the *less bad* bad guys, but you ain't the good guys. You playing the devil's game too." He kicked the motorbike alive and peeled away, leaving a cloud of blue exhaust.

Kara looked at Daniel. Daniel looked at Pat.

Pat said, "Welcome to Liberia."

36: PRAY FOR RAIN

Liberia's rainy season stretches from May to November, giving Monrovia the official title of World's Wettest Capital City. In the month of July alone, Monrovia gets almost twice the rainfall London sees in an entire year. And every year for the past twenty-five, Liberia has earned another dubious title: World's Worst Roads.

Once you get away from the airport, it's all crumbling asphalt and potholes—sinkholes, really—some big enough to swallow a piano.

And once you get away from the city, it's all red mud.

Red.

Mud.

Everywhere.

Red mud beside the dirt road, washed across the dirt road, piled atop the dirt road . . . three feet high in spots. And then you just can't tell the difference, because the road *is* mud.

Pat said, "Kids living out here in the sticks scratch together a living in the rainy season, charging money to dig out cars that get stuck. Nicer the car, the higher the fee. Looming starvation makes capitalists of us all. Gotta give 'em respect, they work hard and earn enough to keep themselves fed and clothed. And their capital investment? A shovel."

"What do they do in the dry season?" said Kara.

"Starve, mostly . . . and pray for rain. Look, sister, it's a shitty place to be born, they do whatever they have to." He gestured at the few wispy clouds in the wide blue sky. "Anyway we got lucky. Hasn't rained for two days, which at the end of August is a minor miracle. These roads are passable. If you feel bad about it, you can always toss some money out the window."

Pat was right, the roads were passable, but it was a slow drive. After two hours, they pulled off and parked in the shade of a large mahogany tree.

"DEET up," said Pat, tossing the gallon jug of industrial-strength insect repellant to Daniel. They were at a higher elevation now, but if the place was no longer a swamp, it was still a steam bath, with frequent swarms of mosquitoes and other evil, biting bugs that fly. And despite his earlier application of the foul stuff, Daniel had already picked up a few bites.

Daniel and Kara shared the bottle, pouring the greasy liquid over their hands and spreading it on their skin and clothes, combing it through their hair with their fingers.

"I may asphyxiate before the critters can get me," said Kara, waving at the toxic fumes in front of her face.

"Beats the hell out of the alternative," said Daniel. He'd caught dengue fever six years earlier in Venezuela and it hadn't been a fun ride. He'd be perfectly content not to add malaria to his list of life's adventures.

Daniel set up a folding card table and three stools in the shade as Pat took his turn with the insect repellant. Kara got some protein bars and Tetra Paks of coconut water from the cooler, and refilled their canteens from one of the large water jugs. Pat used the sat phone to tether his Toughbook to the web, then dialed the phone and spoke into it.

"Hey, Gerald, we're about an hour away. Can your guys get us a live feed? Thanks, dude." Pat tore open a protein bar and ate. He was just starting on his second bar when the satellite came online.

Daniel leaned over to see the screen. The village looked the same as it had the previous day. The ground perhaps slightly less red, having had another day to dry out, but otherwise the same.

"This is live, yes?" he said.

Pat nodded. "Gerald says we've got this satellite for an hour, hour and thirty tops. After that, no eye in the sky until tomorrow morning."

They kept their eyes on the screen as they finished their lunch. Nothing changed.

"Not even a sentry," said Daniel.

Pat said, "Sentry's not gonna stand in the sun—it's 105 out, dude's gonna find shade. We gotta assume whoever's there is just stayin' cool inside or under the canopy."

Daniel squinted at the screen, at something that looked like movement in the trees just north of the clearing. He held out his hand and Pat passed him the sat phone. "Hey, Gerald. Is it possible to get any closer?"

From over forty-six hundred miles away in New York City, Gerald So, the Foundation's chief computer genius, chuckled. "Not piggybacking on *this* bird. It'll be days before we get a better ride. But we're close enough to pick up individuals. There's nobody out there right now."

✦ ✦ ✦

A quarter mile from their destination, Pat said, "We walk from here." He pulled the Land Cruiser around to face the way they'd come, parked it in a shady spot. He put the key in a magnetic box and stuck it behind the bumper while Daniel called Gerald on the sat phone.

Nothing to report, still no movement in the village.

The Browning Hi Power carries a thirteen-round magazine, plus one in the chamber. Daniel and Pat both carried a fully loaded gun and three spare mags. If they couldn't get away while firing a combined 106 rounds, a few more bullets wouldn't help them. Better just to run than to stop and feed bullets one by one into the empty mags. They left the shotgun behind, loaded and accessible. If they were coming in hot, it could be a lifesaver.

They moved very slowly—Pat walking point, then Kara, Daniel covering their rear—guns drawn, staying quiet, stopping frequently, checking through binoculars, seeing no one, taking slightly more than thirty minutes to cross the final quarter mile. By the time they reached the edge of the village, Daniel's shirt was plastered to his chest and back, his arms and the backs of his hands covered by a sheen of perspiration.

Just outside the village clearing, they stopped again. This time it was an odor that stopped them. And it wasn't the odor of bug spray.

"I've spent enough time in morgues to know that smell," whispered Kara.

They scanned the place through lenses once more and, seeing no sign of occupancy, broke past the cover of the trees and walked on the dirt road that ran along the north edge of the village clearing.

And then Daniel saw the camouflage netting suspended above a long rectangular pit dug in the ground—about twenty feet by fifty—the mottled green netting held up by black metal poles. It was the very spot that had drawn Daniel's attention on the satellite feed, where he thought he'd seen something move.

The sour stench of rotting flesh grew stifling as they walked closer, and Daniel could now hear a loud humming, like electricity, coming from the pit under the blind. He walked close enough to see down into the pit and realized the source of the humming.

Not electricity. Flies. A black buzzing cloud of flies stretched from one end of the trench to the other, hovering over piles of human corpses putrefying in the heat, exposed skin split open, yellow liquid oozing from eye sockets and ears, mouths full of maggots.

Dillman's crew had killed the entire village, young and old. Just as Kara had dreamed.

The flies were not the only opportunists to find the pit. Three vultures and a dozen smaller birds were making meals of the dead, squawking and flapping whenever a rival moved in to feast off a body they'd claimed for themselves.

A feral dog, all ribcage and shoulder blades and hip bones, sniffed around the edges of the pit and, beginning to drool, stalked tentatively down the muddy slope to claim a place at the table. But the nearest vulture was having none of it. The vulture let out a piercing screech and launched itself at the dog, talons forward, beating its wings wildly. The dog yelped and ran away, ears down and tail between its legs. It looked back once over its shoulder with resentful eyes, then disappeared into the trees.

Better to go hungry.

They stood silent for a few moments, taking in the macabre scene.

In his years traveling as a Vatican investigator, Daniel had been in war zones and refugee camps, places where ethnic cleansing had taken place, but he'd never been on scene so soon after an atrocity. He knew how to remove himself from the horror of it, how to step back and watch himself watching the horror. But directly below him there was a dead little girl lying with her head resting on a woman's breast, their limbs intertwined, and it reminded him of the skeletal remains he'd seen in the cave in Norway. Of course, it wasn't an embrace, it was just the way their bodies had come to rest after falling into the pit. But there was a tenderness to it that moved him just the same.

Daniel turned away, to Kara's glistening and troubled face as she brushed wet hair behind one ear. Still looking into the pit, she said, "After years in the ER, I thought I'd seen every savagery imaginable. Babies murdered by their mothers, women tortured by their boyfriends, stabbings, shootings, beatings . . . but nothing like this. There was no passion to this slaughter, just . . . efficiency. Brutal efficiency." She repeated the words that had come to her in the field outside the cave in Norway: "The work of men who strive to become gods." She looked to Daniel. "Describes this as well."

"Yeah." He'd been thinking the same thing. "How long have these people been dead?"

"In this heat, it's hard . . ." She looked back to assess the degree of putrefaction. "One or two days, not more. That's the top layer. There are older bodies beneath."

Pat had already turned to their left and was lensing the large metal Quonset hut near the river. "Look like nobody home. Stay sharp."

Pat took point again, gun held out in front of him, Kara about six feet behind, Daniel again covering their rear as they crossed slowly to the Quonset hut. The massive generator and air conditioners stood silent and Daniel could hear no other mechanical sounds as they approached.

He squatted down at the metal door on the north-facing wall and examined the lock as Pat swiveled to cover the area.

"Not so bad," he said, plucking his soaked shirt away from his chest, drawing some air in between, then wiping the sweat out of his eyes.

He tucked the pistol behind his belt in the small of his back, and dug a black leather lock pick case from his leg pocket. He selected a couple picks—a long hook and a jag snake—and a tension tool, and he went to work.

It took almost two minutes.

It seemed much longer.

When the last tumbler clicked home, Daniel turned the knob and opened the door an inch. He put his ear to the opening and listened hard.

Nothing.

He stepped inside.

37: SPLITTING THE ATOM

It was cooler inside the Quonset hut, somewhere in the mid-nineties. Daniel wiped sweat out of his eyes again and searched the wall beside the door. He found the light switch and flipped it up, hoping there was enough solar power stored in the battery array to run the interior LED lighting system.

There was.

It was a medical facility. Evenly spaced rows of hospital beds separated by curtains hanging from stainless-steel rods. Carts with monitors, trolleys full of bedpans, a hamper overflowing with white lab coats . . .

The place smelled antiseptic. Daniel counted the beds as they walked deeper into the facility. He stopped counting at fifty.

Pat waved him over to one of the beds. "Look at this."

Hanging from the chrome rails of the bed were wide leather restraints, just like those Daniel had seen on the soldier in West Virginia. He walked down the row—every bed was fitted with restraints. And hanging above each bed was a boom microphone and a video camera.

They'd been recording the patients. Just as they had the soldier in West Virginia.

Daniel snatched a medical chart off the railing at the foot of a bed, handed it to Kara. "What can you tell us?"

Worry lines deepened between Kara's eyebrows as she read the chart, flipped the top sheet over, ran her finger down the page.

"Daniel, this doesn't make sense."

"What do you see?"

"Give me another."

Pat grabbed one from another bed, handed it over. She read it.

"Same thing. It says these people had *Y. Pestis*—the plague—but . . . they weren't being given proper treatment. I mean, it's the right medication—Cipro—but the dosage is far too low, maybe a fifth of what any qualified doctor would prescribe."

Dozens of them, restrained, held somewhere between life and death, allowed neither to die nor to live . . . no mercy . . . and no relief.

Kara's forgotten dream made terrifying sense now. Daniel said, "If you had patients with the plague and you administered *just enough* Cipro, could you keep them alive indefinitely, without curing them?"

Kara nodded. "I don't know about *indefinitely*, but for a while you could. It would be an incredibly cruel thing to do. Why would you?"

"Okay," said Daniel, "we know the man in West Virginia had the plague—a new strain—and we know he had AIT. There's some evidence from the historical record—scant, it was pre-scientific times—but there's evidence an ancient strain of the plague triggered AIT in a small percentage of people, maybe one or two percent. What if this new strain does as well? Whether it was genetically engineered or a natural mutation, let's say you cultured a sample and grew it. Then you administer it to people, say, in an isolated village in Liberia, and you'd have a test group. You could learn to harness AIT."

"Are you saying this entire village was wiped out in some proof-of-concept experiment?"

"That's exactly what I'm saying." Daniel gestured to the camera hanging above the bed. "You infect the village, then record the patients to determine who has AIT. You run the recordings through software to scan for keywords and phrases, like the NSA does with our phone calls and e-mails. The few who manifest AIT stay here and are given just enough antibiotic to keep them alive and suffering, the others you take outside and dump in the pit. Jacob said this was a village of about three hundred, so maybe you get six positives, but what if you repeated the experiment on a larger scale? Imagine the flood of information you could tap into if you could give people AIT at will. Information about the future, the past, about events taking place across the world."

Kara's face darkened. "You could practically control the future."

"Information truly is power," said Daniel.

"C'mere," said Pat from the other end of the Quonset hut, "you wanna check this out."

It was a glass-windowed laboratory, a room about twenty feet wide, sectioned off from the main area. On a counter along the lab's back wall were four blood spinners—centrifuges to separate plasma from blood, or various components from other solutions. Two desktop computers and two petri-dish incubators the size of small refrigerators. Beside the counter, a large steel freezer like you'd find in a restaurant kitchen.

And hanging on the wall, dozens of gas masks.

Gas masks.

Daniel turned to Pat. "Descia was right."

"Holy shit," said Pat.

"Who's Descia?" said Kara. "And what was she right about?"

"She's a microbiologist in London," said Daniel. "She saw the blood work on the soldier in West Virginia, said this new strain of the plague was probably pneumonic."

Kara stared at the wall of gas masks. "So . . . they could give it to anyone. They could contaminate asthma inhalers, or—"

"Hell," said Pat, "they could release it into the ventilation systems of commercial aircraft. Passengers get sick, disperse at their destination and start coughing all over families and friends and coworkers. They could set off a pandemic if they wanted to."

Daniel said, "And look at the size of that freezer. How many test tubes could you fit in there?"

Pat said, "Didn't leave the generator on, so I'm betting they took the critters with them."

Kara was looking at something inside the lab. A small smile formed on her lips. "But they left their computers behind." She strode to the door, Daniel and Pat close behind, opened it, and stepped inside.

A loud metallic click echoed through the room.

"Stop!"

Kara froze in place and looked down at her feet. She was standing on a square steel pressure plate about three feet wide, placed so anyone entering the room had to step on it. Two wires snaked out from the corner of the steel plate and across the floor and up the leg of a desk, disappearing beneath it.

Daniel said, "Don't move." He didn't go into detail about pressure plate switches and improvised explosives. Kara knew she was standing on a bomb; any further detail was unnecessary.

She looked up at him, her eyes wide.

"I got this," Pat went prone on the floor and crawled under the desk. He rolled onto his back and looked up. Then he reached into his pocket and unfolded a multitool with wire cutters built into the pliers.

With a slight tremor in her voice, Kara said, "It can't really be as easy as just *cut the red wire*, can it?" She reached a hand forward and Daniel held it in his.

"It can," said Pat from under the desk, "but sometimes it's the blue wire, or the green wire, or . . ."

"Not helpful," said Daniel.

"It's okay," said Pat, "I've seen this setup before. Have ya outta here in a jiffy, sister." Pat raised the wire cutters, reached up with his other hand, then stopped. "Uh-oh." He shimmied out from under the desk, stood up.

"What?" said Daniel.

"Second set of wires, runs through a seam in the wall. Hang tight, I'll be right back."

Pat left the room and disappeared around the corner.

Kara said, "Whatever happens, you and Pat have to stop these people."

"Don't talk like that." It came out sharper than he'd intended. "You good here for just a minute? I'm gonna grab the hard drives from those computers."

She let go of his hand. "I'm good."

Daniel crossed to the desktop computer on the left side of the counter. When he touched the computer tower, the shell fell away. He spun the tower around. Where the hard drive should've been, there was nothing but a gaping hole. He checked the other computer and found the same thing.

Pat came back into the lab. His normal swagger was missing and his expression was grim. "Wires lead to a control box in the ceiling—can't get to it. And there's enough C-4 up there to bring the whole place down on our heads. It's on a timer—could be ten seconds or ten minutes, no way to know. If I cut the wires from the pressure plate, it'll defuse the bomb under Kara but it'll start the timer in the ceiling. If Kara steps off the plate, she goes boom and the timer starts anyway."

"No choice," said Daniel. "We cut the wire and run."

Kara said, "No. You have to get out of here. I meant what I said. You have to stop these people."

Pat said, "Kara's right."

"What, are you kidding me?"

"Use your head, brother. If we all die here, nobody stops them. And then how many people die?"

"Fine," said Daniel. "You go. I'll cut the wire and run with Kara."

Kara said, "Daniel, no. Just go."

Pat said, "Dude, when Carter sent me on this mission, he made it clear my primary task, above all else, was to get you back safely. He thinks you're essential to solving this thing. And I agree with him. Don't be stupid."

"Enough." Daniel snatched the wire cutters from Pat's hand. He turned to face Kara. "I am not leaving you behind. End of discussion." Then to Pat, "Just show me which wire to cut and get out of here. We'll follow once you're clear."

Pat sighed and held out his hand for the cutters. "You'd probably cut the wrong wire anyway. Screw it, we'll run together."

Daniel handed them over and Pat slid back under the desk. "We go on three."

Daniel tightened his grip on Kara's hand, and they looked at each other and time just about stopped, the moment stretching out...

From under the desk, Pat said, "Everybody ready?"

Daniel nodded to Kara.

She nodded back. "Ready."

"Ready," said Daniel.

"One . . . two . . . THREE!"

Daniel took off running, pulling Kara along as fast as she could go.

Two strides outside the lab, Pat caught up, grabbing Kara's other hand.

Two more strides and a rapid series of explosions ran along the curved support beams above, a deafening roar, and then lighting fixtures and chunks of steel rained down, crashing to the floor all around them, smoke filling the space above their heads.

Three more strides, dodging debris, now twelve paces to the door.

Another series of explosions, and the entire building shuddered, right down to the foundation.

Ten paces to the door.

A low, agonized groan now reverberating through the metal structure as it deformed and began twisting against itself. The ground below them quaking.

Eight paces—

Something heavy struck Daniel on the back of his left shoulder, knocking him to the ground. Muscle memory from the dojo kicked in, and he rolled with it and came back up still running.

Five paces to the door.

The groaning louder, coming from everywhere at once, joined in harmony by the high screech of shearing metal.

Three paces to the door.

The roof of the Quonset hut gave way, curved sidewalls collapsing into each other.

It all came thundering down behind them as they burst through the door and out into the blinding sun.

38: LITANY AGAINST FEAR

Sprinting through the clearing and into the trees as the world imploded behind them . . . maintaining a fast jog the quarter mile back to the Land Cruiser . . . Pat driving a bit wild for a few miles, then settling into a speed that showed at least marginal respect for the slippery red mud, once it was clear nobody was giving chase.

For the next twenty minutes, they just sat without speaking, listening to their ears ring.

Pat broke the silence. "Well, that happened."

"That it did," said Daniel. He reached for the sat phone.

It was then Kara told Daniel his shoulder was bleeding. He got his shirt off and she examined the cut from the backseat. She grabbed the first-aid kit and told him it wasn't too bad. Daniel chewed a couple Percodan, and she poured alcohol over the cut and sewed it up.

Thus repaired, Daniel called New York and got Raoul on the phone. He reported what they'd discovered and how they'd escaped, and using Kara's estimated time of death for the bodies in the pit, he told Raoul to check all charter flights out of Monrovia for the previous twenty to forty-eight hours. Destinations, registrations, passenger manifests, whatever they could access. Raoul said Gerald would get right on it.

Daniel said, "Dillman's crew obviously bugged out in a hurry, took only what they needed, but they invested the time to booby-trap the place instead of just burning it to the ground. Which means Dillman and Conrad know I'm breathing down their necks. They know if I find the place, I'll investigate, set off the implosion. But it's more than just a booby trap—it's a burglar alarm. They can hack into satellite feeds just like we can. They'll know we found it and they'll move faster. We're running out of time."

"Listen to me, Grasshopper," said Raoul. "You're on an adrenaline rush right now, all three of you, and you're no good to us until you get some rest. There's a suite waiting at the Cape—Pat knows the place. Go. Chill out. We'll keep working it on our end, and I'll have a plane pick you up in the morning."

Within five minutes of checking into the Cape Hotel, Pat was snoring on the living-room couch. He could just turn it off like that. But the adrenaline didn't shut off completely for Daniel and Kara, so after a few hours' nap, they both bounced back with an unnaturally perky second wind.

Seemed a shame to waste it.

✦ ✦ ✦

Daniel and Kara sat across from each other at an outdoor table along the railing of the Cape Hotel's dining-room veranda. On the other side of the railing, the beach at Mamba Point stretched out below them, waves gently lapping the shoreline, moonlight shimmering on the surface of the Atlantic under a canopy of numberless stars. Kara's lips—painted red and wet with wine—sparkled in the candlelight.

Such beautiful lips.

She said, "A business consultant I once knew told me a shared brush with death can cause an intense feeling of intimacy between two people."

"Uh-huh," said Daniel.

"It can be a very difficult feeling to resist."

"So let's not. Resist, that is."

Kara reached forward and clinked her glass against his.

The waiter arrived and took their dinner order. This close to the ocean, they agreed it would be stupid not to have fish, and they both took the leap, ordering it with spicy garlic sauce.

Intense flavors for an intense day.

Daniel stood and excused himself, leaning in for a kiss as he left the table, and Kara tilted her face up and put the palm of her hand on his chest and kissed him back.

Passion simmered just beneath the surface—an acknowledgment of what was to come in the bedroom upstairs. But there was also a sadness in the kiss—an acknowledgment that they'd looked into the abyss today, and seen the depths of cruelty humans were capable of.

They'd come so close to death.

And seen such horror.

The only appropriate response was to do something beautiful and life affirming. So they would stare into each other's eyes over a candlelit dinner under the stars and then go upstairs and, as the British say, shag each other rotten. Probably stare into each other's eyes during that, too.

Today had been a good day to die. But Daniel had stayed alive, and whatever happened tomorrow, tonight he would abide.

He left Kara at the table and walked through the hotel lobby and pushed open the polished wood door, into the men's room.

Like the rest of the hotel's public spaces, it was tasteful and well appointed. Their two-bedroom suite with an ocean-view veranda was better still. Even in a place as poor as Monrovia, the money-men and diplomats and spies demanded first-world luxury. And the Cape Hotel delivered.

Daniel stood in front of the urinal and unzipped, thinking: *What a difference seven hours makes . . .*

The men's room door swung open behind Daniel as he zipped up.

He used the urinal's chrome hardware as a mirror to see—

—a large man closing in fast, so fast Daniel felt the sharp pin jab in the back of his neck before he could even pivot.

His legs turned to rubber.

The room started spinning.

He sank to the floor.

A second man pulled a black hood over his head.

Daniel slipped into darkness.

39: STRANGERS

Upon awakening, Daniel's first thought was *headache*.

Followed by: *Right, the guy in the men's room.*

And then: *Kara—oh God did they get Kara, too?*

He opened his eyes. A naked lightbulb hung about six feet above. He was lying on his back on a bench of some kind, secured to it by straps across the chest and thighs and ankles. His wrists were bound together behind his back, arms stretched under the bench. His shoulders throbbed, especially on the left side where Kara had stitched him up. The place smelled of Dettol antiseptic.

He turned his head to the side. The room was about ten feet wide. Cinder-block walls, unpainted. A small, battered table to his left, and a single folding metal chair. On the table, a two-liter torpedo bottle of Coca-Cola. Nothing else in the room.

He heard a door open and then close behind him. Then footsteps—large man, rubber-soled shoes—coming closer. The man appeared in his field of vision—the first man from the men's room, the one who'd injected him—carrying something mounted on a black tripod. Camera? The man set the tripod about four feet away, to Daniel's right.

Not a camera. A workshop light.

Two thousand blinding watts of halogen light bore down on Daniel, making his eyes water. Worse was the heat. Already a hundred degrees in the room, and within seconds Daniel could feel his skin temperature rising under the artificial sun.

The man walked out of Daniel's field of vision. The door opened again.

"He's awake, sir. We're ready."

New footsteps, leather-soled shoes this time, coming closer, stopping next to Daniel on his left, beside the table.

Evan Sage looked down at Daniel, shaking his head. "You know, you are really starting to piss me off, Mr. Byrne. I thought I made my position clear. Your country needs your help. All you had to do was show up at the American embassy and talk to me, like any patriotic citizen would. But you decided it was a better idea to run away to the Liberian jungle"—he leaned in close and spoke directly into Daniel's ear canal—"and DESTROY THE EVIDENCE!"

Sage dragged the metal chair across the concrete floor, closer to Daniel. He sat. "And that makes you an enemy combatant. Your citizenship no longer grants you any rights. Way things stand, you're looking at a one-way trip to Guantanamo."

The other man moved the tripod a foot closer, tilted the head down, pointing the powerful lamp directly at Daniel's face and chest, close enough to give him a sunburn.

Daniel's mouth was dry. He swallowed. "The place was rigged to blow before I got there."

Sage said, "Well, that's a start." He reached into his shirt pocket, pulled out a pack of cigarettes, and lit one with a Zippo, snapping the lighter shut and blowing a blue stream of smoke directly at Daniel's face. "Rigged by whom?"

"The men you're chasing," said Daniel. "Michael Dillman's crew, I guess."

"And how do you know that?"

Daniel tried to clear his throat but it was too dry. "Water," he said.

Sage glanced up at the man standing in the darkness behind the light, then back to Daniel. "How do you know it was Dillman's crew?"

"Said I *guess*. I don't know." Daniel's throat felt like sandpaper.

"Then why do you *guess* it was Dillman's crew?"

"Because you're chasing them. Because you said they're involved in bioweapons. Because the place looked like a medical lab."

"Don't get cute. You knew damn well who Dillman was, and you knew his crew had something going on in Liberia, knew exactly where to look. And you knew it before I did, so you can cut the *business consultant* crap. And don't give me shit about investigating all that mystical Tim Trinity voodoo." Sage blew smoke in Daniel's face again. "Who are you working for?"

Daniel said nothing.

Sage glanced at the big man in the shadows. The man walked away and Daniel heard a faucet running, filling a large metal pail. After a minute, the tap shut off and the man appeared above Daniel, silhouetted by the workshop light.

The man said, "Back in Washington, they call it *enhanced interrogation*, but that's bullshit. I promise you, it's torture. Got a taste of it myself in training. Once you can't breathe, nothing else matters. Me, I'm pretty tough and I cried uncle after two minutes. Nobody else in my group even made it a full minute." He put the pail down, reached into his pocket, and pulled out a black cloth. He stretched the cloth tight across Daniel's mouth and nose, hooking the ends around something to keep it in place.

Daniel sucked air through the cloth, fighting against the panic rising in his chest, focusing on breathing steady and slow.

The man lifted the pail again. "They say it simulates drowning—that's also bullshit. It *is* drowning, just in slow motion. Drowning puts the body under incredible pressure. Usually when people die, it's because they stroke out or have a heart attack. You don't have a heart condition, do you?" He began tilting the pail.

Evan Sage held up a hand and the big man put the pail down again. Sage unhooked the cloth. "We don't have to do this, Daniel." He dragged on his cigarette again. "Hell, I'm a Democrat, I'm against this shit. I hate it, really." He nodded his chin in the direction of the big man. "Sam here, he likes it. But I will do *anything* to protect my country—your country too, by the way—from *all* enemies foreign or domestic."

"We're on the same side," croaked Daniel.

"If that were true, you'd have come to the embassy," said Sage. "If that were true, you'd already be talking instead of waiting to see what happens next. Well here's what happens next: Sam floods your lungs with water until you tell us everything. Period. You don't tell us, we pick up your girlfriend and you can watch while we do it to her." He dropped the cigarette, ground it out under his heel. Then he pulled the cloth taught over Daniel's mouth and nose.

Sam reached for the pail.

Daniel closed his eyes and slowed his breathing further.

The water came. A splash at first, and against his will he swallowed it, rehydrating his parched throat. Then another splash filled his sinuses and then the water came steadily and his entire body went rigid. He fought to turn his head to the side, couldn't. He tried spitting the water back up, but the cloth held most of it in his mouth and it just kept coming faster, more going in than coming out, and he coughed and gagged, heart pounding against his ribs, muscles spasming, but the water just kept coming.

Daniel was drowning. Each second without air was an hour, and the room began spinning around him. Blind panic set in, the pure animal need for oxygen raging in his chest and in his mind. He wanted to tell Sage everything. He *needed* to tell. But somehow, deep in his mind beneath the panic, there was a place of stillness, and he tried to center his consciousness there. And in that place, he knew telling Sage the truth would only make things worse. Everything Daniel had learned, he'd learned by way of what Sage called *that mystical Tim Trinity voodoo*. From the soldier in West Virginia to Kara's voices and dreams, to the cave in Norway, all the way to the horror of that village upriver. He could tell Sage everything, and Sage wouldn't believe a word of it, and the water, the water . . .

the water would . . .

just . . .

keep . . .

coming.

Daniel hacked up a lungful but the cloth stopped it and it came back into his mouth and he swallowed it and his stomach hurt.

The water stopped briefly, and he choked and gasped for air, inhaling water, his chest burning.

The water started again.

"Stop!" Daniel screamed, forcing what little air he had out of his lungs.

The water stopped. Evan Sage untied the cloth. The other man stepped forward and lifted the end of the bench by Daniel's feet and hooked it to something against the wall, putting Daniel's head about twenty degrees lower than his feet.

Daniel vomited all over himself, gasped for air.

Sage checked his watch. "Damn, that was pretty impressive." He glanced at Sam, then looked down at Daniel. "I'm listening."

"You won't believe me."

"I will if it's the truth."

Daniel sifted quickly through the facts, sorting them into *Tell* and *Don't Tell*. It wasn't just about stopping the waterboarding. He could make up a story, tell them what they wanted to hear, and that would stop the waterboarding. But Sage would keep him detained while checking the story out. The main goal—the *only* goal—was to stop Conrad Winter and Michael Dillman from releasing their plague bacteria into the world. And Daniel couldn't do that from this room.

And as much as he hated Evan Sage right now, Daniel knew Sage was committed to stopping them too. Sage didn't need to know about AIT, whether he'd believe it or not. But he needed to know the threat of an outbreak was imminent, regardless of the Foundation's obsession with secrecy.

Daniel said, "Michael Dillman has possession of a new strain of the plague. I don't know if it was bioengineered or a natural mutation, but it's *pneumonic* and he has a lot of it. And I'm trying to stop him before he releases it."

Sage's eyes flicked to Sam and back. *"Where?"*

"I have no idea."

"Who's backing him?"

"He's working for a man named Conrad Winter. A Vatican priest."

Sage snorted. "You expect me to believe the *Vatican* is behind this?"

"No, not the Vatican. Winter has his own agenda."

"So who's behind Winter? Because you don't finance an operation like this on a priest's salary."

"You'd have to ask Winter."

"Winter's not here . . . if he even exists. I'm asking you."

"I don't know," Daniel lied.

"Don't spoon-feed me. I need it all. Who's behind Winter?"

"I don't know."

"You gotta do better than that. A lot better." Sage stretched the black cloth over Daniel's mouth and nose, held it firm, and nodded to Sam. "Again."

Sam unhooked the bench and lowered it back to horizontal.

Shit shit shit shit shit . . .

Sam lifted the bucket, tilted it.

The water started again. Daniel's sinuses flooded and water splashed against his esophagus and he gasped a mix of water and air into his lungs and his diaphragm spasmed.

Sam tilted the bucket further and Daniel couldn't breathe—it was all water now, water and pure blind panic, heart racing, head screaming, chest ready to explode.

Behind Daniel, the door opened and all at once the water stopped.

A third man's voice said, "Sir, phone call for you. Urgent."

"Christ." Sage released the cloth and Sam tilted the bench, and Daniel coughed and gagged and threw up some more water.

Sage stopped on the way to the door and rested his hand on the torpedo bottle. "You have two minutes to rethink your position. Then we switch to Coke. Nobody holds out after they get a lungful of Coke." He left the room.

Daniel got his breathing under control once more, but he couldn't tear his eyes away from the Coke bottle. How much longer could he hold out? He was right at his limit now, with only water. The thought of Coke flooding his lungs sent a violent shudder through his body, and he suddenly felt not hot, but very cold. He shuddered again.

And then Sage was back in the room with the other man. Rough hands released the straps across Daniel's body and cut the zip ties from his wrists and ankles. Sam hauled him to his feet and kept him from falling until he could get his legs under him.

Evan Sage lit a cigarette, spoke bitterly. "I don't know who the hell you are, but you have friends in very high places. You're free to go."

Daniel walked unsteadily to the door, stopped and looked back, and started to speak.

Sage jabbed his cigarette at the open door. "Just fuck off."

40: DON'T SLOW DOWN

Daniel stood alone in the same men's room at the Cape Hotel where a needle in the back of the neck had made him disappear, thinking, *What a difference seven hours makes . . . again.*

The man facing Daniel from the mirror looked older than Daniel. And he needed a shave. Frankly, he looked a mess. His shirt was disgusting, his hair all over the place, his face filthy and shiny and flushed, his expression that of a man disconnected from himself.

Hollow.

Daniel turned on the tap and splashed cold water on his face. Jerked his face up and spun the tap off.

No water, no thank you.

He took a few deep, centering breaths, got his heart rate back down to normal. He pulled his shirt off. There was a horizontal bruise across his chest where he'd struggled against the restraint. Checking over his shoulder confirmed the quality of Kara's needlework—the wound was an angry shade of red, but her stitches had held just fine.

He rinsed his shirt in the sink, dislodging flecks of vomit, ignoring the sound of the faucet as best he could. He shut off the tap, wrung out the shirt and wiped his face with it, then put it back on. He ran his wet fingers through his hair, dried his face and forearms with a towel, and nodded to the scruffy guy in the mirror.

It would have to do.

Upstairs, he keyed his way into the suite and stopped short in the hallway.

Voices from the living room. Kara and Pat. Arguing.

Kara was saying, "Well I can't just sit here and wait for the phone to ring. We should be out there, looking."

Pat said, "You don't know Monrovia, darlin'. We can't just go wanderin' the streets at 3:00 a.m. Jacob's got feelers out all over town, and headquarters is working it full-tilt boogie on their end. Soon as we get a lead, I'm outta here. I'll get our boy back, I promise. Best thing you can do right now is get some sleep."

Daniel walked into the room. "Pat's right, you do look a bit tired."

"Daniel!" Kara shrieked and ran toward him, arms wide.

Last thing Daniel wanted was his chest squeezed, even by her. His body wanted to pivot away from her, make her miss. But he held firm and braced himself for the hug, guiding her arms down and around his lower back. She kissed him and he kept it short, taking hold of her shoulders and moving her back a step.

"I'm disgusting," he said, putting on a smile for her.

"I don't care," she said. "You're alive."

"'Course I am," he said. "You worry too much."

Pat was talking into the phone, relief audible in his tone. "Just walked in the door. Yup." He winked at Daniel. "Little worse for wear, but I reckon he's okay. Will do. Thanks." He put the phone down, grinned at Daniel. "Everyone back home sends hugs."

"Thanks."

"What happened?" said Kara.

"Just an unscheduled conversation with Homeland Security. I'm fine."

She grabbed his hands in hers and went into doctor mode: "You are not fine. Your hands are freezing . . . pupils dilated . . . eyes unfocused. Daniel, you're in shock. What did they do to you?"

"Kara, stop." He looked her in the eyes, making sure to focus his. "They asked me some questions and encouraged me to answer them. And now it's over. I'm fine, really, just need a shower and some shut-eye." He kissed her forehead. "The worst part of it was missing our date. Now go on to bed. It's been a long day for all of us."

✤ ✤ ✤

Pat stood out on the veranda, under the stars, leaning back against the railing and sipping root beer through a straw, smoke rising from a joint in his other hand. Daniel stepped out to join him, closed the door behind.

Pat said, "She asleep?"

"Will be any minute." There was a bottle of Old Rip Van Winkle beside a single rocks glass on the table. Daniel poured a few fingers into the glass and dropped himself heavily into a patio chair, close enough to reach the bottle for refills.

Pat said, "Figured you'd want something to drink that wasn't water."

"Got that right." He toasted Pat with the bourbon. "*Skal.*" His throat was still raw but the bourbon's burn was welcome.

Pat toasted back with his joint, took a drag. "So how you doin'? Really?"

Daniel thought about it, sipped some more bourbon. "I'm okay. Or I will be, anyway. You ever been waterboarded?"

"Yup," said Pat. "Sucks, don't it?"

"That it does." Daniel topped up his drink. "What'd I miss?"

"You mean other than almost every Foundation resource and asset being diverted to find your sorry ass?"

"Yeah, other than that."

"Lots. Gerald ran down the charter flights out of Monrovia for the time frame you gave him—and got a hit. Twenty-three passengers, destination London, left here a little less than a day before we landed. Twenty of them mercs working for the PMC connected to Dillman." Pat checked his watch. "About ten hours ago, they flew from London to Atlanta. There they split up, but thirteen of them are booked on the same commercial flight from Atlanta to Columbia, South Carolina."

"Thirteen of them. Jesus, they're getting ready to release this shit in the United States."

"Looks that way. And there's more: Gerald figured they didn't pick up three tourists, so he drilled down on the other names on that charter flight. You ever hear of Chickamauga?"

"Civil War battle in Georgia, wasn't it?"

Pat nodded. "One of the bloodiest, about thirty-five thousand dead. Huge Confederate victory. But the Confederates messed up. After the Blue retreated to Chattanooga, the Gray should've pressed their advantage. The winning Confederate generals in Chickamauga were Braxton Bragg and James Longstreet, but only Bragg was sent to Chattanooga. Longstreet was ordered to take his men and attack Knoxville, which gave Lincoln time to send Ulysses Grant down with reinforcements."

"Okay . . ."

"Well, Gerald's geeks have been digging through everything they can find on Michael Dillman, before he went dark. Turns out Dillman wrote his masters thesis on the Battle of Chickamauga.

The focus of his paper was the post-victory tactical error of splitting up Bragg and Longstreet."

Daniel sipped his bourbon. "And the too-clever name on that passenger manifest was…?"

"Bingo. James Bragg. Once Gerald knew Dillman's nom de guerre, he found a credit check for James Bragg, run six weeks ago by a bank in downtown Columbia. Seems Dillman rented an apartment there." Pat grinned, a predator knowing he had the drop on his prey. "Dude, we know where Dillman's hanging his hat. We can get him."

Daniel said, "We have an address?"

"Not yet, but knowing Gerald, we'll have it by the time we get there." Pat took one last hit off the spliff and pinched the cherry off, saving the rest for later. He pushed himself off the railing, put his hand on Daniel's shoulder as he passed. "We're wheels up at noon. Don't drink the whole bottle. Try to get some sleep."

41: THE RICHEST MAN IN BABYLON

Nine miles outside Columbia, South Carolina

Complete destruction in Liberia," said Conrad Winter. "Perfect implosion. But the satellite was out of range when the hut came down, so that's all we know." He paused to take in the empty warehouse around them, only a few tables and folding chairs in the place. "How soon will we be ready to go, Colonel?"

"Trucks will arrive within the hour, we can be set up here by midafternoon tomorrow. The Atlanta and Charlotte teams are scheduled to arrive late morning, airport and train station can be off-line by noon. If you give the order, we can go tomorrow."

Dillman's tone said both that he thought it was the wrong call and that he would follow Conrad's orders regardless.

Conrad said, "In a perfect world we'd have more time, but we're awash in unknown unknowns, and even the known unknowns are daunting. We don't know if it was Daniel Byrne who triggered the implosion, and even if he did, we don't know if it killed him. We don't know what his little AIT harlot might've told him, or how much of that information he communicated back to Carter Ames. That prick has been either incredibly good or incredibly lucky . . ." Thinking: *Should've killed him in New Orleans when you had the chance . . .* "Bottom line: Our window may be closing. The bloody

Foundation is breathing *right down our necks*. If we can do this now, we should do it."

After a moment, Michael Dillman said, "Permission to speak freely?"

"Of course." Conrad forced out a reassuring smile. It must've been a little awkward for Dillman to take orders from the son after serving the father so many years. He was handling the transition well.

"Allowing Daniel Byrne or Carter Ames to dictate our timing seems unwise. The plan was to pause and monitor world events after phase one, choose the timing that was to our best advantage. And right now the timing is not to our advantage. Russia is on the march again, China is pressing its influence wider, the Middle East is a disaster, and now we've got Ebola spreading out of control in West Africa . . . I would think we'd want to wait at least until the disease outbreak is contained. This operation is noisy and messy, even at the best of times . . ."

Conrad knew the level of Michael Dillman's security clearance. But he'd already decided to promote the man when he took the director's chair in the coming months. Might as well start reading him in to the larger game now.

Claim it and own it . . .

"Mike, the Middle East is not a disaster—the Middle East is exactly what we need it to be. We've passed the point where maintaining regional instability is enough. Influence and wealth are shifting faster than we've anticipated. Other players— including Nightingale—are pushing the pace of change, and we've been unable to convince them that our chosen pace is preferable for all of us."

"I didn't realize it was past the tipping point."

Conrad pulled up a chair and sat. He nodded to another chair, and Dillman sat facing him.

Conrad said, "Next year when I become director, I'll be taking you with me to Singapore as my tactical adviser, and you'll be fully read in on the larger game. But you already know the west is bankrupt, the tipping point was a while back. The American era is over, all but for the wailing and gnashing of teeth. Hell, anybody with a calculator and a functioning mind knows it, and the smoke and mirrors aren't working any more. All we've got left to offer them is war. War will prop up the fading empire for another decade or two, and there's still value we can draw out in the time remaining."

Michael Dillman nodded as the bigger picture came into focus. "But the people are tired of war, so . . ."

"Exactly. The chaos and disorder we unleash here will provide cover for our AIT operation, and that's essential but it's not the only game we're playing. It also forces Washington's hand in other ways that help us. Within six months, there'll be an additional hundred thousand troops in the Middle East—a whole new offensive. And when the capital city of South Carolina looks like a third-world refugee camp, spoiled Americans will stop bitching and be glad their police departments are becoming standing armies, and they'll welcome the ascendancy of the surveillance state. They'll decide it's a fair trade for keeping them safe and delaying the collapse of their empire. And they'll be right. So noisy and messy is *exactly* what we want."

Claim it and own it . . .

Conrad put a hand on Dillman's shoulder. "Welcome to the larger game, Mike. We launch phase two tomorrow."

42: HIGHER THAN THE WORLD

Fifty-five thousand feet over the Atlantic Ocean

First order of business was getting the injections done.

As Kara prepared the syringes, she said, "Under normal circumstances, giving antibiotics to people who don't have a bacterial infection would be medical malpractice."

She injected herself first.

Pat said, "Doctors do it all the time."

"And it's killing us." Kara put the syringe down. "Probably responsible for the explosion of disease over the last thirty-five years." She put a Band-Aid on her arm. "People talk about the 'friendly' bacteria that live on us, but they're more than friendly. These little guys quite literally keep us alive. There are trillions—with a *t*—of bacteria living in and on our bodies. In fact, we carry around more living non-human cells than we do human cells. This bacterial ecosystem makes up our own personal microbiome. And we're killing it by overusing antibiotics. That's why we're seeing an explosion of everything from obesity to diabetes to colitis to asthma, immune deficiency, even cancer."

She picked up the second syringe and injected Pat. "The greatest medical discovery in human history, the biggest boon to human existence, and in a few short generations we've turned it into the biggest *threat* to human existence." She stuck a Band-Aid over the injection site on Pat's muscular arm. "For such a smart species, we're incredibly stupid."

Daniel said, "But the bug we're chasing ain't even close to friendly. It'll kill us if we catch it."

"Agreed." Kara picked up a third syringe. "But don't get the idea that this sort of thing is a good idea in general, understand it comes at a cost. We are hurting ourselves."

Pat rolled down his sleeve and grinned. "I'm gonna head up to where the action is, sit in the cockpit and see if I can get the pilot to give me a turn at the stick."

After Pat left, Kara injected Daniel, then reached for another syringe. "Lucky boy, you get two."

"What's the second?"

"Bunch of stuff. We have no idea what creepy-crawlies were living in that water they forced into you."

"I think it was treated," said Daniel. "Tasted like chlorine anyway. Like pool water."

"Not a chance we should take." Kara stuck him with the other needle, depressed the plunger.

"Thanks."

Daniel found a bottle of red wine in the galley, poured a couple of glasses, and settled in beside Kara on the big leather sofa.

Kara sipped her wine. "You really think this strain of the plague causes AIT?"

"Not necessarily *causes*, but *triggers*. In a small percentage of people. There's evidence that an early form of plague triggered it as well. Back then there was no science to speak of, but historical records are strongly suggestive."

"How so?"

"The first records of the connection go back to just before the fall of the Roman Empire, when a plague wiped out entire cities in the Roman colonies of North Africa. Of course, plague victims babble a lot of gibberish as the fever damages their brains, but church leaders noted that a small percentage of these people were saying things about what was going on back in Rome—things they couldn't have possibly known about. Others spoke in foreign tongues they didn't know. The pre-scientific conclusion was that these people were demon possessed. Some scholars at the time concluded that it was a signal of the beginning of the apocalypse, really believed the world was about to end. And in a way, it was. Not the world, but the world as they knew it—the Roman Empire collapsed shortly thereafter." Daniel sipped some wine. "The records were locked away, kept secret, but the church knew about them and when the Black Death hit in the fourteenth century, they saw the same phenomenon and recognized it. That was part of the rationale for the pogroms across Europe. Some in the church thought if they killed the Jews, God would call off what they called the Great Mortality. They thought they were postponing the end of the world."

"Why is it always the Jews?" said Kara.

Daniel shrugged. "Anyway, it wasn't only the Jews in this case. The church's roving thugs also wiped out entire towns, whether or not Jews were present, if they detected the symptoms of AIT— which of course they still considered demonic possession."

"You think that's what happened to the village in Mandal?"

Daniel nodded. "AIT waxes and wanes through history, like ribbons in time, sometimes thicker, other times so thin it practically disappears. To those church leaders, demonic possession was a pre-scientific attempt to understand what was happening.

And after the plague passed, AIT went dormant again. The magic went away. They decided they'd killed enough Jews, or flagellated themselves enough, that God took mercy and gave them protection from the demons."

Kara shook her head, clearly frustrated. "Doesn't get us any closer to understanding the cause of AIT."

"The cause may be something beyond our ability to understand, Kara."

"Oh great. Now we're back to the God question."

Daniel said, "Think of it this way: A dog doesn't understand mathematics, but that doesn't mean mathematics doesn't exist. We don't understand the cause of AIT, but we can observe it phenomenologically, so we know it exists, and there is a cause."

"I can accept it phenomenologically," said Kara, "but even if you could explain the cause by some sort of quantum information leakage through one of the collapsed dimensions like you were talking about, that doesn't begin to address the fact that the whole thing feels . . ."

"Feels what?"

"Intentional. The voices, the dreams, the whole thing. It feels like there's an intention behind it."

Daniel said, "Like the universe is trying to tell us something."

"Yes. And you can't have that level of intention without some kind of intelligence behind it. But I just find the whole concept of God ridiculous."

Daniel laughed. "You won't get any answers from me on that front." He drank some wine. "I was raised by a phony faith healer who neglected to tell me it was all a con, so as a kid I believed in everything. Why wouldn't I? My guardian was a messenger from God, far as I knew. Hell, I saw real live miracles taking place all the time. And when I got a little older and finally saw through the grift, when that house of cards came crashing down, I ran to the church. Eventually I joined the priesthood and spent a decade searching for a real miracle. But in the end, I found something much stranger than what I was looking for."

"But you do believe in God."

"I no longer believe in the God I learned about in the Bible, but I'm humble enough to acknowledge that I don't know the secrets of the universe. I'm no longer chasing faith. I'm chasing truth—and that means accepting uncertainty, accepting that the universe is bigger and stranger than we can even know. Is it possible that the universe acts with intention, with intelligence? Science is learning that it's not only possible, it's likely. But that doesn't mean I believe in an old guy with a white beard in the sky. What I believe is we're able to push the boundaries of our knowledge only so long as we keep our focus on phenomena itself, rejecting metaphysical conclusions and false certainty, however comforting they may be."

"Sounds a little flimsy."

"Existence is flimsy," said Daniel. "Ninety-six percent of the universe is made of dark energy and dark matter. We don't even know what the universe *is*. How can we state definitively that it is or is not intelligent?"

"Wow. You *do* embrace uncertainty. I don't know how many people could be comfortable with that worldview."

"Way I see it, hard-core materialists and hard-core spiritualists are two sides of the same coin, both claiming certainty about the fundamental nature of existence itself, which they can't possibly know. Which in both cases requires a hubris I can no longer muster."

"So if I'm a hard-core materialist, you're a . . . phenomenological existentialist?"

"That's a mouthful." Daniel smiled. "And I guess it's as close as you're gonna get. But the truth is, I'm not an anything-*ist*. I think embracing a label hinders clear-eyed study. I also study Buddhism, but I'm not a Buddhist. I'm just a person trying to find the truth. As are we all. But as soon as you embrace isms and schisms, you're no longer looking out at the world, you're just looking at yourself."

Kara sipped her wine and smiled at him. "You do have an interesting mind, Daniel Byrne."

⚓ ⚓ ⚓

After a second glass of wine, Kara visited the lavatory at the back of the plane. She returned, her eyes a little wide. "Did you know there's an entire bedroom in the back?"

"Yup."

"The outfit you guys work for must have money to burn. It's like a flying apartment."

She sat back down next to Daniel, leaning against his shoulder, then kicked off her shoes and put her feet up on the sofa. Daniel put his arm around her, adjusting to a comfortable position.

He said, "Ridiculous for moving three people, I know. I think they're laying on the extra comfort to try and calm our minds, given all the excitement yesterday."

Kara said, "Do you really think your employers will tell the world about AIT, or are they just trying to monopolize it for their own use like the other guys? I keep thinking about what Jacob said when we arrived in Monrovia."

Daniel had been thinking about it, too. "I've only been in the game a few months, I don't know for sure. But I do know they're trying to stop Conrad Winter's group from releasing this plague, and right now that's enough for me."

"Conrad Winter is that priest you told me about?"

Daniel fished in his pocket and pulled out his smartphone, scrolled through some files, found a photo of Conrad. He showed it to her. "This is him. Memorize his face. If you see him, even if you think just maybe some face in the crowd *might* be him, you let me know right away, y'hear?"

Kara took the phone and looked at the photo for a minute, then passed it back. "So he's the bad guy."

"He and his group."

"But Jacob said the people you work for were just the *less bad* bad guys."

"He may be right. I mean, we're talking about immensely wealthy people doing things in secret. They're plutocrats, they have a vested interest in maintaining the status quo. But looking at what Conrad Winter is aiming to do, I'll give my guys the benefit of the doubt for the time being."

Kara said, "Why would Conrad Winter want to infect an American city? He's got the bacteria, he could just quietly infect people in Liberia or some other place off the radar without drawing attention to himself."

"Good question, and I can see two reasons. The first is simply a numbers thing. Let's say you want to build, for want of a better term, an army of prophets, say, five hundred strong. With five hundred Tim Trinitys, each spewing information about the future, the hidden past, or otherwise unknown current events, you could grow incredibly powerful. You'd have so much exclusive information that you could completely control the financial markets, international banking, the flow of political power . . . nobody could match your power. Remember, Tim Trinity almost destroyed the status quo in the most powerful nation on earth, and he was just one man. Now let's say this strain of the plague triggers AIT in one percent of those infected—could be as high as two, but let's work with one. To get an army of five hundred Trinitys, you'd have to infect fifty thousand people. Even in Liberia, you can't give fifty thousand people the plague and not be noticed, and you'd be stopped before you could get it done, right?"

"Right."

"So you have to stage it as an outbreak, all at once."

Kara said, "Okay, but why do it in America?"

Daniel said, "That's the other reason. The thing is, with these people there's always more than one game at play. AIT is just one game, and the most important one, but Conrad will find a way to play it that supports their other aims."

"Which are?"

Daniel didn't know how to answer that without getting into issues better left alone. "Conrad's group always had more influence with authoritarian regimes than democracies, and they've been pushing the West steadily toward greater government authority for years. But after the Snowden leaks, Americans started to push back. Conrad knows another terrorist attack on American soil would put an end to that pushback. And if it's a bioweapon? The public won't just accept the surveillance state, they'll demand it. I think that's Conrad's plan."

"Sounds pretty extreme," said Kara.

"So does building a machine that beams voices into people's heads. But Michael Dillman built one just the same. And now he works for Conrad." He sipped some wine. "These are not nice people, Kara, and they do not think small."

They fell into silence, Kara's head on his chest, his arm around her shoulder, the muted sound of the jet engines filling the cabin as they finished their wine.

If not now, when?

Daniel touched the side of her jaw and gently tilted her face up.

A long, lingering kiss that grew into something else entirely.

"So." She brushed her lips against his. "What do we do now?"

"We've got eight hours and a flying bedroom in back," he said. "I'm sure we'll think of something."

Kara kissed him again, harder.

✤✤✤

Afterward, they slept for a few blissful hours.

Daniel woke as turbulence jostled the plane. He sat up, put his hand on the bed as the plane again rocked a bit. He could hear rain against the fuselage, but no thunder. He got up from the bed and stood naked, looking out through a porthole window. They were passing through a large raincloud, the entire world a gray fog, water streaking sideways across the window.

"Hey good looking," said Kara.

He turned to face her. "How're you feelin'?"

"Amazing." She smiled. "If a little sore. That was . . . intense."

It had been. Daniel could still feel the lines her nails had carved in his back. He returned to the bed and kissed her. "I mean, about everything. What we talked about before. You know, you can still get off this ride. We're playing against dangerous people. If you want out—"

Kara silenced him with a kiss. "Thanks, no. I'm in and I'm staying in. For six years the whole world told me I was crazy, and as certain as I was, there was also a small part of me that wondered if they were right. Now I know I'm not crazy. And you know, even if drinking too much kept the voices down, it wasn't really helping me cope, emotionally. Right now, I feel pretty strong."

"Okay."

She pushed herself up, sitting with her back against the leather headboard. "I had another dream. It didn't seem like anything, but . . ."

"But what?"

"It was one of those flying dreams, you know the ones. I was just flying through rain with my arms outstretched, but for some reason I didn't get wet and I didn't see any clouds. It was like a rain of fine, dark mist on a cloudless day, and I was flying right through the mist. When I woke up, I saw the rain outside so I figured it was nothing. But then I realized I could still taste cinnamon."

43: CHAIN OF COMMAND

DHS Headquarters—Washington, DC

D on't get comfortable, boss." Janet passed Evan Sage a coffee mug before he could even get his jacket off. "P-DUS wants you in his office right away. And from the sound of Helen's voice, you might want to wear Kevlar." She stuck a file folder in his other hand.

P-DUS was Greg Rundle, principal deputy undersecretary for Intelligence and Analysis. Apparently he'd not enjoyed the memo Evan sent before leaving Monrovia.

Evan sipped some coffee. "Figured as much. Helen texted me to come straight in from the airport. I'll need a printout of the memo—"

"It's in the folder, on top, followed by your previous e-mails on the case in reverse chronology."

"Thanks, Janet. You're the best."

Greg Rundle's office was two floors up. Evan had managed to sleep only four hours on the flight, so he took the stairs two at a time to work up a little energy.

Didn't help much.

He opened the door and stepped into the outer office.

Helen raised her eyebrows at him. "Go right in." It sounded like a warning.

Greg Rundle stood behind the glass desk at the far end of his large office. A tall blond woman stood beside him, her back turned, reading a paper she held in her hand.

Evan closed the door and she turned to face him as he crossed the office.

Shelly Henniger.

Shit . . .

Henniger was CIA—Evan had worked with her twice before. Both times, she'd snatched the case away from DHS just before the win, and the Company took the credit. She was very good. And very ambitious.

"Sir. Shelly."

Henniger said, "Lovely to see you again, Evan." The accompanying smile was pure aspartame. She gestured to the printout she'd been reading. "You've been busy. Running in all the wrong directions, I'm sorry to say."

Evan ignored her and addressed his boss instead. "Sir, I ran a check on flights out of Monrovia and tracked Dillman's PMCs. I believe the target is in or near Columbia, South Carolina." He held Rundle's gaze. "And I believe an attack is imminent."

"Colonel Michael Dillman is one of the most respected men at DIA."

"Yes, sir. And I believe he's gone rogue. This plague first showed in blood work that came from a soldier serving directly under Colonel Dillman. The contractors working that facility in Liberia are all connected to Dillman "

"I've read your reports, don't waste our time."

Not *my* time, *our* time. The clear implication being that Shelly Henniger's time, like Rundle's, was of more value than Evan's.

Henniger said, "You don't actually know anything, do you? You don't know that this plague was created as a bioweapon, you don't know what the facility in Liberia even was—for God's sake, the country's scrambling with an Ebola outbreak that could go pandemic across the region at any minute. Maybe they were testing a vaccine—or maybe it's a legit DIA black op—you don't even have a credible lead on who Colonel Dillman is supposedly in bed with."

"I had a lead," said Evan, "until I was ordered to let him walk out the door."

Henniger smiled again. "Yes, *waterboarding*. Very unlike you, Evan. Honestly, I think you've lost your perspective."

"Look, if Daniel Byrne is one of ours—"

Rundle said, "Daniel Byrne is a business consultant. End of story."

"But—"

"End of story," Rundle repeated. "I need you investigating actual bad guys who actually mean to do this country harm. To that end, I'm lending you to Langley for a week. There's been increased chatter out of Yemen and you've had experience there in the last year."

"*Yemen?*" Evan didn't even try to moderate his tone.

Henniger said, "An Islamist group called the Brightest Dawn—"

"Never heard of them."

"New al-Qaida affiliate. Chatter suggests they've developed a bioweapon of their own."

"Is everyone at Langley *high*? The al-Qaida allies in Yemen are a bunch of kids with Kalashnikovs and suicide vests. They have neither the funding nor the expertise to even attempt a bioweapon."

"So maybe somebody gave them one. And maybe you can help us find out who." Henniger picked up her briefcase and shook Greg Rundle's hand. "Thank you, sir. I'll try to return him in one piece."

Rundle was decidedly not amused. "I'm doing you a favor, young lady. You play nice, or I'll take my man back early."

"Of course. We're grateful for Homeland's help."

She turned on her heel and strode out of Rundle's office, but couldn't resist rubbing it in, winking at Evan as she passed. "See you tomorrow, my place."

After the door closed, Rundle said, "Evan, I appreciate the fact that you're an unorthodox thinker, that's part of your value to DHS—we need more people who think like you. But Shelly may be right. There's a fine line between 'unorthodox thinker' and 'paranoid wing nut' and you seem to be flirting with it. A week at Langley won't kill you and you might actually catch a bad guy. Go over your Yemen files and report to CIA at o-nine-hundred tomorrow. But feel free to slap her down if she keeps on with the snark. I'll have your back on that. If she wants your help, she treats you with due respect. And try to get some rest—you look like hell."

The subject was firmly closed, but Evan had to pry it open again.

"Sir, I'm telling you, we are on the verge of a major bioterror attack on American soil. Never had a stronger gut instinct in my life—and no, the facts I've uncovered so far don't *prove* it, but they sure as hell support it. Even Shelly knows a bioterror attack on American soil is far beyond the current capabilities of Yemeni Islamists. These are American PMCs, all connected to Dillman." He opened his file folder. "And I do still have one lead: Daniel Byrne told me Dillman is working with—"

"Let me put this simply." Rundle snatched the file folder from Evan's hand, dumped it in the wastebasket. He leaned forward, resting his knuckles on the desk. "Conrad Winter does not exist for you. Period. You are to stand down on this investigation. Even if I wanted to let you run with it, I couldn't."

The world's axis shifted, and a knot formed in Evan Sage's gut as he incorporated this new information . . . this new reality.

Shelly Henniger hadn't lobbied Rundle to shut down Evan's investigation at all. It wasn't even Rundle's decision. It had come down to Rundle from higher on the food chain. Much higher.

He said, "Who is this Conrad Winter that he's so untouchable?"

Rundle shook his head. "I wasn't invited to ask. And neither are you." He dismissed Evan with a nod toward the door.

Evan crossed the office and stopped, looking at the doorknob but not reaching for it. He knew he should just walk out the door . . .

He spun around. "A *plague* is gonna hit Columbia!"

Greg Rundle said nothing, just stared him down.

"And you and I will both live with the fact that we could've done something, but didn't."

Greg Rundle said, "Close the door behind you."

Evan stormed down the stairs all the way to the lobby, thinking, *Maybe that bastard can live with it* . . .

By the time he got outside, he'd made his decision. He lit a cigarette and texted his secretary:

Catching a cab to Dulles.

Book me next flight to Columbia, SC.

44: JACOB'S LADDER

Columbia, South Carolina
10:00 a.m.

Daniel and Kara sat parked across from a two-story red brick apartment building on Gervais Street. Gerald had texted the address while Daniel was renting the car at the airport. As James Bragg, Colonel Michael Dillman had a six-month lease on apartment 205.

The rear passenger-side door opened and Pat ducked back into the car.

"Looks like nobody home but can't be certain, interior doors are closed." Pat unzipped his duffel bag, pulled out a hefty black Para-Ordnance .45, and holstered it under his Windbreaker. It was already seventy-five degrees outside, heading for a high of eighty-six, not a cloud in the sky. So a little warm for a Windbreaker, but Pat insisted on carrying the canon whenever possible. He reached into the bag again, handed Daniel a compact stainless Sig Sauer P232.

Daniel tucked the pistol behind his belt in the small of his back. He looked at Kara and said, "Ballcap."

Kara was wearing jeans and a red-and-black USC Gamecocks football jersey. She now added a matching ballcap, tucking her hair behind her ears. Pat handed her a pair of glasses with tortoise frames and plain lenses. She put them on, then reached down by her feet and picked up the small white cardboard box with a courier logo on it.

"Ready," she said.

Pat reached for the door handle. "We go carefully. I'll take the fire escape in back, you guys go up the front like civilized people."

As they crossed the street, Daniel stuck the car keys in Kara's hand. "Like before, stay behind me. Anything goes wrong, you take off, don't wait for us. Call the number I gave you, ask for Raoul, and tell him what went down."

Kara squeezed his hand. "Just don't let anything go wrong."

Pat said, "Knock in five minutes. Starting in three . . . two . . . one . . ."

Daniel started the chronograph on his watch and Pat jogged away, disappearing behind the apartment building.

A young man in running gear walked his dog along the other side of the street, past the rental car. Another man—middle-aged, suit, tie, leather briefcase—walked in the opposite direction on this side.

Both men, if they glanced at the building, saw Daniel and Kara walking hand in hand, slowly up the path. Just a happy couple on their way to visit a friend. The closer man might have heard Daniel say something about Georgian architecture while pointing at the decorative molding above the front entrance.

The men kept walking, leaving the block empty for the moment.

At the front door Daniel reached into his back pocket, handed Kara a folded street map of Columbia. "Gimme a screen." She unfolded the map and held it open just above waist level and started musing aloud about the local attractions they might visit after lunch.

Daniel examined the lock and bet himself he could pick it in a minute-thirty. There was also an electronic combination keypad of no better than average quality. The landlord had gone cheap with the hardware, he'd probably also gone cheap with the installer. And half-assed locksmiths often forgot to erase the factory code while adding the combination supplied by the landlord.

Daniel pressed 0-0-0-0-#.

The door buzzed open.

They climbed the stairs to the second floor, passing no one along the way.

The second floor hallway was equally empty.

Daniel took his position beside the door of apartment 205. He counted down the final thirty seconds on his watch, then nodded to Kara. She held the box in front of her, knocked on the door.

Silence.

She knocked again. "Delivery for a Mister Bragg. Gamecock Couriers."

Silence.

After a minute passed with no sound from inside, Daniel stepped forward and checked the locks. The deadbolt was better than the lock downstairs. Might take three or four minutes. He kneeled, put his pistol on the floor, concealed it with his right foot, then pulled out his lockpicks and went to work.

Without warning, the deadbolt clicked open from the inside and the door swung wide. Daniel dropped the picks and scooped up his gun and raised—

"Don't shoot, broheim." Pat grinned down at him from inside the apartment.

"Jesus," said Daniel. "Give a guy a heart attack."

Pat shrugged. "Got bored waitin'. He's not home, c'mon in."

The place looked like one of those long-term executive rentals, everything high quality, everything generic, safe, the framed prints on the wall selected for their pleasant blandness, no risk of offending anyone's taste. That is, beyond the small minority offended by pleasant blandness.

Daniel headed for the bedroom, checking closets and drawers. All empty. Nothing under the mattress, either.

"Doesn't look like anybody lives here," said Kara as he returned to the living room. "The fridge is completely empty, cupboards bare."

"But look." Daniel pointed through the open wall into the kitchen. "There's a bowl and a glass in the drying rack." He crossed to the kitchen. There was also a single spoon in the rack, like someone had had cereal and juice for breakfast. But nothing in the fridge, and no cereal box to be seen.

He checked the living room, under the couch cushions and tables, above the entertainment center, behind furniture. He looked through the hall closet.

Nothing.

Pat came in from the bathroom. "Clean. Not even a toothbrush. But the towel is still damp. Dillman was here this morning, and it don't look like he's plannin' to return."

Daniel felt a chill run down his arms. He looked at Pat. "It's going down today."

Kara strode over to the phone, hit the speakerphone, and pressed Redial. The phone rang four times and went to voice-mail.

The message started with a few seconds of Frank Sinatra singing "Come Fly With Me." Then a man's voice with a thick Carolina accent: "You've reached Emmett's Flight School, where we help you grow your wings! Sorry we can't get to the phone, means we prolly up in the air right now. But you'll wanna leave a message. Soon as we touch down, we call ya right back. Bye-bye."

Daniel said, "A private airfield."

Kara's eyes went wide, her expression turning to horror. "The plague they've got is pneumonic. They're gonna cropdust the city with it."

A rain of fine, dark mist on a cloudless day.

45: A HARD RAIN'S A-GONNA FALL

Northbound I-77
Near Great Falls, South Carolina
11:00 a.m.

The rental car had an electronically limited top speed of 110, and Pat had it pegged.

"Goddamn nanny state," he said.

"Ninety-seven's coming up," said Daniel. "Take it westbound toward Chester."

"Ninety-seven to Chester, got it."

Daniel turned his attention back to the phone.

Raoul said, "We're back-channeling through an ally in the governor's office, but with an election coming up, he's not gonna declare a state of emergency and risk looking like a fool if nothing happens."

"I thought you guys had influence everywhere."

"We do—that's what *back-channeling through an ally* means. But until we have some proof that an attack is underway, the governor's not gonna budge. We've also got ranking members of the state police and South Carolina National Guard. They're on alert, but again, until we know it's going down for sure, they can't deploy. They've called some snap drills for this afternoon, so their troops will be as ready as we can make them. Soon as you know for sure, text me 999 and I'll get them deployed."

"Not good enough," said Daniel.

"For the moment, it's going to have to be," said Raoul. "The Foundation does not reveal itself, you know that. *Whatever* happens. Our power resides in our ability to leverage the systems that exist. We pull levers, call governors and generals and ambassadors, nudge the systems that are already in place. And that's how we win the long game. Soon as we reveal ourselves, we're out of the game entirely, and then we'll have *no* influence on the future. So just keep your shit together."

Daniel looked outside at the clear blue sky. "It's going down today, Raoul. I *know* it. Kara dreamed of a rain like dark mist from a cloudless sky. The plague's pneumonic, it's aerosolized. At least twenty of Dillman's mercs flew into Atlanta yesterday, at least thirteen to Columbia—that's just the ones we know about—and Dillman's last call before cleaning out his apartment was to a private airfield."

"And if you're right," said Raoul, "we'll pull the trigger, and the military will scramble jets and deploy troops. But if we pull the trigger and they deploy on a false alarm, we lose influence with our allies the next time we need them. More importantly, we give Conrad Winter the chance to restage this thing somewhere else. The fact that Dillman cleaned out his apartment today does not prove that the attack is happening today."

Daniel said, "I'm gonna call Evan Sage."

Raoul said, "You're kidding, right?"

"He needs to know. Maybe he can do something. And he already knows I exist, so you can relax—I won't be revealing your existence by calling."

"Daniel, give your head a shake. It's like you've developed the world's fastest case of Stockholm syndrome. The prick tortured you."

Not helpful.

Daniel took a deep breath and blew it out, fighting against the flood of images and sounds and feelings, fighting them off before they got out of control.

He took another breath. "I don't see how that's relevant. I'm not asking him to wear my frat pin."

Raoul said, "The answer is no," and broke the connection.

Daniel looked at Pat. "Screw it. I'm gonna call Evan Sage."

Pat said, "Raoul will lose his freakin' mind."

"I don't care."

"Good. Then call him. Just don't be any more sharey than you need to."

"Don't worry about it." Daniel fished Evan Sage's business card from his wallet. He dialed the number for Sage's cell.

"Sage here."

"It's Daniel Byrne."

There was a pause. "What do you want?"

"Like I told you before, I want the same thing you want. I also want to break your nose, but that'll have to wait for later."

"Understandable," said Sage. "Go ahead, I'm listening."

"The target is South Carolina, probably Columbia."

"I'm *in* Columbia," said Sage.

"Then you need to get shot up with Cipro. I think you're at ground zero. They're flying out of a small private airstrip near Chester, less than sixty miles north of Columbia. Emmett's Flight School, Dillman's last phone call was to there. We think they're gonna cropdust this shit."

Sage said, "The target could be anywhere within flying distance of that airstrip."

"It'll be Columbia," said Daniel. "I know Conrad Winter, how his mind works. He appreciates the value of symbols, the grand gesture. He'll choose the capital city—the democratic seat of government—over a military target or commercial center or tourist town. He wants to put the weakness of democracy on display."

Pat swerved for the Highway 97 exit, wheels skidding on the ramp, shooting past the sign to Chester. Ninety-seven was a two-lane blacktop in good condition with no traffic in sight. Pat kept their speed up.

Daniel said, "I'm less than six miles from the airstrip, no planes yet. Will let you know. Meanwhile, get the government ready for a disaster. If I don't get there in time, you need to drop a net over Columbia. You can't let those people spread it outside the state."

"You just get there in time," said Evan Sage.

"You're an asshole," said Daniel, "and I'm still gonna break your nose." He ended the call.

Pat slowed as the airstrip appeared up ahead on the left.

A large grassy field with a landing strip paved down the middle, no fence around the property. An airplane hangar loomed at the far end of the strip, probably large enough to house a dozen single-engine aircraft. Closer to the road, a fairly new double-wide trailer served as the office. Wooden billboards lined the driveway on both sides. Handpainted on a red background:

EMMETT'S FLIGHT SCHOOL

COME FLY WITH US!

WE HELP YOU GROW YOUR WINGS!

The logo above the office door featured a smiling cartoon Carolina Gamecock piloting a cartoon spitfire with Confederate flags painted on its wings. There was a white Ford F-350 pickup, also new, parked next to the entrance.

Pat stopped next to the double-wide, shut off the engine, and twisted to face Kara in the backseat. "Hand me the shotgun."

Kara opened his duffle on the seat next to her, rummaged inside.

"The big one, for God's sake. Hand me the big one."

"Don't bite my head off, I'm not a gun girl." Kara handed Pat the shotgun. It had a pistol grip and a short barrel, but it was the biggest gun in the bag.

Pat propped the shotgun up in the passenger footwell next to Daniel's legs. "Okay, this is our fallback position. We leave the keys in it and the doors open, 'case we be leavin' in a hurry."

They left the car, doors standing wide. Daniel adjusted the pistol in his belt and glanced at Kara.

Kara said, "I know, stay behind you."

Pat unzipped his Windbreaker. They climbed the three wooden stairs and stepped inside the trailer.

The man standing behind the counter was huge—even bigger than Pat—so big his head looked like it had been transplanted from the body of a much smaller man. He wore oil-stained coveralls and a week's growth of beard. He grinned at the visitors.

"Howdy, folks. What can I do ya for?"

Pat said, "I got my pilot's license with me. Can I rent a plane? Wanna take these folks up."

"Sorry. Not the way it works. We got rules, you gotta be a member, gotta fly with me first, get checked out."

Daniel said, "Any flights leave outta here today, Emmett?"

"I'm not Emmett," said the man. "Emmett's home sick."

"Sorry to hear it," said Daniel. "Any flights leave outta here today?"

"Sure, a couple."

"May I see the flight logs?"

The man looked at Daniel for a long moment. "Sure, sounds awright. Got 'em right here." He reached under the counter and came up fast with—

—the top half of the man's head exploded, gore splattering across the map pinned to the wall behind him. A shotgun clattered to the floor, and the man's lifeless body crumpled, disappearing behind the counter.

Pat reholstered his pistol, turned to Kara. "Had to be done."

Kara blew out a long breath. "How did you know he was going for a gun?"

"Mercs are pretty good at recognizing each other. He pegged me, too, soon as I walked in the door. Saw it in his eyes. From there it was just a matter of who was gonna draw first. Daniel gave him the perfect excuse."

Daniel said, "A guy with a licensed airfield is not gonna just show his flight logs to some guy who walks in off the street and asks."

Kara said, "So I'm the only one who didn't know we were about to be in a gunfight."

"That's about the size of it," said Pat.

It was then Daniel heard the sound of engines from outside.

Aircraft engines.

"Look!" Kara pointed out the window.

A line of single-engine Cessnas taxied out of the hangar and onto the tarmac, single file.

Six of them.

Daniel sprinted through the door, straight for the car.

Pat passed him, yelled, "You drive!" and ran for the passenger side.

Daniel jumped in behind the wheel as Pat slammed his door and grabbed the shotgun. Daniel cranked the engine. Kara was in the backseat before he put it in Drive. He mashed the pedal to the floor, tearing across the grass field toward the paved airstrip.

Pat yelled into the backseat, "Stay down. Find the box marked *Slugs* and get ready to pass 'em to me one by one."

They were perpendicular to the runway, still thirty yards away, and the first plane was already passing in front of them.

Then the second.

At ten yards, Daniel could make out the cropdusting hardware—pipes and nozzles mounted under the wings.

"We're not gonna make it," he said.

The third plane passed.

"Just step on it!" said Pat.

The forth plane passed.

Daniel said, "My foot's on the floor! Goin' as fast as it'll go!"

They hit the tarmac just behind the last plane and Daniel wrenched the wheel, skidding in line behind the procession.

Now on pavement, the car finally gained speed.

Pat braced himself against the door, leaning his head and shoulders through the window, holding the shotgun on target. "Closer!"

The last plane shifted slightly to the right. Daniel dropped down a gear, and they lurched forward and left, their front bumper now parallel with the plane's tail.

At the front of the line, the first plane went airborne.

Pat unloaded, not at the plane beside them but the one directly ahead of it. It skidded a little, almost took them both out, but then righted itself and pressed on.

The second plane took to the sky.

Pat pulled back inside. "Slugs!"

Kara handed the shells to him, and Pat fed them into the shotgun.

The third plane left the ground.

They were gaining, the car's front wheels now parallel to the last plane's tail. The pilot turned his head to look down at them, and for a frozen moment he and Daniel held eye contact.

Michael Dillman.

Maybe twenty years older than in the photo Gerald had dug up, mustache now gray, face now deeply lined, but it was the same man.

The fourth plane took off.

And the fifth.

Daniel edged to the right, bringing the car's engine compartment gently against the fuselage and clipping the plane's tailsection, shoving it farther to the right.

The plane lurched, tilted, and went over on its right wing, showering sparks along the runway, shuddering violently as the end of the wing snapped off, finally lurching to a stop, resting on what was left of its right wing.

Daniel slammed the brakes, turning the wheel and skidding to face the wreckage. He jumped out and drew his pistol, using the car door for cover.

On the other side, Pat did the same.

The door on the right side of the cockpit fell open and Michael Dillman dropped down twelve feet to the ground, came up with an assault rifle leveled.

At this distance, the chances of Daniel hitting Dillman with the little .380 were slim, and Dillman's rifle had a significant advantage over Pat's larger pistol as well.

But Dillman didn't pull the trigger.

Instead, he just stopped and stared down. The payload tank had ruptured, and he was standing in a dark purple, viscous liquid. It was all over his pants, his shirtfront, his hands and forearms, his neck. He was covered in it.

Michael Dillman looked back up at Daniel, his face a frozen mask of abject terror—no amount of antibiotics could protect him from this deluge.

Dillman put the barrel of the assault rifle under his chin and pulled the trigger.

In the distance, five single-engine Cessnas flew low over the horizon, straight toward the capital city of South Carolina.

46: ONE MAN ISLAND

DHS Field Office—Columbia, South Carolina
1:45 p.m.—One hour and thirty-two minutes
after contamination . . .

Evan Sage stood facing the crowded bullpen through the window in the inner office's door. Twelve Homeland Security agents and five support staff, the governor's chief of staff, the Columbia PD chief and his deputy, the local FBI special agent in charge with three of his underlings, four representatives from FEMA, and another dozen or so emergency workers Evan had not yet identified.

The big dog in the room was Major General Sanders, who commanded the eleven thousand troops of the South Carolina National Guard. As Evan looked across the room, he noticed that Sanders was the only person not talking.

Everyone else was talking at the same time, not to each other but *at* each other, each voice staking its claim with ever-rising volume, demanding to be heard amid the growing din, each making it impossible for anyone at all to be heard, should anyone shut up long enough to listen.

And these were the professionals. There'd been so much brain drain—so much talent siphoned off by the corporate world. Everybody had chased the dollar.

And where were they now, when their country needed them?

Air raid sirens continued to echo across Columbia, muted by the building's double-glazed windows, almost drowned out by the voices of constrained panic inside, but Evan could hear them when he listened. One long blast every minute since the planes passed overhead at 12:13—so low it looked like the middle plane might clip the flagpole on the State House dome—leaving behind a fine, dark mist to settle like a blanket over the city. A few minutes later, three F-15E Strike Eagle jets screamed across the sky from north to south.

Evan had arrived to the office two minutes after noon. That was when his phone started buzzing with a series of one-line text messages sent from the number Daniel Byrne had used to call him earlier:

Now heading your way

5 Cessnas with dusting gear

Disabled plane 6

. . .

Pilot was Dillman

Send biocontainment team

Dillman ate his gun

Evan immediately called up a biohazard team and directed them to the private airfield south of Chester. Government bureaucracy being what it is, *immediately* meant three separate phone calls and two lengthy waits on hold.

He was still on hold when the planes appeared in the distance, growing larger, flying in a V formation like a small family of Canada geese heading south for the winter.

Evan watched the planes through this window, standing in this office, impotent to stop them from releasing their poisonous black rain, the telephone receiver still in his hand.

Ten minutes after the planes had passed, the governor appeared on television and declared a state of emergency. The governor assured the citizens of South Carolina (and the rest of the country—his statement was carried live on CNN and Fox News) that he'd been in contact with the White House, that the National Guard had been activated, and that he'd ordered all state and local police and emergency personnel to report for immediate deployment. He calmly ordered all citizens to get indoors and stay indoors until the particulate matter sprayed from the planes had been identified, and he suggested duct-taping the seams of their windows and doors and boiling their water.

And the citizens responded by running wild in the streets, looting antibiotics and first-aid kits from pharmacies, bottled water and canned goods from grocery stores, firearms and ammunition from every Walmart in the state.

Others simply packed up their cars and left town.

They were turned back by National Guard troops in biohazard gear.

The Guard had set up roadblocks with astounding speed on all highways and major roads, effectively sealing most people inside a radius of about ten miles from the edges of Columbia. No way to block all the small roads, but with the major arteries sealed, gridlock took care of the rest. Upon seeing the gridlock, most aspiring evacuees realized getting indoors was their best bet after all, and turned back.

Evan Sage's phone vibrated with the text he'd been waiting for.

But not the result he'd been hoping for:

Confirmed.

He turned to the doctor standing to his left and started to speak. His tongue resisted the command, as if saying the words would somehow make it real.

But it was real, and there was not a goddamn thing Evan could do about that. He removed his jacket and hung it over the back of the chair and rolled up his sleeve. "It's confirmed."

The doctor administered the antibiotic shot, taped a small cotton ball over the injection site. Evan buttoned his cuff and nodded thanks to the doctor. He slipped back into his jacket.

Evan opened the door and stepped into the cacophony of the bullpen. He clapped his hands together. "Ladies and gentlemen, please, your attention for a minute."

Every voice fell quiet, every face turned toward him, every phone call put on hold as they awaited the verdict.

Evan cleared his throat. "Our intel has just been confirmed by the BioWatch system. The detectors show positive for pneumonic plague."

A woman in the back of the room let out a low moan, and a large man near the front started weeping. Another man's voice said, "God help us."

"Be assured, no one in this room is going to get sick." Evan looked at the doctor, now standing at his side. He drew a blank. He was usually good with names but today was far from usual.

Rock Around the Clock . . .

Bill Haley and the Comets . . .

No, not Bill Hailey . . . Phil Hawley.

Evan said, "Dr. Hawley will take it from here," gesturing for the doctor to take the floor.

Hawley stepped forward and addressed the room. "Each of you will receive an injection of either doxycycline, tetracycline, or ciprofloxacin, depending on your allergies and medical history. They're all effective prophylactically against pneumonic plague, but you'll need an additional shot every twenty-four hours for the next seven days—do not miss a shot."

"What about our families?"

"All essential emergency personnel will be treated prophylactically, and the CDC teams will be arriving shortly, but we simply don't have the supply to treat the entire civilian population *just in case* they catch it. Those who become symptomatic will of course be treated. Best thing you can do for your families is convince them to stay indoors and away from other people."

"For how long?"

"The good news is, the *Y. pestis* bacterium is sensitive to sunlight, so it dies pretty fast in the open air. Aerosolized, it's viable for one to two hours without a host. But until right now, we didn't have a live culture of this particular strain to study. It's possible this one has been bioengineered to last longer, perhaps as long as six hours. With about six hundred thousand people in the affected area, we may see as many as a hundred thousand become symptomatic in the next twenty-four to forty-eight hours. Our biggest challenge is to keep those initial carriers from spreading it to the greater population, so we must keep the area sealed off and enforce the governor's curfew to keep the local population from mingling with each other as much as possible. This plague is pneumonic; it is essential that emergency personnel wear surgical masks, gloves, eye protection, and gowns if possible when dealing with the public after the initial infection period from the cropdusting has passed. Pneumonic plague presents similarly to inhalational anthrax, so your teams should be on the lookout for symptoms such as fever, persistent coughing, labored breathing or shortness of breath, chest pain, and of course hemoptysis as the condition worsens—"

"In English please," said a voice from the back.

"Yes, sorry. Coughing up blood. We'll begin to see that in about forty-eight hours, or as soon as twenty-four in people with compromised immune systems. Some patients will also present with nausea and vomiting and/or diarrhea . . ."

Evan's cell phone vibrated. He glanced at the screen—Greg Rundle calling from headquarters in DC.

Evan left Dr. Hawley to finish the briefing and stepped back into the office, closing the door behind.

Greg Rundle said, "Jesus Christ, Evan. You're supposed to be at Langley. If the attack hadn't happened, you'd be facing a disciplinary hearing for gross insubordination right now."

"Lucky me," said Evan.

"Watch it, you might still face sanctions before this is over. Just had my ear chewed off by a four-star general. Colonel Michael Dillman has been leading a black ops team to try and stop the terrorists, and he may have died in that effort today. Shelly Henniger was right—you've climbed up your own ass on this thing. Soon as you're medically cleared to leave Columbia, get your ass back to Langley. Turns out she was right about the Yemeni al-Qaida cell."

"I don't believe it."

"Start believing it. Analysis of the chatter out of Yemen matched keywords picked up by our cousins at GCHQ from a small Islamic center in the East End of London. CIA and MI5 staged a joint raid early this morning. They found aerial maps of South Carolina, contact information for the private airfield in Chester, and traces of the weaponized bacteria. Also a supply of antibiotics. Henniger was right."

"Bullshit," said Evan. "This smells like a cover-up. I'm telling you Dillman was behind this." He started to mention Daniel Byrne's frantic call and text messages, but stopped as a new thought made his blood run cold. He took a breath. "Sir, when I called the local airport and train station to shut them down, they told me they'd already been shut down. They'd both received bomb threats followed by power outages, fifteen minutes *before* the planes flew over the city."

"So the terrorists are well organized. We already know that."

"But why go to all the trouble to mount an operation like this and then shut down transportation? Whoever did this took steps to keep the outbreak contained."

"What are you getting at?"

"Simply that al-Qaida wouldn't do that—they'd want the outbreak to spread and cripple the whole country." Evan knew he was heading into dangerous territory. "And I've run through my list of contacts—no one has even heard of this group, the Brightest Dawn. Frankly, I don't think it exists." What the hell—in for a penny, in for a pound. "Sir, I hate to even consider this possibility, but are we sure this isn't us? Some kind of false flag operation?"

"Are you out of your fucking mind?"

"I'm just saying, if you look at the facts that my investigation has—"

"Your investigation is dead. This attack was the work of Yemeni Islamists connected to al-Qaida, and your job is to help CIA uncover the evidence that will enable us to bring the perpetrators to justice. Period. If you value your career and your country, you will leave that paranoid conspiracy shit alone. Are we clear?"

Evan Sage swallowed his first response.

"Yes, sir. We're clear."

47: SILENCE

"It is in the thick of calamity that one gets hardened to the truth—in other words, to silence."

—Albert Camus, *The Plague*

48: TEARDROP

Columbia, South Carolina
12:13 p.m.—Twenty-four hours after contamination . . .

Kara, please."

"No. Daniel, this is bullshit."

"I promise you, we're working on it."

"Working on it? We're watching TV and ordering room service and swimming in the hotel pool. What we are *not* doing is working on it."

"Gerald's team is scanning the city electronically, every CCTV camera, every ATM camera, Internet traffic, e-mail traffic, cell phones—the works. And we've got National Guard and state police allies keeping an eye out. Columbia's still under curfew. What would you have us do? Wander the streets calling, 'Yoo-hoo! Conrad, where are you?'"

Pat hurled the book he was reading hard against the wall and stood up. "That's it, I'm out." He strode toward the door. "I'm gonna go smoke a joint up on the roof-deck. Kara: Fight fair. Daniel: Stop being a dick. It's a lovers' quarrel, not nuclear frickin' war."

Pat jerked the door open and marched out of the suite.

Daniel said, "He's right. I'm sorry for the sarcasm. There was no call for that. Not me at my best."

Kara nodded acceptance of the apology. "So this is our first lovers' quarrel," she said.

"I guess it is."

"And that would make us . . . lovers."

"Of course we are—c'mere." Daniel opened his arms, Kara stepped close, and they held each other for a minute without speaking.

Kara said, "I stopped drinking enough to keep the voices away back in Norway. Didn't get drunk in Liberia and haven't had a drop since we landed. It's like I've laid out a bloody welcome banner for the voices. So where the hell are they?"

Daniel kissed the top of her head and thought about what to say. The voices had abandoned Tim Trinity, too, a few days before his death. But that was not helpful information.

He said, "You had the dream on the plane. That was something."

"But what's the point? I get tortured by voices for six years, I lose my daughter, my marriage. Career, friends . . . everything, my whole life. Then you come along, and suddenly this AIT kicks into high gear, adding dreams and fainting spells and—*goddamnit* what for? So we can be just *a little bit too late* to stop an atrocity? What's the point of it? Because it's starting to feel like a lesson in random cruelty. What could the universe possibly be trying to tell us in this ridiculous manner?"

Kara looked up at him as a teardrop slid down her face.

Daniel wiped it away with his thumb and said, "Now who's looking for God?" She took it as intended and smiled back at him. He didn't know what to say next, except the obvious. "I can't even begin to imagine what it's like to be in your shoes, so I know this is a case of easy-for-me-to-say, but—"

She stopped him with a finger to his lips, then turned and walked to the window and looked out at the sun-drenched city.

He followed and stood beside her, and she took his hand in hers.

The streets below were completely empty. It brought to mind an old horror movie, Charlton Heston tearing through the deserted streets of dead Los Angeles in a convertible, machine gun by his side, ready to blast away at anything that moved.

But this horror was real.

Kara said, "It's so quiet out there."

Daniel said, "My monkey brain wants to endlessly re-examine the last week looking for everything I might've done differently to get us here just a little sooner. But I didn't know then what I know now. Even if I could reverse time, I'd just do the same things all over again. So I tell my monkey brain he's a narcissist, and he goes away for a while. Then he comes back and tries again."

Daniel looked down and across the block to the Columbia Museum of Art's courtyard, all red bricks and young trees and a gleaming steel sculpture rising above a blue fountain. The kind of fountain kids studying fine art at USC would sit around to eat their lunch on any other day.

Today there was just one man. A white-haired old man in an old black suit, shuffling through the courtyard with his dog and then stopping to sit on the edge of the fountain.

Kara said, "You see him?"

"Yeah. I see him."

At first glance, Daniel had thought the man homeless, but now he looked closer. The suit was at least thirty years old and shiny from too many pressings, but it was spotless and the cuffs were not frayed. The white mane was a little wild, but clean.

And the dog looked healthy and well fed.

The old man glanced up and down Main Street, then patted the edge of the fountain. The dog jumped up and in, splashing around for a minute, then back out again, where he shook water all over his master's pant legs before turning in a circle and lying down in a small patch of shade.

The old man's shoulders shook as he was seized by a coughing fit that lasted so long the dog eventually got up and came over to check on him. He patted the dog and continued coughing for another minute, then reached into his breast pocket and produced a silver flask and drank deeply from it. He put the flask away, and the coughing started again, even more violently this time. The coughing stopped and the man worked to catch his breath. Then he wiped his hand on the side of the fountain.

There was blood on his hand.

The man now lay on his back along the fountain's edge and stared at the blue sky above, his chest rising and falling very slowly.

The final lines of T.S. Eliot's "The Hollow Men" came to Daniel's mind unbidden:

This is the way the world ends
This is the way the world ends
This is the way the world ends
Not with a bang but a whimper.

Kara said, "There's already fifty thousand at the stadium—this thing is stronger than anyone anticipated and they just put another call out for all available doctors. This is what I do, Daniel. I have to go. I can help. I need to help."

Daniel said, "I know you do." He squeezed her hand. "Just be careful."

"I will. And I'll have my cell. If anything happens—voices, visions, any kind of episode at all—I'll stop what I'm doing and call you immediately."

"I know you will."

49: LIAR'S CLUB

12:13 p.m.—Forty-eight hours after contamination . . .

My fellow Americans: Two days ago, our homeland was savagely attacked by terrorists using weapons of mass destruction banned by every civilized nation on the planet. These bioweapons were smuggled into this country and used to unleash an aerosolized plague bacteria on the great state of South Carolina—on civilians going about their daily lives—mothers and fathers, children, grandparents, police officers, teachers, young men and women striving to earn a university education.

"Since I spoke to you last evening, we have learned a great deal more about the barbaric group of cowards behind this attack on our citizens. I want to acknowledge the courage and dedication of the men and women of our intelligence services who have worked and continue to work around the clock to bring those responsible for this atrocity to justice.

"And make no mistake: We *will* see justice done. To those who committed this unpardonable sin and those who supported them financially, I make this promise: Your days are numbered. America will not rest until you are made to answer for your crimes. We know who you are, we are coming for you, and there is nowhere you can hide. We will hunt you to the ends of the earth. And you will burn in hell. For there is no God of any religion who would condone or forgive the evil you have committed against humanity.

"Let me be clear: America will stand strong through this terrible ordeal, and we will emerge even stronger. We will never allow cowards and extremists to change our way of life nor turn us away from prosecuting the war on terror. We are, and will remain, one nation under God, indivisible, with liberty and justice for all."

The president turned from the podium and walked back into the White House.

Pat said, "At least he didn't tell us to go shopping."

An animated graphic swept across the television screen to the sound of a military snare drum with a lot of reverb added. The graphic read: *Bioterror America* and featured the map of South Carolina under neon-red crosshairs.

There followed a video package including cell phone video of the planes flying over Columbia trailing dark mist behind their wings, fighter jets streaking across the sky, shots of smashed windows and looted stores, army Humvees driving through downtown streets, soldiers ordering civilians off the streets at gunpoint, and finally an aerial shot of five Cessnas left on a stretch of two-lane blacktop, surrounded by military vehicles.

The newsreader said, "The terrorists abandoned the single-engine planes used in this horrific bioterror attack on a stretch of highway just outside of the city limits, and those planes are now being examined for forensic evidence. The city of Columbia remains under quarantine, although the CDC insists that the air is safe to breathe and says the quarantine is to prevent the spread of disease from those already infected."

A shot of the football stadium came up on the screen, with a large CDC mobile command center parked in front.

"Williams-Brice Stadium, home of the Carolina Gamecocks, has been set up as a central intake facility, and the governor has issued the following statement: 'If you or a loved one is showing signs of infection that include fever, go directly to the central intake facility where all arrivals are screened. Anyone with plague symptoms will be turned away by area hospitals and redirected to the stadium. If you are in the quarantine zone but are not sick, you should stay home until the curfew is lifted. National Guard and FEMA personnel will be patrolling the streets to assist people back home and prevent looting.'"

The newsreader introduced a retired general and a former CIA Middle East analyst on split-screen, and asked them to shed some light on the situation.

The former CIA analyst said, "Out of necessity, the government is keeping most of the intelligence data back—we can't tip our hand to the terrorists—but our sources have confirmed that the group behind this vicious attack is a little-known but well-funded al-Qaida affiliate based out of Yemen that calls itself the Brightest Dawn, and they staged the attack out of an Islamic cultural center in London with the help of British jihadists."

The retired general said, "The weaponized plague bacteria certainly didn't come from Britain, most likely was engineered in Iran or Syria, possibly Russia or even North Korea. We are truly fighting a global war on terror, and at this point it is impossible to say where the next front in that war will be. We'll just have to wait and see where the intelligence leads."

"Liars." Daniel sailed his empty beer bottle across the room and into the trashcan. "I can't believe they're selling this as an al-Qaida plot. And they're gonna get away with it."

Pat muted the television. "Notice how the network calls these people 'retired general' and 'former CIA analyst' but neglects to mention that they're now getting rich on the payroll of the military contractors who'll make billions from the war they're selling. Journalism is truly dead, my brother. Of course they're gonna get away with it."

Daniel said, "So that's Conrad's endgame. They're not just trying to shore up the surveillance state, they're trying to start another war. We should've seen it sooner."

"Yup." Pat nodded. "We got played. We freaked out about the possibility of a plague outbreak, just as Conrad knew we would, and we underestimated the size of the other game he was playing. It wasn't just about plague, it was also about war."

Daniel said, "Plague or war, two sides of the same coin."

"What's the coin?"

"A message from the universe, maybe. Plagues and wars, both pretty clear testimony that we're badly mismanaging our affairs as a species."

"Shit. We don't manage anything *as a species*." Pat got up and grabbed a root beer from the fridge and another beer for Daniel. He sat back down. "How's our girl doing?"

Daniel said, "She's been going round the clock, sounded exhausted when we spoke this morning. She hasn't answered her phone since. I hope she listened to reason and took a nap. She said it's madness down there, people are still streaming in. The stadium is full and they've got army cots spread across the parking lots. She said they'll probably have a hundred thousand by the end of the day."

Pat gestured with his root beer toward the muted television: an aerial view of the stadium from a helicopter, hundreds of white

Red Cross tents covering the football field and filling the parking lot outside. A near-constant stream of cars and pickup trucks, people dropping off their sick loved ones or neighbors. Ambulances and military people movers dropping off those redirected from area hospitals.

Pat said, "Can you imagine? If they have a hundred thousand infected down there, there could be one or two thousand Tim Trinitys among them. Wish I could be a fly on the wall, hear what they're all babbling about."

Daniel's stomach turned to ice. "Oh shit."

"What?"

"That's it." Daniel grabbed his phone. "Conrad faked us out once. Now we're seeing his war game, we're taking our eye off the original ball. He's faking us out a second time."

"I don't follow."

"Okay, we already figured Conrad would use an outbreak to create a bunch of Trinitys all at once and cloak his actions."

"Right. Going from one tiny African village to the next might let you fly under the radar for a while, but it would just take too long and the risk of exposure grows, the longer you're there. Gotta use an outbreak."

Daniel said, "What if he's not just trying to *create* them all at once, but also *collect* them all at once. Think about it: Kara said it's complete chaos down there—she just showed up and told them she was a doctor and they put her to work. Her medical license has been suspended for three years but they don't have time to vet volunteers, they're in full crisis mode. Conrad and Dillman's men could move through the place as volunteers, culling out people who show signs of AIT before the situation calms down. With a big enough team, he might get five hundred or more."

"Damn," said Pat. "Ballsy play."

"Just the kind Conrad likes," said Daniel. "You think he'd pass up this opportunity?"

"No, I don't."

Daniel speed-dialed New York. "Raoul, listen. I need you guys to get us onto a satellite over South Carolina."

"Hold on while I patch Gerald in," said Raoul. In a few seconds, Gerald So joined them on the call.

Daniel said, "Michael Dillman had over twenty mercs fly into Atlanta with him. But they only needed six to fly the planes, including Dillman, plus one in the trailer at the airfield, and maybe a few more to pick them up where they ditched the planes. So where are the rest of them, and what are they doing?"

"Don't make us guess," said Raoul.

"They're gonna cull the infected who get AIT right out from under our noses. I bet they set up a place to take them ahead of time. Gerald, I need every video feed you can get, traffic cameras, satellite, everything. Zero in on Williams-Brice Stadium, look for panel vans, trucks, even ambulances, anything picking people up instead of dropping them off, anything making return trips. Follow them, find out where they're going."

"On it," said Gerald So. "Give me a half hour to hack into the satellite feed, the rest is already up and running."

Daniel dialed Kara's cell again, got her voice-mail again. "It's me. Call me back soon as you can."

50: CHAOS AND DISORDER

The parking lot outside Williams-Brice Stadium was a sea of army cots, IV stands, wheeled carts . . . and the white blur of lab coats, doctors and nurses in constant motion. Kara Singh stood to full height and stretched her lower back. She lifted the yellow plastic splatter shield and wiped her face and neck with a cool wet cloth, then left the cloth resting on the back of her neck and stretched her arms above her head.

Even with the white gazebo tents giving shade, it was over ninety degrees in the lot with so many bodies radiating heat. Add to that a long-sleeved lab coat, latex gloves pulled up over the cuffs, and the splatter shield/headband combo . . . no wonder three doctors and two nurses had passed out in the last hour.

Everyone was ragged, nobody was getting enough sleep, and the place was starting to look like a war zone refugee camp. Which, Kara supposed, it sort of was.

God, she was tired.

Cots were also set up in the stadium's dressing rooms and workout rooms, so emergency workers could grab an hour's sleep here and there.

Kara glanced at her watch. Not yet one o'clock. She'd been here almost twenty-four hours, hadn't taken a nap yet, despite Daniel's urging when they spoke around breakfast.

Not smart, girl. You'll do nobody any good if you crash . . .

But even bone-tired, Kara was in the zone, doing what she did best: delivering medical aid to people who needed it. It felt like a victory. It felt like staking a claim to the woman she had long ago been—and still had a right to be.

A doctor. And a damn good one.

Still, she needed to get some sleep. Soon.

The patients with high fevers were taken inside the stadium to the cots set up on the football field, where giant fans blowing across tubs of ice water lowered the air temperature. There were also misting stations inside where you could stand under the nozzles and cool down fast. Three hours ago, the man from FEMA promised they'd get a similar setup for the parking lot, but they hadn't expected this many people and the extra fans and misters were being brought up from Charleston.

When they'd get here was anybody's guess.

Help one more, then go inside and get cool. Then a caffeine nap . . .

Problem was, for every patient sick with the plague, there were almost a dozen with psychosomatic plague, what used to be called *hysterical* symptoms. Convinced they had the plague, they felt the shortness of breath, chest pain, and incessant need to cough. Some felt nauseated and some of those even vomited. And subjectively, they reported feeling feverish and their bodies complied by breaking out in extra sweat, but they couldn't think their way into a genuine fever of any significance.

Hysterical or not, they still had to be screened.

Kara lowered her splatter shield and walked to the next row of cots. A black man in his forties lay on the nearest cot. One look and Kara knew he had a high fever. The man was completely soaked, his eyes bloodshot and skin flushed. He thrashed around a bit, mumbling, coughing, only half-conscious. A young woman in her twenties squatted next to the man, dabbing his forehead with a cloth. She had a bandana tied over her nose and mouth, no gloves, no eye protection. Her eyes looked frightened.

Kara bent down and used the electronic ear thermometer to check the man's temperature.

The girl said, "My father."

The thermometer read 103.8.

The girl said, "He gonna live?"

Kara said, "Tell me about his symptoms. Has he coughed up blood?"

"No, ma'am, he cough a lot but no blood. An' he upchuck after breakfast, say his chest feel tight. He gonna die?"

"No, I don't think so," said Kara. "How about you, how are you feeling?"

"M'okay," said the girl. "Just scared is all."

"You live with your father?"

"Uh-huh. Breast cancer take my momma five years ago next month. Just him and me. You sure he ain't gonna die?"

Kara looked at the girl and saw more than just regular fear in her eyes.

"Come on, girl. Out with it."

The girl's gaze shifted to her father. "I tell you, you'll think I'm crazy."

"No, I won't."

"Well it sound crazy, but this morning he start talkin' funny. I can't understand him at all. Then I realize he talkin' in French." The girl looked up at Kara. "Only, he don't know any French."

Kara stopped dead, a chill spider-crawling up her arms.

Daniel was right. This strain of the plague did trigger AIT.

She looked down at the man again, wondering what it was like inside his head, if it was like her voices and vision-dreams. She felt a surge of emotion, a strange kinship with the man. She reached forward and took his pulse.

The girl said, "Please don't tell nobody what I said, they'll send me to Bull Street, put me in a padded room."

Kara smiled at the girl. "It'll be our secret," she said. "We're gonna take good care of him, I'm sure when he gets better he won't be speaking French anymore."

"Thank you."

"You go home now, try to stay away from people as much as you can for the next few days, and don't get anywhere near anyone who's coughing." Kara reached into the pocket of her lab coat, pulled out a pair of latex gloves and a surgical mask, and handed them to the girl. "Wear these whenever you have to be near other people, okay?"

"Yes, ma'am. Thank you."

The girl walked away and Kara signaled for a couple of volunteers—big boys who were on the football team here—and they brought a stretcher and carried the man inside the stadium.

Kara followed, almost staggering at the temperature change when they passed through the doors. In the battle between caffeine and exhaustion, exhaustion was clearly winning.

The boys put the man down on a cot near one of the big fans on the field, then took their stretcher and headed back out. Kara stepped over to the nearest nursing station and removed the splatter shield. She popped a couple of Wake-Ups, guzzling them down with a whole bottle of spring water. Then she loaded a syringe for the man, and put the damn shield back on.

But when she returned to the cot, the man was gone.

Kara looked around to see if he'd wandered off, as unlikely as that might be. He hadn't seemed strong enough to even sit up, much less stand and wander. She didn't see him, but she did see the nurse working this row of cots.

She removed the face shield, caught the nurse's eye, and waved her over, hoping the woman's name would come to her before they were face-to-face.

It did, just in time.

"Maggie, I put a man in this cot not four minutes ago . . ."

"Oh yeah, I saw him. A couple of doctors with CDC lab coats took him."

"Took him?"

"Uh-huh. When I first saw the priest leaning over him, I thought he was getting last rites, but then the priest called the doctors over and they loaded him on a gurney and took him."

Priest . . .

Kara said, "Took him where?"

Maggie pointed to the tunnel where the football players ran out from under the stands at the beginning of a game. "That way."

Kara ran down the row, cut three rows over where there was a break between cots, then down another row, three rows over, and so on until she was almost at the tunnel and could see the men in lab coats wheeling her patient into the building under the stands.

The priest was still with them. He was tall and thin and blond with a slightly receding hairline.

The same man Daniel had shown her on his phone.

She settled into a fast walk, still closing the gap behind the men, grabbed the cell phone from her pocket and hit speed-dial.

Daniel answered before the first ring was over.

Kara said, "Listen: The priest you said to keep an eye out for—Conrad Winter. He's here."

Daniel said, "Sure it's him?"

"I'm sure."

"When did you last see him?"

"Daniel, I'm looking at him right now. He just took my patient—who I think has AIT. The priest is working with a couple guys in lab coats with CDC logos on the pockets, but—"

Kara ducked behind one of the big fans as Conrad Winter turned his head in her direction.

She said, "They don't strike me as doctors. They could be real doctors who happen to lift weights for fun, but to me they look more like Pat's type—"

Conrad Winter turned away and said something to the men in the lab coats, and they started wheeling the gurney farther inside the dark tunnel.

"They're on the move. Gotta go."

Daniel said, "Kara, we're on the way to you. Hang back, do not follow Conrad."

"I'm just gonna see what room they're taking him to, I'll be careful. Text me when you get here."

"No, Kara, don't—"

She ended the call and slipped the phone back in her pocket.

The men had disappeared into the blackness of the tunnel. Kara picked up her pace to close the distance. She entered the tunnel and slowed long enough for her eyes to adjust. Then continued to the end, where a curved hallway ran left and right under the stands. She looked both ways, but the men were out of sight. She listened for their footfalls, for the sound of a squeaky wheel on the gurney.

She heard nothing from either direction.

A fifty-fifty chance.

She chose left. Moving along the curved hallway, past framed photos of South Carolina college football legends evenly spaced along the glossy white-painted cinder block.

She stopped to listen. Now she heard their footsteps on the concrete floor ahead, echoing back through the hallway.

She passed a sign on the wall:

→ LOADING DOCKS 1-4 →

They weren't taking her patient to a room at all. They were taking him away.

Kara slowed as the hallway opened up to a large empty shipping/receiving area, with four loading docks where big trucks could back up and make deliveries.

Shifting to one side, she ducked behind a stack of packing crates.

After a few seconds, she peeked around the corner.

The two men in lab coats were loading the gurney into a large white cube van parked at loading dock number three. Six other patients were already loaded into the van. She couldn't see the priest. Maybe he was already behind the steering wheel waiting for them to finish.

As one of the men stepped across to the deck of the cube van, his lab coat pulled open. A black submachine gun was slung under the man's armpit. It looked just like the guns the mercenaries had carried in Norway.

Kara pulled back behind the crates.

A man's voice spoke quietly, just behind her left ear. "I really wish you hadn't seen that."

She spun around. The tall blond priest stood not two feet from her.

"I was just looking for more sterile bandages, Father. I think they're in these crates but—"

"No," he said. His expression was pained, full of sadness. "I'm sorry, Dr. Singh."

Kara's eye caught a glint of light off the blade in his hand, too late to react.

Conrad stuck the blade between her ribs.

51: BAD CARD

New York City

D aniel was right," said Gerald So, entering Carter Ames's office. "We've identified four cube vans and six panel vans, running back and forth from the stadium to a warehouse north of town."

Ayo and Raoul looked at each other. Raoul started to speak, but Carter spoke first.

"How many have they culled?"

Gerald said, "At least two hundred so far, maybe as many as three if the vans are running at full capacity. And they're still at it. My guys are keeping track."

Raoul said, "We can't let the Council have—"

Carter raised his hand. *First things first.* "Gerald, get Daniel on the horn, let him know. Then come straight back."

Gerald nodded and left the room in a hurry.

Raoul, clearly burning to make his case, jumped right in where he left off. "Three *hundred* Trinitys? That'll be game over, they'll control the future. We have to do it. You both know we do."

Ayo shook her head. "It's a step too far, Raoul. There must be another way." She turned her appeal in Carter's direction. "What about Daniel and Pat? Shouldn't we at least give them more time? Daniel might be the key here. You've been saying that all along."

Raoul said, "Despite everything, Daniel is still a rookie, and he's still made mistakes. We can't bet *everything* on him . . . and frankly, what else can we do at this point? We've been dealt a bad card, but we've gotta play it."

"You're both right," said Carter. "All our indicators say Daniel is at the very heart of this thing—that's why we scouted him so intensely. We don't know when it's going to happen or what it's going to look like . . . but perhaps this *is* the time."

Raoul started to protest, but again Carter raised his hand. "If it were any other operative down there, we'd already be taking action. But it isn't. I want you to brief Contingency, have them prepare our response. Don't deploy without my order. We'll give Daniel a little more time and see how it plays out. But we'll be ready to shut it down."

Ayo's expression softened, and Raoul reluctantly nodded acceptance. Raoul said, "What parameters should I give Contingency?"

Carter Ames let out a breath. "If we go, we go all the way."

52: SAFE FROM HARM

Daniel and Pat got off the elevator and strode into the Marriott's parking garage, Daniel leading the way, car keys in hand.

They were twenty feet from the car when Evan Sage stepped out from behind a concrete pillar, pistol aimed straight at Daniel's chest.

"Either of you moves, I will put Daniel down."

Pat said, "Easy there."

Daniel said, "We don't have time for this."

Evan said, "Fuck you."

Daniel said, "Coming as it does from a waterboarding torture monkey, that doesn't wound me a whole lot, Evan."

Pat said, "Man's got a point."

Evan said, "You think you're off-limits? *Nobody* is off-limits, not while my country is under attack. So you two bastards are gonna tell me exactly what you know. Right now."

Pat shrugged. "I thought the Yemenis were behind it. Saw it on TV, must be true."

"Put the gun away, asshole," said Daniel. "You wouldn't be standing here asking us if you had a goddamn clue."

Evan Sage held his position.

Daniel said, "Can't live with the company line, huh? Can't swallow the big lie? You're off the reservation and you need my help. Again. You won't get it at the point of a gun."

Evan thought about it. He looked tired. He holstered his pistol.

"Good," said Daniel. "Here's the deal: Conrad Winter is at the triage center at Williams-Brice right now, but I don't know for how much longer. You wanna come with us, fine, we can use an extra man. You don't wanna come, that's fine too. But you try to stop us, we'll have that gunfight right here."

Evan Sage said nothing.

"Make a decision. You wanna find the truth or not?"

Sage looked from Daniel to Pat.

Pat said, "What he said."

Sage thought for another minute, then decided.

"I'll follow you in my car."

✢ ✢ ✢

"Gerald, we're about two minutes out, what've you got?"

Daniel checked over his shoulder as they burned rubber around the corner onto Bluff Road. Evan Sage was having no trouble keeping up with Pat's daredevil driving.

"I see you," said Gerald So, no doubt watching a satellite feed. "Just past the stadium hang a left onto Berea, then another left on Key Road. Last van pulled out a few minutes ago. Right now the loading docks are clear."

Daniel relayed the directions to Pat and a minute later they skidded to a stop in front of the football stadium's vacant loading docks. Evan Sage skidded to a stop in formation beside them. All three men approached the loading docks with guns drawn.

Pat turned to face the lot, covering their rear. Daniel hopped up and inside the building, moving slowly as his eyes adjusted to the light. There was something on the floor near a stack of shipping crates.

A body.

Evan Sage jumped up and moved to Daniel's left, toward the hallway.

Daniel walked closer to the body on the floor.

No no no no no . . .

Please no. Don't let it be—

—Kara, curled up on the concrete floor, blood pooling under her torso.

Oh, God no . . .

Daniel dropped to his knees and gently rolled Kara on her back and cradled her head in one hand.

Looking for any rise and fall in her chest, seeing none.

"Come on, baby, come on, please, I know you're in there . . ."

Searching for a pulse in her wrist, finding none.

"Kara, stay with me, don't you dare leave now . . ."

Blinking away tears, dropping her wrist, moving his hand to her neck.

"Come on back, baby, you know you're not done yet . . ."

Searching her neck for a pulse . . .

not finding a pulse . . .

then finding it.

Weak.

Slow.

But beating.

Behind Daniel, Evan Sage ran into the hallway. "Medic! We need a medic here!"

Daniel tilted Kara's head back and put his mouth on hers and breathed air into her lungs.

53: BULL IN THE PEN

Conrad Winter walked through the blazing sun and into the air-conditioned warehouse. He tugged at his clerical collar to let some cool air in, then thought, *What the hell?* and just pulled the thing off completely.

Bobby McCue greeted Conrad just inside the door. McCue had been Michael Dillman's trusted right-hand. With Michael gone, he was now ranking officer of the mercenary teams.

The warehouse held ten rows of army cots—thirty per row—and most were occupied. Rich and poor and middle class, black and white and brown, young and old, all lying side by side in neat rows. The plague did not discriminate, and neither, it seemed, did plague-triggered AIT. It was of no consequence what god you worshiped or didn't, what moral code you lived by or didn't.

The plague was the great equalizer.

Fifteen former army medics in gloves and splatter shields moved along the rows, tending to the infected herd. In addition to the medical carts, there were about fifty camcorders set up on tripods and connected to laptop computers, each camera pointing down at a patient in a cot.

"A lot of them are babbling," said Bobby McCue, "so we've started recording the ones saying anything we can understand."

"One of the men just brought in is speaking French. I want a camera on him without delay."

"What's so special about him?"

"He's talking about the near future."

"Roger that, will set it up, stat."

Conrad scanned the rows of cots once more. "What's our current total?"

"Including the ones you just brought in, we're at 263."

"I thought we passed 270 on the previous delivery."

"Some were false-positives, turns out they didn't have a fever." Bobby McCue offered a grim but reassuring nod. "We'll be sure the bodies are never found."

So they had 263. Not quite the walk-off grand slam Conrad had dreamed of in his perfect fantasy scenario, but a decisive victory, nonetheless. A very big win, indeed.

Provided they got away clean.

Bobby McCue was saying, " . . . destinations are prepped and the semis are being brought in and fueled, we can pull out tomorrow morning. We should have at least four hundred by then."

"Negative," said Conrad. "We're blown. No more runs to the stadium. Have your men ditch the vans, then pack everything up and get everyone on the road. Understood?"

"Yes, sir. We'll get out well before sunrise."

"See that you do." Conrad started to walk away, turned back. "Oh, and Bobby?"

"Yes, sir?"

Conrad dug in his pocket and pulled out the knife, still stained with the blood of Kara Singh.

"Make this disappear."

54: EVERYTHING COMES DOWN TO THIS

Daniel sat alone in a private waiting room at Providence Hospital . . . not moving, not thinking, just staring at his hands and feeling the oppressive weight of complete and utter silence.

He wore Kara's blood all over his hands and forearms and shirtfront, where it had dried almost to the color of rust. But he couldn't stand the thought of washing it off—washing *her* off—of seeing her blood turn pink and dilute and then disappear down the drain.

He pushed the image away and returned to the silence.

The emptiness.

The waiting.

⚜ ⚜ ⚜

"I've got to be honest, Mr. Byrne," said the lantern-jawed doctor, "she's not out of the woods. We lost her briefly—it still could go either way."

"Lost her?"

The doctor nodded. "She arrived to the ER in cardiac arrest. There was a great deal of internal bleeding and commensurate loss of blood pressure, and she flatlined for several minutes, during which time her brain was denied oxygen. She's out of surgery and we've moved her to ICU, but she's in a pretty deep coma and she's not breathing on her own. I wish I could give you better news. All we can do now is wait and pray."

The doctor excused himself and left the room.

And the silence pressed in again.

8:13 p.m.—Fifty-six hours after contamination . . .

Pat Wahlquist stepped out of a conference room on the hospital's fifth floor and put a hand on Daniel's shoulder. "I pleaded your case, but Raoul's 'bout ready to spit nails."

Daniel entered the room. Ayo Onatade and Raoul Aharon and Carter Ames stood around the table. Nobody looked particularly happy.

Carter Ames said, "I'm terribly sorry about Kara, Daniel. I understand you two have grown quite close. How are you feeling?"

"I'm fine," said Daniel. "Good to go. When do we move on the warehouse?"

"You've been through enough," said Ames, "we'll handle it from here."

"Don't be ridiculous. After what Conrad's done, no way I'm sitting this one out."

Raoul said, "It's not negotiable. First of all, Conrad Winter isn't even in the country anymore. And even if he were standing in this room, he's off-limits."

"That's bullshit."

"No, that's the real shit. You're benched, Daniel. That's it. I know you want payback for Kara's death—"

"She's not dead."

"Yet," said Raoul.

Daniel glanced at Ayo, who looked like she desperately wanted to be somewhere else.

Raoul shrugged. "Point is, until you can play by the rules, you're no good to us in the field. You're a promising operative and you still have an important role to play with the Foundation, but you've proven you're not ready. It's that simple."

"Easy to say from a high-rise in New York. If I hadn't improvised, we never would've even gotten this close."

"This may be hard for you to hear, but the *only* reason Kara got knifed is because you read her in—against my explicit orders. If she hadn't recognized Conrad, she wouldn't be circling the drain right now. So if you want to find the man responsible for her death, look in the mirror. She deserved better."

Daniel forced his fists to unclench. "I swear, if you refer to her in the past tense again—"

"Stop it." Carter Ames stepped forward, between the men. "Raoul, take a walk, get a coffee or something."

"Fine," said Raoul. He pointed at Daniel. "But you're on leave. Stay here, mourn your girlfriend, get your head together. When you decide you're ready to be part of a team, come see me in New York."

Raoul walked out and closed the door hard behind him.

Carter said, "I'm sorry, Daniel, but he's right. Not only did you read Kara in, but you brought a Homeland Security agent in, and God knows what you told him."

"Jesus, Carter. I didn't tell him a damn thing about your Foundation."

"*Our* Foundation. Which is exactly Raoul's point. You don't see yourself as part of this, not fully. And until you do, we can't risk your continued involvement in the field. Don't misunderstand—we're incredibly grateful for your work and we don't want to lose you. Really this is my fault for rushing your training."

"So there's nothing I can say. I'm benched."

"I'm afraid so. Stay here with Kara, and when this is all over, come back to New York and we'll finish your training." Carter Ames offered an avuncular smile. "As valuable as you are, I'm confident we can handle the warehouse without your help."

Daniel said, "And what about the larger issue? The Foundation's gonna let Conrad have his war?"

Ames said, "Such are the consequences of losing. This time the Council won the game. We just have to face that fact and be better next time, nothing else we can do."

"We can tell the world the truth. That it wasn't Yemeni terrorists, that it was a rogue American military officer working with private contractors, that it was the work of the Council—"

"With what evidence, Daniel? The soldier in West Virginia is gone, probably dead, the lab in Liberia is gone, the bodies of Colonel Dillman and the mercenary Pat shot at the airfield were removed before authorities arrived, Descia Milinkovic is dead—"

It felt like a gut punch. "Descia's dead?"

"Yes. She and five of our other top allies in microbiology, plus a couple who were Council allies. Conrad Winter had it all planned out ahead of time, they tied off all loose ends, didn't leave us anything. They even hit Kara's flat in London, burned it to the ground. All her journals, gone. We have nothing. No evidence to leak, at least not without revealing ourselves to the world. And you know that's not an option."

"So Conrad gets his war."

"Yes, he does. Those are the stakes we play for."

"And Conrad remains untouchable?"

"Yes, he does. I'm sorry."

Daniel turned to Ayo. "Do you agree with this? You think Conrad Winter should be off-limits?"

Ayo stood silent, looking into Daniel's eyes with such naked sympathy it made his chest ache. Her look told him everything—that she agreed with him, she'd argued his position, and she'd been overruled.

"I am truly sorry, Daniel," was all she said.

55: WE DO WHAT WE'RE TOLD

So we ridin' the pine, you and me." Pat took one last hit off the joint, tossed it over the edge of the Marriott's rooftop, and looked out over the moonlit city. "I got benched, too, for lettin' you reach out to Evan Sage."

Daniel took a swig of beer. "It was still the right thing to do."

"That it was."

"I can't believe Carter's gonna let this war happen."

"They play a ruthless game, you knew that when you signed on. They're cold when it comes to cuttin' their losses, stayin' alive to play the long game."

"But there's gotta be a point where you go all-in."

Pat shrugged. "This ain't that point. Not for them."

"Well, I don't see how much larger the stakes can get." Daniel swallowed some more beer without tasting it. "I mean, what's the endgame? We let this go, the Council nudges America closer to fascism, breeds xenophobia, and then we drop more bombs on the Middle East, killing tens of thousands, maybe hundreds of thousands, mostly civilians . . . we flatten entire cities. In the end, we create another generation of Muslims who've seen their families murdered by the West, another generation of broken kids who'll be manipulated to sign up for jihad."

"That's about the size of it."

"And the cycle just continues—it's like these people never heard of *blowback*."

"Hell, they *invented* blowback, they *manage* it while gettin' rich off war. You gotta stop thinkin' in terms of nations and regions. For these guys, it's all about power and money."

"Then Jacob was right. We're not the good guys, we're just the *less bad* bad guys. We're playing the devil's game, too."

"Yup."

"And we just let Conrad walk away from it."

"Hey man, I warned you back in New Orleans, I told you not to join up."

"You told me it would get me killed. You didn't say it would cost me my soul."

Pat shrugged. "That part was implied." For a moment, he seemed lost in thought. "You know why I like being a mercenary better than being a soldier? It's not the money, although the money is way better. It's the choice. As a soldier, you just do what you're told, even when your leaders conflate national security with economic security, and you end up going to war because it's in the interests of oil men or finance men or defense contractors or god knows what. But I only fight the battles I deem worth fighting. That's why I stayed a Foundation ally, never joined as a full member. But now I've seen what the Council is willing to do, I say: *Screw all that*. Sometimes the ends really do justify the means, and if letting Conrad Winter walk away helps us win the long game, I can live with that."

Daniel's phone buzzed with an incoming text. He checked the screen. It was from Ayo.

Remember how you said you'd take me to Barbados for a vacation when we had time? Now's the time. Go to Barbados, scout the west coast for a place we can stay. Do it now. xoxo—A. O.

But Daniel had never suggested a vacation to Ayo, and he'd never even been to Barbados.

He put the phone away.

Daniel turned to his best friend. "I'm gonna go back to the hospital, check on Kara," he lied.

Pat nodded to Daniel with what might've been a knowing smirk, or might've been nothing at all. "Catch you on the flipside, brother."

56: HELL IS CHROME

11:13 p.m.—Fifty-nine hours after contamination . . .

If you ignored the complete absence of people and cars, it could've been any quiet night in downtown Columbia. Daniel sat at the top of the South Carolina State House steps, just outside the beam of the floodlights, a palmetto tree rising from a planter to his left.

When Daniel heard the leather-soled footsteps approaching, he didn't turn around. The footsteps stopped just behind him. He still didn't turn around.

"You gonna join me?" he said.

Evan Sage sat to Daniel's right. He fished a pack of cigarettes from a pocket and lit one and blew a stream of smoke at the stars. He said, "Is this the part where you try to break my nose?"

"No," said Daniel, "this is the part where I ask for your help."

"So now we're *both* off the reservation, is that it?"

"I suppose it is."

"Lemme guess, Conrad Winter is off-limits." He held Daniel's gaze. "Yup, I was told the same thing by my people. And I'm sick to death of being jerked around by people who know things I don't, including you."

"Maybe I should've waterboarded you instead."

Sage shrugged. "Fair point. But I don't owe you a favor."

"I didn't say favor, I said help. Conrad Winter was responsible for this plague. What's stopping him from cooking up another batch and releasing it somewhere else? I know where he is, I just need a quick off-the-books flight there. All I'm asking you for is a lift. Some jet fuel." Daniel looked out across the silent, empty streets, watched the traffic lights change for no one. "It comes down to this: I don't want to live in a world where someone can do this and still be *off-limits* . . . and I'm betting neither do you."

"What are you gonna do if you find him?"

"You know what I'm gonna do."

"And you're gonna be okay with that?"

"Conrad killed my uncle, he killed that entire village in Liberia, he infected over a hundred thousand Americans . . ." Daniel started to add Kara to the list, stopped himself. "It may not be self-defense, but it's not revenge, either. The man has to be stopped."

Sage sat and smoked and thought about it, and Daniel let him. He'd made his pitch, there was nothing else to say.

"I'll get you the plane. But that's all. After this, I'm out."

"Thank you," said Daniel.

Evan Sage said, "Send the bastard straight to hell."

57: IT'S NO GAME

St. Michael, Barbados

Conrad Winter hadn't expected fanfare. He hadn't expected a victory party. But he'd expected *something*. Maybe a quiet celebratory drink on the pool deck while the old man offered awkward congratulations for a job well done.

Something.

Instead he found a note on the dining room table.

Gone to Singapore.

That's it.

Fine. He'd celebrate alone.

Conrad opened a bottle of Dom and took it to the living room. He toasted his reflection in the blank screen of the plasma television.

He could declare victory on all three levels. There would now be a war that would dwarf Iraq, Middle East oil secured for another ten years at least. Dissent in America would look like treason, the surveillance state locked in for a generation. And the Council had collected 263 people with AIT—263 sources of secret intelligence that would be the Council's alone. No telling what they would be able to do with that information.

Would've been nice to have more, but Kara Singh might've called it in to Daniel before Conrad spotted her, so he'd had to shut it down. Anyway, 263 would be plenty, for now. Conrad had left South Carolina while the trucks were being refueled for transport out of state. By now, those people would be in ten different locations across six different states.

He'd done it. This is what victory felt like. In a few short months, he would take over the director's chair. Unfortunate that Michael Dillman wouldn't be there to advise—worse than unfortunate—but important victories rarely come without sacrifice.

Conrad made a silent toast to Dillman and refilled his glass.

Claim it and own it, the old man had said.

Conrad had done just that.

He looked out through the French doors to the pool deck. He'd avoided this place for years, but now he saw it differently. Now it was something he'd earned. *He* would be director now, perhaps he'd keep this place as a winter home.

Why not?

The phone in his pocket vibrated and the screen showed it was coming from the director's plane.

"Good morning, Father," Conrad allowed a little swagger into his tone. He'd earned that, too. "Sorry you couldn't stick around for the debrief. We had to cap the AIT project a little early but we've got 263, which is plenty. All other aspects were a complete success."

The old man cleared his throat in Conrad's ear. "You don't even know, do you?"

"Know what?"

"You're sitting around my house, drinking my champagne and congratulating yourself like a child," the old man growled. "And you don't even know."

Conrad felt sick. "What?"

"Turn on the damn television."

Conrad grabbed the remote and turned on CNN. It was an aerial shot of the warehouse north of Columbia.

Or what was left of it. A smoldering ruin, surrounded by fire engines and police cars and National Guard vehicles.

The director said, "Carter Ames knew somehow, took it out with a drone strike, *before* your men got the people out. You were too cocky, Conrad." He cleared his throat again. "Charles has been cleaning up your mess. He seeded a cover story with our allies in the federal government. It'll be used to support the al-Qaida story. But you've lost the directorship. The board of advisers met this morning and gave Charles a five-year term."

Conrad's father ended the call without another word.

Conrad watched the champagne bubbles rise with his temper, felt the pressure building in his head, then hurled the glass against the wall.

Shit. Piss. Damn.

He turned up the television's volume.

The newsreader was saying, " . . . details still coming in, but government sources tell us that late last night, acting on intelligence gathered by the CIA, a joint FBI–Homeland Security task force tracked the al-Qaida terrorists to this warehouse north of Columbia. Rather than surrender, the terrorists detonated the building, committing mass suicide. Six Yemeni passports have been recovered from the site, apparently ejected from the building by the explosion, but it will be some time before authorities can move in and comb through the wreckage for more forensic evidence . . ."

Conrad turned off the television.

He drank some champagne straight from the bottle. It was bitter on his tongue.

Five years until he might get another shot at the directorship.

Five years he'd have to serve under Charles Carruthers.

He'd come so close.

And failed.

Conrad wept.

✣ ✣ ✣

The west coast of Barbados lay to Conrad's port side, glimmering in the midday sun, palm trees swaying in the breeze blowing in off the Caribbean Sea, luxury hotels dotting the shoreline white and pink, waterski boats dragging rich tourists in their wake, WaveRunners buzzing like water insects closer to shore, a couple of dive boats at anchor over popular reefs.

Conrad stood up on the flybridge, piloting the luxury motor cat down the St. James coast, toward Dottins Reef. He'd stop there and drop anchor for lunch, maybe take a dive in the afternoon.

Being out on the water would bring perspective, would clear his focus.

In time.

But for now it would hurt. It had to. Bottom line: The last major event of Conrad's life before his father's death was a failure. And there was nothing he could do about that.

Knock off the self-pity, be a man. Reframe it, find what you can use, and plan the path forward . . .

Okay. It wasn't a total loss. In fact, it was still mostly a victory. The board of advisers would see that. Yes, Charles would get the director's chair, but Conrad would be right there next to the seat of power, and he'd find a way in.

It wouldn't take five years, either, dammit. Charles would make a mistake in his first year—Conrad would make sure of it, and jump on the opportunity. Meanwhile, he would plan another way to tap into the power of AIT. He still had the formula to engineer the bacterial strain and there were plenty of desperate places in the world to set up another lab.

Once he had enough . . . there would be another chance.

It would *not* take five years.

Dottins Reef was unoccupied as Conrad approached. He eased back on the throttle and moved in to drop anchor.

Then his engines quit.

He knew he had plenty of fuel, but maybe there was a pinhole in the fuel line system, probably the filter. Mechanical fuel pumps were prone to shutdown with the tiniest amount of air in the line. The boat was new, and there were usually a few bugs to work out, even in the best yachts.

They were temperamental mistresses.

Conrad dropped anchor and walked down to the deck. At the lower helm, he grabbed the keys, then opened the hatch and climbed down the aluminum steps to the starboard engine room, switching on the LED lights on his way down.

The engine room was gleaming white, no fuel leak, no moisture on the line or the floor below the pump. He followed the line and found the culprit.

The fuel had been shut off.

Shut off.

The valve had been turned, manually.

By someone.

Someone on the boat.

And Conrad's gun was back in the cabin, at the main helm station.

Shit.

Conrad crept slowly back to the hatch, wrench in hand.

Then up the steps and onto the deck, silent as a shadow.

There was a man standing in the cabin, at the helm, his back to Conrad.

Conrad inched forward, wrench held high, as his eyes adjusted to the bright light and the man came into focus.

The man turned around to face him.

Daniel Byrne.

Holding Conrad's gun.

"Put the wrench down, Conrad."

"Hello, Daniel," Conrad dropped the wrench. "You coming out, or am I coming in?"

Daniel walked forward, out onto the deck, the barrel of the gun never leaving Conrad's chest.

Daniel said, "Did you really think I wouldn't come after you? After what you've done, did you think I would let *anything* stop me?"

"Carter Ames would never sanction this."

"What Carter Ames wants is immaterial."

"This is not how we play the game."

"It's no game."

"You do this, it'll be all-out war. And we've got more resources than you do. Think about it."

"I don't have any resources at all," said Daniel. "I've just got your gun, and a keen desire to stop you."

"I know you, Daniel, you're not a murderer."

"You don't know me."

There had to be a better angle, another approach. *Play for time* . . .

Conrad said, "Look man, it's all messed up, I understand that. But this solves nothing, just makes everything worse." Then the better approach came to him. "You know what Carter Ames did last night, right?"

Daniel's expression didn't change, but there was a flicker in his eyes. He didn't know yet.

Conrad said, "Your Foundation's Department of Contingency hit that warehouse with a drone strike, killed 263 innocent people along with my men. You really want to work for an organization that would do that to a warehouse full of innocent civilians?"

"You put those people there."

"Yeah, I put those people there. But you didn't save them, Daniel. You killed them. And now you want to kill me? It won't change anything, but now you'll be a murderer. And that won't wash off, you'll carry it with you forever."

"Maybe I don't care."

"You care. You're better than this. I know you are, and so do you."

✤ ✤ ✤

Daniel shot Conrad Winter twice in the chest.

Conrad looked surprised. He opened his mouth to speak, but his heart was no longer pumping blood, and after standing still for several long seconds, he spasmed once and collapsed to the deck.

Dead.

No, it wasn't self-defense. It was defense of the entire world.

Could Daniel live with that?

He thought he could.

58: CLAMPDOWN

Central Park—New York City
Two weeks after contamination . . .

Carter Ames entered Central Park from Seventy-Fourth Street and strolled past the copper-roofed boathouse, past the model sailboat pond, toward the statue of Alice in Wonderland. The pond was busy today, dotted with a hundred white sails, grandparents and children elbow to elbow along the shoreline clutching radio-control transmitters, eager to get some model sailing in before the weather turned crisp.

He continued on through Bethesda Terrace to the Bow Bridge, a graceful cast-iron structure spanning sixty feet across Central Park Lake. The man standing in the middle of the bridge looked much older and smaller than Carter remembered him, and his hair was gone.

Even from a distance, it was clear that the director of the Council for World Peace was a dying man. Carter walked to the middle of the bridge and stood beside him.

The old man cleared his throat for a long time. "I didn't know you had it in you, Carter. A drone strike? Not exactly Foundation protocol."

"You didn't leave us any choice, Tom."

"There's always a choice. Even when there are no good options, there's still a choice."

"Then let me put it this way: The Foundation's choice is to draw the line right here, however poor the options."

"Dark times ahead," said the old man. "If you don't embrace change, you can't influence it. You'll get run over."

"That's a poor excuse for collaboration. No thanks, we'll fight it."

"You know what's coming, Carter. The shift has already begun."

"And your policies are accelerating it. Which is why I cannot allow the Council this advantage. Hundreds of your own pet prophets? I won't allow it."

"You can't stop us."

"Actually, I think I can." Carter looked out across the lake. Couples walking along the shore, hand in hand. Old people feeding the birds. Kids playing catch. All of them unaware of how close the whole system was to collapse. He said, "I'm sorry about your son, Tom. Our man went rogue, we tried to stop him . . . we got there too late, he was already gone. But we gave the boat a thorough going-over, and we have Conrad's computer."

The old man stared at Carter but didn't speak.

Carter said, "Yes, we decoded the recipe. And now we can do it, too. We've already cooked up a batch, a very big batch, which will stay under lock and key in our labs. We won't use it to our advantage, and you won't use it to yours."

The old man said, "Mutually Assured Destruction?"

"Something like that, yes. The strain is contained and it'll stay that way. But if even one case of your designer plague appears on our radar anywhere in the world, we will raise our own little army of prophets. See, your problem is that you only considered the massive advantage it would give you, never the massive *disadvantage* if we had it. Now we do. If we both deploy, it will be utter chaos—AIT isn't predictable, and your wealth advantage can't ensure that your prophets would be equal to ours. It could even tip the scales in our favor. So we will both stand down, and neither of us will force nature's hand."

"You call it nature. You don't know what's causing it any more than we do."

"No, but I know that *we* won't be causing it. And neither will you."

The old man thought for a long time, then nodded once and cleared his throat again. "All right. The plague goes on ice—for both of us. We'll continue fighting over what 'nature' sees fit to give us. But your man has to pay for my son. That can't go unanswered."

"No. That's off the table."

"What?"

"I am sorry for your loss, but Conrad overreached and he paid the price. Daniel is not to be touched."

"You're willing to risk everything just to protect this man?" The director of the Council held Carter's eyes, perhaps looking for some sign of a bluff.

But Carter Ames wasn't bluffing.

"Everything. The crossover is coming and . . . Daniel Byrne may somehow hold the key to a future for us all. You go after him, it'll be all-out war between us. You may very well win that war, but I'll do everything in my power to see that you come away from it permanently crippled, if not mortally wounded. I'll burn us both to the ground if necessary."

59: WHAT ABOUT NOW

Bathsheba, Barbados
Nine weeks after contamination . . .

*T*oday is a good day to die. But I've decided to stay alive until tomorrow.

Daniel ended his meditation, opened his eyes, and watched the waves roll in from the Atlantic Ocean and break against the massive coral rock formations. He stood and stripped out of his shirt, ran down the beach and into the surf.

He swam hard until his muscles let him know they'd had a good workout, then eased over onto his back, past the breakers where the water was calm, sculling along the surface, feeling the morning sun bake his skin. When his skin got hot, he flipped over and kicked his feet and dived down into the cooler water, swimming a few feet down for a while, then breaking the surface again, facing shore. The colorful little hillside town of Bathsheba beckoned him back, coconut palms waving at him in the tropical breeze. He headed back in, thinking about lunch and the afternoon ahead.

For the last nine weeks, this had been his life. Breakfast of papaya and pineapple and coconut and coffee in his rented seaside cottage, followed by meditation on the beach and a long swim. Some days he'd bicycle down the coast to the calmer waters and more secluded beaches at Skeetes and Kitridge and Harrismith. He'd buy fish from the Rastas at the open-air markets, sometimes stop at a rum shop for a drink and a game of dominoes with the regulars, sometimes he'd hike into the hills and share his food with the friendly green monkeys that were ubiquitous in Barbados.

When he didn't feel like cooking, he'd visit the nearby Round House or the Atlantis Hotel, or Merton's Place up in St. Lucy.

He bought a small car with a snap-off canvas roof and no doors—locals called it a Moke—and when he felt like it, he'd drive across the island for the more pampered lifestyle and placid waters on the west coast, stopping at Mullins or Holetown, eating at The Tides or Sandpiper or Coral Reef Club, scuba diving with the dive shop there.

Most evenings were spent back in Bathsheba on his front porch with a book and a cigar and a glass of good rum, chatting with neighbors, listening to reggae.

It was a beautiful life. A sane life. Daniel loved the routine, the sameness of the days, the consistency of his mood, the peace he'd found. He loved his bronzed skin and the salt in his hair, which he'd let grow out a little longer. He loved the pace of life here and the ease with which people smiled and laughed. He loved the music and the rum and the green monkeys and the ocean and the nocturnal symphony of tree frogs.

But he had no idea how long it could last.

Raoul Aharon had come to visit three weeks after Daniel killed Conrad Winter. Raoul told him the Foundation considered this a paid leave of absence, told Daniel to take his time and come visit New York in about six months. And sure enough, his salary continued to accrue in his bank account every two weeks.

But Daniel had no intention of returning to the Fleur-de-Lis Foundation. Not in six months. Not ever.

He'd had a few bad nights dealing with what he'd done, a few bad dreams about murder—the kind of nightmares where you're battling a monster, only in these dreams Daniel *was* the monster—but the dreams had faded recently.

And it *was* murder—he didn't try to tell himself otherwise. But even so, he found that he could live with it. He wasn't sure what that said about him, but as the days passed, he thought about it less often.

✣ ✣ ✣

Daniel showered the salt away and dried off under his bedroom ceiling fan. He dressed casually and combed his hair with his fingers, then checked his watch—something he did less often these days, but today was not the usual routine.

It was time.

He removed the Moke's ragtop and drove under the afternoon sun, all the way down the Atlantic coast past Crane Beach, turning west into Christ Church.

He pulled to a stop at the curb in front of Grantley Adams Airport, checked his watch again.

Ten minutes later, Kara walked out of the airport pulling a wheeled suitcase. She wore a floral sundress and big Jackie O sunglasses.

Gorgeous.

Daniel took her slowly into his arms . . .

✣ ✣ ✣

They lay naked on top of the sheets under the ceiling fan, covered in a sheen of perspiration, catching their breath, unable to speak.

After a few minutes Kara said, "That was acceptable."

They both laughed.

Daniel ran his finger along the raised scar between her ribs. He leaned forward and kissed it, tasting the salt on her skin.

✦ ✦ ✦

After dinner they sat on the wicker loveseat on Daniel's front porch and watched the waves roll in under the moonlight.

Kara sipped her rum. "I can't think of a more beautiful place."

"Even more beautiful since you arrived," said Daniel. "You could stay, you know."

Her expression darkened a little. "Daniel, let's not do that. I don't even know who I'm going to be next. I don't want to plan ahead."

"Yeah, okay. I just mean, stay as long as you like."

Kara smiled. "You've got me for two weeks." She leaned forward and kissed him softly, then reclined and put her bare feet up on the coffee table. "Kara Singh is dead, the Foundation gave me a whole new identity. My name is now Maya Seth. I was born in Montreal, I've got a medical degree from the University of Toronto, and I'm licensed to practice medicine in Ontario and Quebec."

"But that's not what you're going to do next?"

Kara shook her head. "Next, I'm going to volunteer for a few months with Doctors Without Borders in India. I've made no decisions beyond that. Frankly, I'm still trying to get used to the silence in my head."

"The voices never came back?"

"No. I have no idea why they came or why they left. I thought maybe because I flatlined again after Conrad stabbed me, but the voices were gone a few days before that . . . which also doesn't mean much, since they would often disappear for days at a time during the six years I had them. I guess I'll never know."

Daniel said, "The voices abandoned my uncle, too, a few days before he died. Like you, he fought against them for a long time, then fought to define them, interpreting them, misinterpreting them . . . until finally he accepted them. Embraced them even, and found some peace when he did. And then they just went away. It was as if they'd accomplished what they needed to." He smiled. "But of course, that goes back to intention, and we don't know if there's intelligence behind them, do we?"

Kara thought for a minute before speaking. "I think there is. I don't mean a god, but I can't believe they were totally random, either. Remember what you said before? It's like the universe was trying to tell us something." She brushed it aside. "Anyway, I'm glad they're done with me and I hope they never come back. For the first time in six years, I'm the sole inhabitant of my own head, and it feels terrific." She laughed. "You should've seen me in the Atlanta airport, though. I passed one of those places that sells cinnamon buns, and when the smell hit me I just about freaked out. If I never taste cinnamon again, it'll be too soon."

❖ ❖ ❖

They made love again, gently this time.

Kara fell asleep immediately afterward, and Daniel enjoyed watching her sleep.

He had her for two weeks; he wouldn't ruin a second of it wishing for more. Maybe after she'd decided who she wanted to be next, they'd reconnect. Maybe not. It didn't matter.

What mattered was right here, right now.

This very moment was all that mattered, all that existed.

And in this moment, Daniel was happy.

✤ ✤ ✤

A storm rolled in sometime during the night, while they slept.

Daniel dreamed the fury of the storm, rain lashing the metal roof, thunder booming so close it shook the little cottage. In the dream, it wasn't just a storm. It was a malevolent force, and it wanted to kill Daniel.

In the dream, he jumped naked from the bed and ran to the window, forcing the storm shutters closed, latching them as lightning flashed outside. The front door banged open and he ran to the living room. Wind howled through the open door, blowing the rain inside. Daniel ran to the door, the wind so strong he had to lean into it. He got to the door and started to close it.

And that's when a bolt of lightning hit him right in the chest.

Daniel woke up, gasping for air, covered in sweat. He looked across the room, through the open window to the tropical rain sheeting down in the moonlight outside.

The storm outside was just a storm, that was all.

He got out of the bed, careful not to wake Kara, who slept peacefully beside him unaware of the storm.

He crossed to the window and looked down to the sea.

Just a storm.

He reached forward and closed the shutters, and a woman's voice behind him said:

Daniel. Pay attention.

He turned around. Kara was still asleep.

Daniel's mouth filled with the taste of cinnamon.

THANKS AND PRAISES

Life occasionally throws you a curveball. This one came in the form of injury (I really need to fall down less often). So the first *thank-you* goes to the many readers who stuck by me during the long wait and even sent e-mails to remind me they were eager for the next book. You guys rock.

Dan Conaway never wavered in his support, both as an agent and as a friend. I couldn't ask for better, on either count. Thanks also to Simon Lipskar, Maja Nikolic, Taylor Templeton, and everyone at Writers House. And to my film agent, Lucy Stille, at APA.

Alison Dasho is both an incredible editor and one of the finest humans I know. Alan Turkus was steadfast in his support and a joy to work with. Jacque Ben-Zekry may in fact be superhuman. Really, the whole team at Thomas & Mercer is beyond amazing. Gracie Doyle, Tiffany Pokorny, Timoney Korbar, Dan Byrne, Kim Bae, Andy Bartlett, Terry Goodman, Mikyla Bruder, Daphne Durham, Jeff Belle—I feel lucky to know you all.

Marjorie Braman, *editrix extraordinaire*, brought her usual keen eye and sharp intellect to the dance, for which I am very grateful. And Lindsey Alexander's copy edit was simply terrific. Thanks also to Bethany Davis, Karen Parkin, Paul Barrett, and Marc J. Cohen. And special thanks to Luke Daniels.

Early readers are often acknowledged in these pages, but these three people are more than early readers—they are early collaborators. Without them, this book would not exist. Marcus Sakey (bosom buddy and lifelong pal), Agent 99 (love of my life, apple of my eye, gorilla my dreams), and Barbara Chercover (best mom and friend in the history of moms and friends).

Knut Holmsen is more than just an awesome father-in-law. He and his extended network of Norwegians provided invaluable assistance. If I messed up the Norwegian stuff in this book, blame them (kidding—any mistakes are my own).

Jeff Abbott provided the gift of music when I needed it most.

Paul Guyot and Keith Snyder (great people and great writers, both) got me back on the bike. I owe them for that, big time.

Greg Seldon, my oldest friend, has done much to keep me sane (or happily insane). Love to you, my brother.

A whole bunch of talented people helped put me back together and enabled me to avoid major surgery. Dr. Jayne Davis, Dr. Doreen Campbell, Nicole Westlake, Dr. Vanessa Nobrega, Dr. Mark Ellingson, and the whole team at Balance Fitness.

Jon and Ruth Jordan exemplify the love of the crime fiction community—to know them is to consider yourself lucky. I am more than lucky; to me, they are family. Thank you, Jon and Ruth, for keeping the home fires burning during my absence. It's great to be back.

Finally, to Agent 99 and Firedog. You are the reason I get up in the morning.

ABOUT THE AUTHOR

Sean Chercover is the author of the bestselling thriller *The Trinity Game* and two award-winning novels featuring Chicago private investigator Ray Dudgeon: *Big City, Bad Blood* and *Trigger City*. After living in Chicago; New Orleans; and Columbia, South Carolina, Sean returned to his native Toronto, where he lives with his wife and son.

Sean's fiction has earned top mystery and thriller honors in the US, Canada, and the UK. He has won the Anthony, Shamus, CWA Dagger, Dilys, and Crimespree Awards and has been short-listed for the Edgar, Barry, Macavity, Arthur Ellis, and ITW Thriller Awards.

You'll find him at www.chercover.com or @SeanChercover on Twitter.